UP TRAIL!

A Desperate Cattle Drive Out of Texas During The Great American Civil War

Dann Wallis

authorHOUSE®

AuthorHouse™
1663 Liberty Drive
Bloomington, IN 47403
www.authorhouse.com
Phone: 1-800-839-8640

First published by AuthorHouse 1/27/2010

ISBN: 978-1-4490-6806-6 (e)
ISBN: 978-1-4490-6805-9 (sc)

Library of Congress Control Number: 2009914355

Printed in the United States of America
Bloomington, Indiana

This book is printed on acid-free paper.

This book is dedicated...

to the memory of **Eric S. Buharp** (1970-2008). Eric was a loving husband and son, a devoted father, a student of Civil War history and one of the most authentic and energetic Civil War re-enactors I had ever met. He always took the time to share his considerable knowledge of this most important period in American history with anyone who would but ask a question. Eric was a great friend and a truly a man's man; one who was taken from us much too soon.

in honor of my two precious grandchildren, **Chelsea Savannah Campbell** and **Nicholas McDaniel Hawthorne.** It is my prayer for them that their intelligence, love of country and energy will cause them and their generation to leave this nation a much better place than the one our generation left for them. I pray that with their devotion to the principles of the nation's foundation they may truly lead America to become the "Shining City On The Hill" that President Ronald Reagan saw for American.

"I have lived Sir, a very long time and the longer I live the more convincing proofs I see of this truth: that God governs in the affairs of men. And, if a sparrow cannot fall to the ground without His notice, is it less probable that an empire can rise without His aid?"

Benjamin Franklin…Address to the Constitutional Convention, June 28, 1787.
Mr. Franklin died April 17, 1790.

"With malice toward none and charity for all…"

Second Inaugural Address…President Abraham Lincoln, March 4, 1865.
President Lincoln was assassinated on April 14, 1865.

"Mr. Johnson, thank God that you are here Sir. Mr. Lincoln had too much of the milk of kindness to deal with these damned Rebels. Now they will be dealt with according to their deserts!"

Benjamin F. Wade, United States Senator from Ohio…Upon greeting the new 17th. President on April 19, 1865.

"It is time that we adopt some definite plan upon which the future prosecution of our struggle shall be conducted."

Jefferson Davis, President of the Confederate States of America…Address to his cabinet in Abbeville, South Carolina, May 2, 1865.
President Davis was captured by the Fourth Michigan Cavalry on May 10, 1865 at Irwinsville, Georgia

"War is the supreme test of man in which he rises to heights never approached in any other activity!"

Major General George S. Patton of World War I and II fame. (1885-1945)

Acknowledgements...

This is the location in the book where novelists advise their readers that the events and characters of this novel are fictional and spring from the imagination of the writer. I can not do that! I am passionate about the history of the Civil War and have gone to great lengths in my research to insure that I was not reinventing any of those events about which I was writing. Further, I have walked every battlefield and significant location included in this story. Though the story is a product of my imagination; the history is as accurate as I can make it.

As to the characters, with two exceptions, they also are the result of my creation. The two are **Bernard Craig Tierney**, often called BC, and the Union Army officer Thomas Moore. These names were "borrowed" from real people as a means of paying my respect to them. BC Tierney, first introduced in Chapter Eight was my closest and best friend throughout our navy days and much of our later life; and as a trusted warrior during our fourteen months in the Korean War together. Sadly he passed from this life in 1995...but not from my memory.

Thomas Moore is, and remains, a good friend and one who's own Civil War research I have shamelessly borrowed in this book and in the prequel, **"Burnin' Daylight!"**. An example of that research can be found in the Author's Notes at the end of Chapter Seven in the piece about the raid of Union Colonel Benjamin H. Grierson. Tom served this nation for 34 years in the United States Army and retired as a Colonel from the 81ˢᵗ Regional Support Command. He was originally introduced in the prequel with the rank of Colonel in the battle of White Mountain, but when I reintroduced him in Chapter Fourteen of this book I thought it time for his promotion and thus I awarded him his first star as a Union Brigadier General, correcting that obvious oversight by the U.S. Army.

I also am indebted to the many people who read various drafts of this story and suggested changes and corrections, and especially to my dear friend **Ann Shambo**. Ann spend many hours reading and suggesting changes that all served to make the story stronger. The errors which may remain are all mine, not theirs and certainly not Ann's!

And, I will forever be grateful to my Great Grandfather, **John Wallis**, who during this Civil War served as a Private in Company E, the 19th Iowa Volunteers of General Ulysses Grant's Army of the Frontier. As influential and inspiring as his experiences became to me, it was my daughter **Gina Lynn Wallis** who did the initial research on the history of his regiment and from that first sparked my curiosity about Grandpa John and his wartime experiences, some of which have found their way into these two books. Thank you Gina!

Last, but certainly not least is my **"Little Brother" Roger** who led me through the formatting changes required to get this book in print. He is the technology expert and tireless consultant who made this book a reality!

I do hope you approve of these results and enjoy this story.

UP TRAIL!

Coming Forward From

BURNIN' DAYLIGHT!

This novel, *"Up Trail"* is the sequel to *"Burnin'Daylight!"*. While it is the author's hope that you would have first read *"Burnin'Daylight!"*; if you have not done so, perhaps this "Forward" will help you catch up on the adventures thus far.

In the year of our Lord 1861, the reader will meet John Michael Kelley, the 17 year old son of a southeastern Iowa homesteader. Like many 17 year old young men, John is filled with wanderlust and a desire to see what adventure might await him just over the next hill. With his Pa's blessing, John volunteers in Fort Madison, Iowa, for one year of service with the Iowa 14th Volunteer Regiment and will become part of newly commissioned General Ulysses Grant's Army of The Frontier. In the next thirteen months, he will be a part of five major battles in the great American Civil War's western campaign, and distinguishing himself, will be promoted to Corporal. His service eventually leads him to the most costly battle of the entire war in the west; the two-day battle which the Union called Pittsburg Landing but history would name simply "Shiloh". *"Burnin'Daylight!"* begins as John regains consciousness on the battlefield at night following the second day's fighting; during which, his squad was over-run by elements of the Confederate army. John decides the time of his muster is more than expired and the army just forgot to say, "Thank you", and tell him he could leave, so he prepares on his own to do so.

While scavenging the now deserted and ghostly battlefield for the supplies for his trip into the west, John encounters a severely wounded Confederate Lieutenant, Andrew Glenn McCord from the Hill Country of Texas, serving in the Arkansas 6th. Resisting his training to kill this enemy, John and Glenn make an uneasy pact to help each other; Glenn to return to his home in Texas before he dies of his wounds and John to his imagined new life in the west.

Along the trail west these former enemies must employ all of their training and daring to elude capture by either of the two warring armies, or the bands of bounty hunters roaming the frontier; each day brings a new danger and a new challenge to their freedom. The two spend their nights by the campfires questioning each other's understanding of "The War" from two very different backgrounds. Weak from lack of sleep and nourishment and nearing the end of their endurance, the two are taken in and aided by the young widow of a Confederate Captain, who was killed in a battle in which John fought for the Union side. As the men recover sufficiently to ride on, John realizes he has fallen in love with her but leaves her behind as he fulfills his pledge to see Glenn home.

In their further adventures, they will team up on the trail with a very pregnant woman escaping from Vicksburg, aided by her newly freed slave. The four will attempt to break her husband, a captured Union Naval Officer out of the largest prisoner-of-war compound west of the Mississippi River; Camp Ford in Tyler, Texas.

Upon arriving at Glenn's family home in Texas, John will write a letter to the Confederate widow he left behind in Arkansas, confessing his love for her and asking her to marry him, but as the story closes he has no answer.

Now you are ready for the young men's adventure to continue in *"Up Trail!"*.

Enjoy!

Up Trail – THE PROLOGUE

During the winter of 1862 and the spring of 1863, the former enemies, Union Corporal John Michael Kelley and Confederate Lieutenant Andrew Glenn McCord began their slow recovery from their wounds and the fatigue of war in The Hill Country of Texas; as the Great American Civil War labored on without end in sight. The Union armies and river navy continued to successfully prosecute the war in the west, while President Lincoln began to use up Union Generals trying to find one who could out maneuver and ultimately defeat Confederate Generals Robert E. Lee and Stonewall Jackson in the eastern campaign. The first to be fired was George McClellan, he the much-heralded successor to the hero of the Mexican War, General Winfield Scott. President Lincoln once wrote to General McClellan, "If you and not going to be using the army I would like to borrow it". The fired McClellan would in 1864 run against Lincoln for the Presidency. McClellan was followed by General Ambrose Burnside, and though he contributed little toward a Union victory, he would at least be the cause of the word "sideburns" to be added to the lexicon as the name for the bushy, mutton-chops hair growth down his cheeks. General McClellan and Burnside each would fail repeatedly to press their timely advantage, their superior numbers and their superior armament to hasten the war's end. Each would be consistently "out-generaled", especially by Confederate General Lee, who most often had to defend with vastly inferior numbers.

On December 12, 1862, after numerous delays caused by his indecision, Burnside would attack Lee at Fredericksburg, Virginia, bringing on a crushing Union defeat that cost the Union almost thirteen thousand causalities to Lee's less than five thousand. Burnside would be fired by President Lincoln three weeks later on January 25, 1863, and replaced by General Joe Hooker. Hooker would last but three and one-half months until May 1, 1863, when his poor judgment would cause a disastrous Union defeat this time at Chancellorsville, Virginia, against a force one-half his size that would inflict eighteen thousand Union causalities. General Hooker was known not to discourage the hordes of female camp-followers who moved with his troops. Thus, the word, "hookers" would come into common and permanent use in the language. Following his defeat, General Hooker would be fired as Lincoln suffered yet again with McCellan, who Lincoln would again fire in favor of General George Meade. Meade would serve in command of The Army of The Potomac until the end of the war. On October 9, 1863, Lieutenant-General Ulysses Simpson Grant came east and was appointed as the Commanding General of all Union armies. His orders to General Meade were simple and to the point, "Where Lee goes, you will go with him!"

Prior to Grant's new appointment however, on December 28 and 29, 1862, General William T. Sherman, acting under orders from General Grant would open the Vicksburg campaign for the Union by being soundly defeated by Confederate General John C. Pemberton at Chickasaw Bluff, Mississippi. After failing in five attempts to reroute the course of the Mississippi River away from the guns of Vicksburg, in April, 1863, Grant would execute a brilliant tactic and march his troops around Vicksburg on the west side of the Mississippi River through the bayous and swamps of Louisiana to the village of Hard Times, well south of his prize. Here, utilizing the barges and transports that had run downstream under the Confederate guns on the river cliffs protecting Vicksburg, he would again cross to the river's east side at Bruinsburg, Mississippi. In rapid succession, Grant would win battles at Port Gibson and Raymond and capture the Capitol of Jackson from General Joe Johnston. Grant's forces would cut all railroad supply lines to Vicksburg and prevented the Confederate forces there from being supplied or reinforced. General Pemberton failed to halt Grant's advance at Champion's Hill and the Big Black River bridges and on May 18, 1863, the door to Vicksburg was slammed shut and the siege began. Forty-seven days and nights of constant bombardment of the city from the land and the river would follow until the unconditional surrender on the Confederate forces on July 4, 1863. As Grant watched the defeated Confederate army exit the city, he again considered his decision to halt all exchanges of prisoners with the Confederates. The reason; of the nearly 20,000 who surrendered and were able to march out of Vicksburg, he again saw many of the same faces who had surrendered to his forces at Fort Donelson, Kentucky, on February 16, 1862, and had been then pardoned to their homes. Men from 28 states would fight at Vicksburg, with numerous units from the state of Missouri fighting on both sides, and opposing each other.

On January 1, 1863, President Lincoln would issue his Emancipation Proclamation freeing the slaves in those states then in revolt against the United States. This was the Proclamation that John and Glenn had first heard about while at the Camp Ford prison compound in Tyler, Texas. Horace Greeley, the Publisher of the New York Tribune, would comment in an Editorial; "Lincoln freed those slaves he could not reach and left in bondage those he could have reached." The value of the slave population held in the south at the time of the 1860 census was estimated at $4 billion (in 1860 dollars).

On February 7, 1863, Lincoln refused an offer by the government of France to mediate the end of the war.

On February 16, 1863, the United States Senate passed the Conscription Act to begin the drafting of men into the Union army; the Act would be finally approved on May 3. However Northerners could avoid military service by paying $300 for a "substitute". Such legal 'draft dodgers' would include future United States President

Grover Cleveland and the father of future President Teddy Roosevelt. The Confederate States had begun their draft one year earlier on April 16, 1862, also with a great number of exemptions.

On February 26, 1863, the Cherokee Nation National Council declared its support for the Union. This, after fighting on the Confederate side from March 1 through March 8, 1862, in the losing effort at the largest land battle west of the Mississippi River, the Battle of Pea Ridge, Arkansas, called Elkhorn Tavern by the forces of the South.

In the spring of 1863, Confederate General Robert E. Lee would begin planning his second invasion into the north; the first having ended at Antictam, Maryland, where on September 17, 1862, America would experience what would become 'the bloodiest day in all of the Nation's history'. Lee would march into Pennsylvania on June 3 leading to a 3-day battle in early July at Gettysburg involving 155,000 men from both sides. Lee would take 20,451 causalities, fully 1/3 of his invading force; a blow from which the Army of Northern Virginia would never recover.

"The War to Save the Union", or "The War of Northern Aggression", or sometimes just "The War" as though no other had ever been fought, would drag on until the surrender of the last Confederate General, Stand Watie on June 23, 1865, eleven weeks after Lee's surrender at Appomattox. Brigadier General Watie was a member of the Cherokee Nation.

Officially the war's causality count would be set at 640,000 Americans, more than all of the Nation's other wars COMBINED. However, because of the poor recordkeeping, most historians now place the final count closer to 720,000. Prior to the American Civil War, it was considered correct grammar to refer to this nation as, "The United States are…" denoting the nation as a loose federation of sovereign states; following the war that phrase would become, "The United States is…", almost 250 years following the landing of the Pilgrims the United States would finally become, **One Nation under God…".**

Chapter One

The Hill Country of Texas, April, 1863

The Decision

John's eyes were open; wide open! He had actually felt them fly open like a runaway window shade. He lay there attempting to focus on something familiar in the dark that surrounded him, because this dark suddenly scared the hell out of him! His body was beaded with sweat and whatever he was laying on was damp with what he had already been shed. He mind was racing to sort it all out; was this real…had he been awake or just reliving this nightmare? Whichever, he was truly scared by what he had 'seen'; as he had been every time he had been forced to 'live' it. Had he screamed out, was that what had wakened him, if so, what about the others in the house…had they heard him? It was all so clear, so detailed, but then it should be…because at least once it had been real!

It was now night on April 7, 1862; the battle of Pittsburg Landing was just over. The Union must have won, if you could call it that, at least the Confederates had withdrawn into the late afternoon sun of Middle Tennessee. He had just come to in the dark, curled up next to Chester's headless body. He and Chester, *what was that boy's last name anyway,* had exhausted all of their powder and were moving back from their position when that Reb. Cavalry rider had charged his horse into them. When John looked over his shoulder, all he could see was the glint of the sun flashing on the wildly swinging saber and the broad chest of that gray horse nearly on top of them, riding them to the ground. The rider had been right handed so it was Chester's head that rolled away as his body had tried to keep running; John was ridden to the ground as the big gray stumbled over the fallen body. Had that rider been left handed, well John wouldn't be here trying to sort out these nightmares.

He sat up, legs over the side of the narrow bed and rubbed his eyes to make the images fade away…for now. He had sent a letter asking Sarah to marry him, *how would she ever handle something like this… how would he ever even explain it to her without scaring her away?* Well he hadn't had an answer to his letter of four months ago; maybe she would just turn him down, likely be better for all of 'em.

* * * * *

"Alli Viene el Cartero! Alli Viene el Cartero! Miss Lucinda, the Post Rider, he comes!"

"Howdy Ma'am. I have here a letter for Mr. John Kelley, he still be a guest of y'all?"

"Yes. Yes he is. Thank you. May I offer you a drink of cool, spring water before you travel on?"

My Dearest John,
March 5, 1863
Ouachita County, Arkansas

It gave me such pleasure for the Post Rider to come to my door-yard with yours of January 7. The letter made the trip from Texas in but seven weeks and you will note that I have stopped to write immediately as the Post Rider promises to return and stop by in two days hence. Matt, since you were here he will no longer answer to Matthew, and I are relieved at the safe arrival and rapid recovery of you and Glenn. Thank you for your kind words regarding my care, but I believe it was your determination to fulfill your pledge to see Glenn home that caused you both to recover.

Before you and Glenn had topped the first rise to the west, the emptiness of your leaving had already settled into my life. Matt and I watched for some time in the hope you would return and ask us just once more to go with you. Yet I knew you well enough to know you would not. You had said your piece once and I knew you would not ask again. Had you, my answer would have been very different that second time. My Aunt who raised me in Little Rock had always told me she believed for every woman, God would provide one good man. During my life with John Henry, I was certain she had lied to me. Then you rode up my lane with Glenn in tow, both of you more dead than alive, and with you, the hope of her words slowly began to return to me. I watched helplessly as you put your life at risk to protect me from the renegades, and later saw you react when Mr. Simcox put his hands on me. I knew then that my Aunt had spoken the truth, for no man had ever stepped forward to protect me before. Your letter said your Mother called this Devine Intervention. I never thought of it that way before, but that is truly what it is; part of God's plan for our lives. And, I stood quietly by the gate, tears in my eyes, and watched as His plan for me rode off to the west.

I find I am much less able to maintain and protect the farm than I thought to be. I am afraid much of your hard work is no longer in evidence. The roads have been full of retreating and deserting Confederate soldiers. They are such a sorry lot; poorly clothed, poorly equipped and so poorly fed. At first I felt such concern for their plight and tried to help, but quickly became overwhelmed by their number. They broke into the barn for shelter and used the siding to start fires for warmth. At some point they stole one of the renegades' horses and our milk cow from my pasture. During a lull in the traffic, Matt and I moved the other three horses and your two calves into the back pasture where they can not be seen from the road, but I do not know how long they may be safe. I fear as I write this there may now be two men camping in the barn. Matt, Duke and I stay safely barricaded in the house during the day with the scattergun; I am certain you remember your introduction to my scattergun! Then we take care of our water, food and other needs at night.

John, if you have not figured it out by now, my answer to your wonderful proposal is most definitely YES! And, thank you for wanting us in your life. In the interest of time, I would come to you. But given the current conditions, I would be fearful for our safety on these roads. So I hope you will want us enough to come for us as we are oh so ready to be with you.

It is with great love and anticipation that we wait.

Yours Forever...Sarah

* * * * *

It was unusually cool in the west Texas Hill Country for an evening in early April in this year of our Lord 1863. It had been a wet spring and the grass on the prairies was already almost belly-tall to a Longhorn...had there been any Longhorns nearby to measure it on. Oh there were a few still held by the corral...Mr. McCord says in Texas you couldn't call yourself a rancher if'n you ain't got no cattle. But, with all of the men of Texas off fighting Indians or Federals, the cattle had all gone wild and run off the ranches to hide in the brakes and the draws and just propagate. For the most part, it wasn't even worthwhile going after them...there was no gold to be had for their sale and with the inflation of the confederate money; it became more nearly worthless each day. No one would ever trade anything of value for a cow, if they needed one for food they would just go off and fetch one out of the canyons.

The bluebonnets were spectacular, and because the warm, wet weather had come early and stayed late, everyone said it was the most beautiful spring they could remember…but people said something like that every year. The meadows and the wagon roads were alive with color. Even the normally grassy strip in the center of the wagon tracks were solid blue. John had wished his mother could see this picture as she loved flowers so. He would have welcomed the chance to show them to Sarah also. Sarah was just very much back in the front of his mind again, and now that her letter had finally arrived, he was both relieved and comforted to read just how she felt.

Angus McCord and John had sat for some time across from each other with the welcome warmth of the fire in the sunken pit in-between. Neither had spoken for some while. Angus looked over the top of his whiskey glass, the fire dancing in the remaining amber liquid his glass held. He thought John had been dozing, and then as he took a sip, the tip of John's cigar began to glow a brighter red. Angus kicked the remnants of a log back onto the fire with the toe of his boot. As the flames leaped and the glowing sparks were swept up into the black night sky, he used the fire light to study the face of this ex-union Corporal slumped across from him. Never in all of his life had Angus felt such a debt to another human being. This enemy soldier had brought his severely wounded, his only son, home from the Shiloh Church battlefield in Tennessee. He knew if this Yankee soldier had followed his training and the instincts honed during 13 months of bitter war, he would have killed Glenn as his enemy; or at least left him to die of his wounds as he saw to his own needs. *Thank you God that he did neither!*

This young man he now saw over the fire was still a boy really…just a tall, gangly, not-yet-done-growing-up boy; just over six feet but still too thin for his frame. But the things he'd seen, the things he's been called upon to do, had rushed him to manhood long before his time; things that would likely haunt him in the years to come. It was the hard look around the eyes that gave away the fact that his youth had been too-early and too-harshly taken from him. Those eyes were always moving, looking for danger…seeing around him what many others would miss. That instinct had kept him alive, and had kept his son Glenn alive during those long months they spent on the trail between the two warring armies. It seemed strange to think of his son as a "Glenn" when he had always been called, "Andrew". But he came home from the war called by his middle name and since it had always been the favorite with his mother, the name would stick. Angus thought of his own war experiences with General Sam Houston during the fight for Texas Independence. It was damn scary to him then, but it was next to nothing compared to the slaughter these young men had been a part of in but a few short months; why the Austin paper has said there were over twenty-four thousand casualties in just two days at Shiloh Church. Angus remembered when General Sam had come to their campfire one evening and a soldier ask him, "General, just how far are we gonna run backwards before we stand and fight the Mex.?"

Old Sam had studied their eager, young faces for a moment and said, "Just until Santa Anna gets tired of chasing us and has to stop to rest. Then we'll turn and kill him!"

 "But we're out numbered five to one, what makes you think we can kill him?"

"We'll get 'er done 'cause we're fighting for our homeland and because we **believe** we can do it!" And so they had!

John stretched and his cigar glowed again, so Angus offered, "I seen the Post Rider come calling by yesterday. That's twice since you arrived he's stopped by; believe his last visit afore you came was maybe years before that."

"I got an answer to one of those letters I wrote when I first got here. You'll recall that one to my folks you said I had to write, or move on? Well I haven't heard from that one yet, but then it had to cross through two armies. But when we find some time, I'll be talking to you about the message in the one that did come."

Somewhere back in one of the wings of the rambling, single story adobe house a baby cried out. Angus smiled at the pleasant sound, had been a very long time since such a pleasant sound came from within the house of Angus and Lucinda McCord. They had thought to never hear such coming from their house again…what with their son in the war and a daughter too independent for any man to corral. That would be three month old Master Michael Glenn Wagner announcing it was time for him to be fed. He had been born within a very few hours after John had driven Mrs. Lewis Wagner's team and wagon into the McCord's dooryard back in December. John said he was more scared about that baby comin' early on the trail than he ever had been in battle with the Confederates! Mrs. Wagner, Savannah, was a true Mississippi Belle, the daughter of Alexander Clayton, a Vicksburg delegate to the Secessionist Convention in Montgomery. Her daddy had the vision to see the eventual value of Vicksburg to the Union and the battle that would follow for control of the Mississippi River. He wanted her out of the city before it erupted. The real wonder was that she could convince John and Glenn that if they would help her and her newly freed slave, the four of them could get her Union Naval Captain husband out of the largest Confederate prisoner-of-war compound west of the Mississippi. These two boys saw those flashing eyes, the beautiful smile, and likely the tight bodice and said, "Sure, we can do that!" Angus wondered how many fool adventures had been started on less…likely a few wars, as well. Well, they got him out only for him to die in her arms a few days later…but maybe that's not such a bad way to go; to die in the arms of a beautiful woman who loves you. Then in a bit of the war's irony that Yankee Captain was buried in the family cemetery plot on the home site of Mr. John H. Reagan, the former Congressman from Texas and currently the Postmaster General of the Confederate States of America. Havin' a Yankee in among 'em was likely disturbing the eternal rest of Mr. Reagan's kinfolk.

Glenn McCord came through the arch still limping slightly, moving toward the two men and the warmth of the fire. Angus noted his son was wearing that same moon struck look on his face that he'd worn for months, almost since the moment Mrs. Wagner had arrived. *Damn, but I think that boy's in love.* Glenn hooked a chair with the toe of his boot and pulled it up to the fire ring. His Pa looked over and inquired, "How's it happen you're not in with Mrs. Wagner and your god-child? That's where we usually find you".

"Michael Glenn's gotta' eat, so Ma and Suzanne bid me to get out."

"So, you figure what...that's somethin' those three women can't do proper without your supervision?"

"If you two would quit jawing each other and give me a chance, I'd like to talk a little about the letter from Sarah that came this morning and what I'm aimin' do about it."

At which point Glenn piped-up, "The Post Rider come today? I didn't seem 'em."

"Son of mine, you ain't been out of that room long enough lately to even see sunshine! Since John's helped you acquire a taste for it, want a little sour mash with us?" Glenn and John both nodded in unison and Angus reached and filled glasses for them and of course his own. Angus kind of thought they might all could use a taste while John unraveled his news.

John took a taste of the liquid, puffed his cigar back to life, exhaled and started in. "I'm fixin' to go back to Arkansas! In her letter, Sarah allowed as how she may have made a mistake by them not leaving with us before, and she's just having lots of problems keeping the farm going. I thought it might be best if I went and took a look for myself."

"Boy, you plannin' on staying there or what have you got in mind?"

"I knew the minute I rode down her lane and turned that gray mare's head west to bring Glenn home, that I loved her and wanted to ask her to marry with me. So I aim to go do that proper. I think she's ready to throw in with me now and so, I'd like to get the two of em' and bring em' back to Texas so's we can be startin' a cattle ranch of our own someplace around here."

Glenn stood up and looked at John, "I'll be goin' with you!"

"I figured you to say that and, Glenn I do appreciate it, but it's my belief I should take Joshua along. If we're gonna try this wild-cow hunt when I return, the one Miss Lucinda keeps calling 'Angus' fool errand', you need to continue to rest up and recover. Besides, like the rest of us, Joshua ain't doing nothin' to earn his keep 'cept practice with that Colt all day. And, I know your folks, and especially Mrs. Wagner, would like it better if'n you were here. Anyway, that's the way I figure."

Glenn stood tall and took in a big breath to start his protest, but Angus held up his hand for silence. "I think that's sound reasonin' John. How long do you figure to be gone?"

"If we push hard, don't find too much trouble along the way and ride at least 30 to 40 miles a day, we can get up there in about 15 days. Probably the better part of two weeks to get Sarah and Matt ready to travel and the farm closed up…so I figure we'll be back here by mid-May, and ready to go down in the breaks wild cow-hunting shortly after that."

"And leaving here when?"

"I've been kind a gettin' organized in my head for the last two days, so the decisions are mostly made. I need to talk to Joshua and we need to load some .44's since Joshua's been blowing up the hillsides, but I'd say in a couple of days.

"John, we've got plenty of .44's loaded. You're welcome to take whatever you need."

"My experience with ammunition is; I've always found its best to have more than you'll likely need…for if you're caught with less than you need, somehow things have a way of not working out well. Gonna also have to find me some .56's for my Spencer. I figure when you begin a journey like this you should always expect the worst; that way you're never gonna be disappointed!"

As Angus was about to comment on that, Lucinda came through the arch to join the men, "Boy git up and give you mother your chair!" As the group all settled in around the warmth of the fire pit again she added, "John, I see you received a letter yesterday, I've been going to ask you about that but haven't seen much of you since, except at meals."

"Momma, he was just telling us it was from the lady in Arkansas, Sarah, who nursed me back to health, and he's fixin' to take Joshua and go fetch her and her boy."

"I thought as much from the look on his face since. I'm pleased you're not taking Glenn along. He's not ready to travel yet." Glenn scowled, but he knew to keep his tongue.

Angus felt the need to take back the conversation again, "John I'm gonna' give you and Joshua a new Henry .44, 16-shot repeater rifle and you can leave that Spencer here for one of my hands."

"Where'd you get two Henrys…they're not even in general issue to the army yet?"

"I've been to Austin to talk about our cattle drive with my friend from the War for Independence, S. G. Haynie. He offered up a case of 'em, and I couldn't disrespect his generosity by saying no."

"Lucinda said firmly, "So that's who you've been seeing on these trips to Austin the last few months, I was beginning to think you had a wild woman stashed away up there!"

"There's more wild women on this here ranch right now than any one man would be wise to try to handle. And with John's news, sounds like another one might be coming!"

"And Angus McCord, don't you ever forget it! Mrs. Graham and her boy would certainly be welcome as long as we have a roof. Who is this S. G. Haynie any way…he got a real name?"

"He's a Doctor, name's Samuel Garner, he's the Mayor of Austin for the second time, and we served General Sam together in '36. Besides that, he knows just about everything that's going on, especially in this part of the world, and got his hand in most of it."

"So I suppose you told him all about your "fool's errand" and he just thought it was a splendid idea?"

"Well he didn't think it a bad idea given' we got lots of cattle and no gold, while the Yankees' got lots of gold and no cattle. However he wasn't too excited about a drive into Missouri and I was intendin' to tell the boys about that when you come waltzin' out here and took over the men's conversation."

Even in the dimming fire light, the untrained eye could see Miss Lucinda's French-Creole blood coming to the surface. Angus just loved to get her started, but contained his smile and went on, "S. G. points out that going to Missouri would take the drive through both the Union and Confederate armies, likely more than once, and across the Nations and through the five tribes. Someone in all of that is just gonna have to try to take that herd away from us and we're likely not going to have enough men to stop them. If we even get to Missouri, they had a ban just before the war on Texas cattle 'cause of the Texas tick fever, so we'd likely have to fight them too while lookin' for a buyer with gold…just likely more than we'd be able to handle with a small crew. Oh, it could be done alright, been done before. Was called the Shawnee Trail in the 1840's, and later the Preston Road; and went clean to St. Louis. But S.G. thinks it's an unnecessary risk. There ain't no war in the Colorado mining camps and there's plenty of gold to buy our cattle. So S. G. had me go talk to the Butterfield Stage drivers who run from Austin up through the New Mexico Territory towards Santa Fe. After one get's across the desert, the trails not too rough and with good water and grass much of the way. The Confederate army was driven out of New Mexico Territory in '82 and the Union has a number of garrisoned forts needing cattle; and there's plenty of gold coming in from the Colorado and California fields to buy with. Just seems like the way to go. And, that's what I've been thinkin' on. With John and Joshua on the trail for a spell, it'll give us time to get a crew and equipment put together. Then when they return we'll be ready to go to the Johnson and Midland River Draws cow-huntin'"

"Its good thinkin' Pa'; how many men you figure we gonna' need?"

"Well, we use to figure a rider for every 200 head, plus probably two men for the horse remuda, a cook and maybe a cook's helper, and a trail scout. This being our first drive with wild cattle and given who we're trying to sell to, I'd like to hit the trail with about fifteen hundred head. So that's, let's see…eleven or twelve men. With Joshua, there's four of us plus Pedro's five, so we've got some recruitin' to do and I already spoke to Pedro about some of his family goin' with us and maybe getting' some horses from them. Problem is folks are gonna' have to throw in with us for shares at the end of the drive 'cause there ain't no money around that's worth a damn."

"What about horses, how many of them we gonna' need?"

"Well, I recon' at least two per rider cause a drive will just plain wear out horse flesh. Need a four-up on the chuck wagon plus a change. So were looking at about 30 head, now we got some of these and most riders will have one mount of their own, but we're gonna' need to find about 20 head I would figure, plus a chuck wagon, so we plain got us things to do while John's in Arkansas. But I think all of these are doable, and for me that makes it a go!"

Angus looked for a moment at the face of each one assembled around the fire and no one was shaking their head 'no'…Lucinda didn't like the idea, but she had no better one to offer to save all that they had worked so hard for. After surveying the faces, Angus topped off the men's glasses and poured a taste for his beautiful wife; then he raised his glass toward the dying fire and said, "Here's to our goin' ***up trail!***"

"What's that mean goin' up trail?"

"Back in the days before the war with Mexico, men trying to start a new and better life in this new territory would go into Mexico to get cattle; likely some of them cattle even got paid for. They'd drive 'em back to the Texas Territory and since that was goin' north it was called going up the trail. Well in time it just naturally got shortened to "up trail" and became the cattle driver's call ever since, regardless to which direction he was a goin'.".

And, the three raised their glasses with him, touched them together as they echoed, *"up trail!"*

Author's Note...

During each month of the entire Civil War, three or four ships would set sail from San Francisco loaded with millions of dollars worth of gold...wealth that would fuel the Union during the long and costly war. In the ten year period just prior to the start of the war, more gold came out of the California mines than the total amount the **entire** world had produced in the preceding 150 years! All of that started when on January 24, 1848, James W. Marshall discovered a large gold nugget in a stream at Sutter's Mill in northern California...that find would launch the gold rush of '49. California, however, came very close to becoming part of the Confederacy...an alliance that perhaps might have changed the entire outcome of the war.

Many Californians had been born in southern states and maintained their sympathies with the southern cause. In the election of 1860 Abraham Lincoln had only received 32% of the votes cast in the state. But an effort to join with the state of Oregon in forming the "Pacific Republic" and then later joining the Confederacy were both defeated in favor of joining with the Union. The reasons were mostly economic; the miners, regardless of where they were born, did not want to compete against the use of slave labor in the mines, or against the companies who would use slave labor in their mines.

The battle to control California (and Colorado) gold began in earnest early 1862. Confederate Brigadier General H. H. Sibley assumed command of the Confederate forces on the upper Rio Grande

River and in all of the territories of New Mexico. Almost without opposition Sibley captured Tucson in February and by March 1, Albuquerque, and Santa Fe, and having established The Confederate Territory of Arizona, he then headed out northeast to capture the last remaining Federal strongpoint at Fort Union. Filled with the same concerns as their California counterparts, 900 Colorado volunteers, mostly miners, joined with the Union forces and in a bold raid on the Confederate supply depot at Pigeon's Ranch destroyed all of Sibley's supplies. Without ammunition, food, fodder, or replacements the Confederates retreated to Santa Fe, and then fled ahead of the pursuing Union forces through Albuquerque and back into Texas. Thus for the remainder of the war ending any hope the Confederacy might have held of conquering the Southwest and gaining access to the rich western mines and gold fields.

Chapter Two

THE WAY TO SARAH

John hurried through the kitchen on his way out the back door, his new Henry rifle slung casually over his shoulder as he held the barrel for balance. He noted Lucinda sitting on a stool at her work space peeling and slicing apples, and stopped to watch. He had paused mainly because he just loved to look at her, he thought her such an elegant lady. She was a slight built woman who appeared taller than she actually was because of her slight frame. Her features were dark, in part from working for years beside her husband in the hot Texas sun, and part would be her French-Louisiana ancestry showing through. Her shinny black hair that now was heavily streaked with gray, was as always, pulled tight and captured behind her head. As she sensed his presence and looked up, he smiled at her and said, "I remember when I was a small boy watching my momma peeling our apples. I would always challenger her to peel the whole apple without letting the peeling break."

"And, could she peel the entire apple without it breaking?"

"Yes, but she would only do it once just to show me she could. Said it was wasteful 'cause she had to peel it thicker; and in my family, we tried hard not to waste anything! She would have a tin cup close by and when she had a 'specially fine apple, she would save the seeds. Later we would soak them in water for a spell and then plant 'em, first in the hot beds and later moving the seedlings to the ground; most of our orchard came that way. I remember Momma telling me, "Anyone can tell you how many seeds there are in an apple, but only God knows how many apples there are in a seed.""

"There's a special way your face lights up when you talk about her, I noticed it before. You must have been very close, you and your Mother."

"Yes Ma'am we surely were, and I do miss her. She was a teacher back east 'fore she married Pa and she taught us boys to read and write, and to do ciphers so we could get more pleasure from the world. Every day she would get out the Bible and that blue New England Primer she had from her teachin' days and we'd do our readin' lessons."

"What are you doing with the new rifle, you goin' hunting?"

"No ma'am, Joshua and me are gonna sight 'em in."

"Now what's that all about?"

"These Henry's are military rifles so they have an adjustable rear sight. We'll set the sights to hit dead center at about 200 yards. Then if your target is further away or closer than 200, we just adjust our eye up or down on the notches in the sight. Though if it's much over 200 yards, most of the time you're just wasting the lead anyway."

"Oh, I see," Though from the expression on her face, John seriously doubted that she did. He picked up his Henry and again started for the door. "John, when do you plan to leave to go for Sarah?"

"I think just at first light tomorrow. I want to get there and back so's we can start our cow-huntin'!"

"Alright, much as I hate for you to leave, I do understand your need to do so. I have a few food items for your trip that I will get together today then. You be certain that nice lady and her son know how much we want to welcome them here! I can't get over what she did for you and Glenn. John, is it alright for me to go into your room put out some things?"

"Ma'am, a couple of things…about the food items, please remember we're a traveling by horse back, so all we have is a couple a saddle-bags. And, of course you can go into my room, this is after-all, your house!"

"John, you are a member of this family and I would not violate your privacy anymore than I would Glenn's without at least asking first. Among that wagon load of things that Dr. Haynie sent home with Angus were some new and different men's trousers that look to be more comfortable and cooler than those wools you wear. Seems there is a maker of sails for sailing ships in San Francisco, German man named Strauss, who started making trousers for the gold miners. He uses dyed cotton sail cloth, double stitches the seams and puts rivets at all of the pressure points. Doctor Haynie told Angus they wear like iron, and I thought you and Joshua might like to try them on your trip. Most of the time I think that Doctor is a crazy old coot, but he does like Angus and every once in a while he stumbles on a good idea, though I **do not** think this cattle drive is one of them. But like Angus, I can't think of anything better."

"Ma'am, I'd be pleased to try 'em and thank you. As for the other, much as I hate to say it to you, I do not believe the Confederates can, or will, win this war and most especially if England and France stay out of it. But it's going to be a long process of just wearing each other away and in that process the south will be bled dry…not only of her manpower, but her wealth as well; you can see what's happened after only two years, Confederate money's not worth a tinkers. Then after the South surrenders, the Federals will bring down an occupation army that'll stay for a long time. Any Southerner with property who can't physically protect it and can't pay the taxes on it will lose it, and by pay taxes, I mean in Federal dollars, or gold. That's the harsh truth of it…if we don't get our hands on some real Yankee gold and get enough to put some away, this place…this life's work of yours will be gone, likely to someone who has not yet even arrived in these parts! We paid the taxes on Sarah's place for a couple of years, but there's no way she can protect it, probably not even if I was there. As I've heard said, we should enjoy the war cause the peace will be terrible! No Ma'am, I've thought on it long and hard and as desperate as this roundup and drive sounds, it's about the only chance we've got to get ready for what's coming…just a sure as tomorrow, it's comin'! Now, if I could steal me a piece of that apple, I'll be gettin' to it."

Lucinda used her paring knife to spear a peeled half of apple from her bowl and held it out for John. He took it, and as he smiled at her his whole face just lit up; picking up the Henry he moved on out the kitchen door. *God I love that boy,* she thought.

* * * * *

This evening the temperature was becoming more pleasant, but still the fire blazing in the hacienda fire pit felt good. Again, the three men had gathered, this time for their last nightly drink together for some time. Finally Angus broke the silence, "What time you figure to leave in the morning?"

"Plannin' on just before first light. That should have us at Marshall's Ford on the Llano River about dawn."

Angus followed, "You satisfied that you know the way to the Graham's place?"

"Glenn and I pooled our thoughts today and drew a map from our memory, then had Mrs. Wagner look at it also. I'm right hard to lose after I get things straight in my mind, 'sides I've got this compass that'll help."

"Let's see that boy, that's a fine looking instrument. *'Captain Jonas P. Markum'.*" Angus turned the shinny brass compass in the firelight as he read. "You know this Captain Markum?"

"No Sir. I don't, but when I picked it up, he surely wasn't going to be using it any more."

Through all of the exchange, Glenn remained silent, and struggled to keep his mouth shut. Finally he could stand it no longer and snapped, "Pa he took it off a dead Confederate Officer at Shiloh 'fore we left."

"Well it's too good a thing to just leave lay on the ground…especially when the owner is no longer gonna be using it. It's just one of the parts of war Son, where do you think the bay horse that carried you home came from? Get over it!" Angus added.

"How about your gear? You and Joshua got all you need?"

"We got our bed roll with an oil slick ground blanket, some cookin' gear, plenty of .44 cartridges and I'm gonna take the scattergun also. Glenn let Joshua take the pack he was using when we arrived. And, I have no idea how much food stuff we'll be hauling; Miss Lucinda's been in there packing for us all day."

Angus reached behind him and brought out a near-new wide brim, western hat with a black leather band and extended it to John. "I'd like you to wear this hat instead of that old beat-up thing you've been a wearin'."

"Well I appreciate the offer, sir, but that's your hat and I couldn't take it, I might just decide I like it and never give it back, or worse, might get a hole shot in it."

"I want you to have it, you and I are partners now and well, you see out here in Texas with cowboys it all starts with the hat…a man won't be taken as a serious cowboy unless he's wearin' a cowboy's hat, otherwise folks might think I've thrown in with an Iowa sodbuster and I can't be doin' that to my reputation."

"We both wish you God's speed boy and we'll be watching for your return." Then Angus added, "Now go get 'er done, Yankee!"

* * * * *

As first light approached on April 14, 1863, while John and Joshua are trying to again trail break their horses, Union troops engaged the Confederates at Bayou Teche, Louisiana. During this engagement the Union forces bombarded and destroyed the former Union vessel *Queen of the West*, now in Confederate hands. This is the ship, named for the city of Chicago that Mrs. Wagner's husband, Captain Lewis Wagner, had commanded prior to his capture by the Confederates; that had followed with his internment at the Camp Ford prisoner-of-war compound where his wounds brought him near death.

* * * * *

The dawn sun was just balanced on the eastern hills as the two men reined up at the Ford. John pulled down on his new cowboy wide-brim hat to offer some relief from the glare. The morning fog still lay in the low areas around the crossing as the water ran cold and swift in front of them. The recent rains upstream had raised the water above the normal level. John said, "We'll cross first, then water the horses from the other side, I want to get a look at the ground on the other bank." The gray mare was back to her old ways and very skittish as she approached the swift running stream. John put his heals into her flanks and finally she took a first tentative step off of the bank. Finding it not to her liking, she danced sideways all the way to the opposite side. John dismounted, handed the reins to Joshua so he could water, and moving away from the crossing, he studied the ground. "Been some unshod ponies cross here, I'd say not long ago…maybe five or six of 'em heading out to the east."

"What do you make of that Mister John?"

"First Joshua, don't give me any of your 'Mister John' crap! You and I've been 'John' and 'Joshua' since we shot our way out of the German's saloon in Texarkana and you kept that Roberts brother from back-shootin' me, so you don't get to go 'house-boy' on me now. We clear on that? I'd say Indians, five or six of 'em a few hours ahead of us heading down our trail; in this area they'll most likely be Comanche. We're going to have to be watchful...very watchful." Both men pulled their Colts and checked the loads for the fourth time since riding under the McCord's *A-L* sign.

"John I'd like to learn to read a sign...seems a good way to stay alive in this country. Will you show me what you see?"

"Alright, hunker down here with me. Look at this man-track; it's clearly a moccasin print, most likely Indian, but some whites do wear 'em also. See how the sand is darker around the foot print...that's from recent moisture, since we've had no rain today; it's most likely this morning's dew. Now look down in the bottom of the print; the sand is much lighter 'cause it's dry; a man stepped here after the dew had already fallen. When we were getting our horses packed in the dark this morning, the dew was wetting our clothes; so this man has walked here since then. Looking at the eastern horizon, the sun is not yet full up so I'd say it's about half-past six now. So that print was made within the last two hours, putting 'em close in front of us."

"How do you know if'n it's Indian or a white man?"

"You've gotta' read what your given. The horses are unshod; if he was a white man, his horses most likely would be wearing shoes. Also, look at the hoof marks; they are narrower and not as deep in the sand as our horses. Indian ponies are usually lighter and smaller. Then look again at the moccasin prints. See how they go forward in a straight line one behind the other; a white man will walk with his toes pointed slightly out while an Indian, as the trackers say, always walks pointin' north and south."

"How'd you know many there are, with the tracks all jumbled up?"

"Well, I try to find matching pairs of front hoof marks, and when I do that gives me one horse. Now look here where they came out of the stream, there are clearly four good sets and this other set is where the horse stumbled. I make it most likely five, but maybe six…but, no more than that. That's how I think I know there are five or six Indians less than two hours ahead of us, going along our trail."

All that day the young men constantly scanned the hills, looking for the Indians they knew were close by…but to no avail. That first night camp on the trail was a nervous one with out much in the way of sleep. They had a cold camp and were up and moving with the first light of day.

* * * * *

John and Joshua spent the day continuing their close watch of the nearby hills for the five that they knew were still trailing just ahead of them. Hundreds of miles to the east twelve river gunboats, under the command of the young Union Admiral David Porter, sailed through the bombardment of the Confederate batteries at Vicksburg. This was a critical initial step that would seal the ultimate loss to the South of Savannah Wagner's hometown and with it, final control of the vital Mississippi River.

* * * * *

They did not stop for the noon meal, but slowed to a walk for their biscuits, cold bacon and water. Each man had been watching the crest of the hills around them for any signs of 'company' but seeing none, had now begun to relax. They were about two hours into the afternoon when Joshua first spotted the silhouettes of the riders paralleling them on the crest of a hill to the north…there were five riders in single file visible against the afternoon sky and making no attempt to hide. "John, what do ya' think that means, what are they up to?"

"Well. I'm no frontier Indian fighter, but given they obviously have us five to two; they're certainly showing us no fear, figuring they can take us whenever they want…whenever they get ready. They are most likely after the horses and our weapons…and likely our scalps. If it was me, I'd wait till after we settle in for the night, come callin' on us, then grab our horses and take whenever they fancy…likely including some hair. We'll just watch 'em for now, I don't think they are gonna come at us till after dark. I also think should they, these 16 shot Henrys may present a hell of a surprise, especially if they was to try us out in the open. If they do come charging us, the Henrys'll kind of help equalize the numbers. Now knowin' they are there and what their likely up to, we'll have a chance to rig a little welcome for 'em after dinner, if they decide to wait that long."

The two men rode at a mile-eating lope keeping a careful watch on their company, until the sun had dropped out of sight and by then the trailing Indians had just as suddenly disappeared. Then, while the sun was still offering a little light to the ground, the men moved off the trail and into a draw with a narrow, quick running stream in its base. The small canyon ran back from the opening about two hundred yards, then where a spring fed the stream, the ground rose sharply to the bluff above.

"Joshua, this looks like a good place to camp and wait for our 'visitors', if they're comin'. We'll build our fire at the mouth of the draw, and then after dark we'll wait back down here beyond the fire light. The breeze is moving up the draw, so that's the way they'll come up on us; from down wind so's not to spook our horses. Alright, let's set up our camp, get a quick bite of food, and then look over our field of fire while we still have the advantage of the light."

The young men hobbled their horses in the good grass just outside of the mouth of the draw, and then gathered plenty of wood for a large fire. They laid out their bedrolls propped up against the saddles with their hats tilted over the ends, put on some coffee and with the Henrys and Colts fully loaded, pick the best places of concealment to wait…wait for whatever might come down the draw and into the circle of firelight.

"Joshua, put your big skinning knife into the top of your right boot next to your leg where you can get at it. They'll most likely send at least two bucks down to do us in…maybe if we're lucky, three or four might come into the fire light, but at least one will be left to stay back and we'll have to hunt him down after."

"Why won't they just go for our horses and then take off?"

"These are young Comanche bucks that will mainly want our weapons and our scalps to sing about at their campfires, 'sides they figure they can get our horses anytime after they get us. Now get comfortable and quiet and be prepared to wait 'em out."

And, they waited…and waited as they heard the braves "call" to each other in the draw. "Sounds like night birds", Joshua noted.

"You can trust me on this; those night birds are wearing feathers alright, but also likely braids and moccasins!"

About an hour before the moon set, the Indians began to move cautiously forward, stopping first at the edge of the diminished fire light. John had caught himself snoozing a couple of times during their long watch and as the 'guests' finally started forward, was again nodding with his eyes closed. He jerked awake as Joshua's elbow found his ribs. When he looked at his companion, he could see the whites all around Joshua's eyes, and with a nod of his head toward their camp, Joshua pointed out the reason why. Three braves had come cautiously into the remaining circle of light, while a fourth was just visible at the beginning of the darkness. As the men watched, the three moved toward the sleeping forms with lances raised, and the fourth now followed them further into the camp. With his hands, John indicated the two he would take and the two Joshua was to take. The poised braves stopped then slashed their lances downward into the forms made by the piled blankets, then looked up expectantly; John nodded and the two Henrys spit fire in unison, once then twice, and the four were on the ground. "Joshua, use your Colt and be damn certain they're finished, I just heard the fifth one step in the stream up the draw. I'll see if I can stop him."

Behind him, John heard the Cold fire four times in rapid succession. As he came into a clearing at the mouth of the draw, John heard, and then saw the running pony as he charged up the hill. For a brief moment at the crest, horse and rider were silhouetted against the waning moon. Doubting he could hit the rider at such a distance, John instead shot the hard running horse. In full gallop, the horse crashed to the ground and the rider went airborne over the head of the falling animal. John took off on a run toward his kill. The Indian had been propelled into a stand of young pine trees and had died instantly with a broken neck; the horse was floundering with a chest wound and a broken front leg. John made no apology to the Indian, but did to the horse just before his Colt fired to end the animal's suffering.

When he returned to the camp, John found Joshua just sitting quietly, back against a tree, looking at the four dead Indians. They were all young, likely just in their teens, out to make their reputation with the elders. "I certainly hope we don't run into any rain." Joshua observed.

"Why's that a bother at a time like this?"

"Well just look here, they done slashed our bedrolls and our ground blankets all to hell. If'n it rains, we're gonna' get wet".

"Likely that's a small price to pay. Least it'll be raining on the tops of our heads and not in our dead, upturned faces."

They pulled the dead, young braves out of their camp area and into the dark beyond, then sat and drank the coffee they had made earlier. John decided Joshua's coffee would be much improved with a little sour mash and retrieved the bottle from his saddlebag. "You want to try some in your coffee?"

"Does it help the taste any?"

"Joshua, I'm Irish and we learn young in life there's not much that whiskey can't make better...and even if you should find something it can't, it damn sure won't make it any worse! You know, according to Saint Timothy, the Lord said, *'Take a little wine for thy stomach's sake and thine other infirmities.'* Had they had any good sour mash Irish whiskey in those days, I'm certain The Lord would have said, *'Take a little Irish.'"* With that assurance, Joshua extended his cup.

"This would be the first whiskey I've had since you served me that drink in the German's saloon in Texarkana after the shoot-out, when that old barkeep wouldn't serve me."

"That surprises me; I know there's drinking goin' on in the bunkhouse where you've been staying. Don't they offer you any?"

"Oh sure, but all the Mexicans just drink Tequila, so that's what I been drinkin'."

"Never had any…what's it like?"

"Well its mostly clear…maybe a little cloudy yellow cast to it, and got a damn good kick. It'll flat sneak up on a person. The Mexicans told me it's made from the sweet sap of the Magueys plant, a kind of Agava, that's then fermented. It's called for the town in Jalisco where it was first made…good stuff and cheap; that's why we drink it…more kick for the dollar."

Taking a deep pull from the sour mash bottle, John said, "You know Joshua; there is much to be admired about Indians. They are the finest cavalry in the world, why they will ride a horse till he drops, stop and eat 'em, then go fight on foot or steal another horse. Many of their beliefs are so simple, yet so pure. The Indian believes that the tree, the flower and man all have the same soul. That it matters not if you live 100 years, or but one day; before the gods all are equal and each has had a full life."

"How come an Iowa homesteader would know so much about Indians?"

"I grew up living next to the "Half-Tract" area in Iowa, that's an area the whites set aside for Indiana half-breeds as they took over the Territory. My best friend growing up was a boy about my age named Eye-Of-The-Hawk who had a white father and a Sac mother. Most of the things I know about Indians, he explained to me including how to read tracks."

"But, that's done, now getting back to our travels, Joshua; I think we should plan on stoppin' and make our manners to Mr. Friel when we get to Texarkana, I know the German would feel bad if'n he heard we just passed him by and didn't at least say 'howdy'. I'm sure not gonna stop on the way back with Sarah and Matt with us. So, what do you think?"

"Well, it would be worth the ride just to see the look on his face and watch him go through not serving me again! But, how'd I know you're not just gonna get us in trouble?"

"If you want to go, I promise I'll not start anything…I'll be just as sweet as my momma raised me to be."

Joshua gave John a look that suggested he may not fully believe him, but nodded and said, "Yeah, let's do it. Let's go make a nice social call on an old friend!" By the dying fire, the bottle was passed more than once. Eventually, in spite of the excitement of the evening and the tattered bedrolls, the young men slept well during what was left of that night.

Author's Notes…

Confederate money would become one of the most notorious examples of bogus currency in history. In the four years from 1861 to 1865, the South printed over twice as much paper money as the North. The Confederate government began to issue money from the first capital in Montgomery, Alabama on April, 28 1861. However, only 4,426 notes were issued there before the capital was moved to Richmond, Virginia, where the Confederacy started to print money in large quantities. By the end of 1864 these issues totaled nearly two billion dollars! In addition, the individual states, territories, banks, municipalities and even associations all began to print their own money; over 150 unique individual bonds were issued. As a result, Confederate money suffered devaluation by a factor of over a thousand before the war's end. After the South had won the war, the promise was to have been interest paid at the rate of 2 cents per day for each $100 denomination. When first issued in 1861, the Confederate dollar would traded for 95 cents in gold. By 1863, the value had dropped to only 33 cents and by the time of Lee's surrender on April 9, 1865, it was trading for only 1.6 cents value in gold. On May 1, 1865, the last active trading day, it took 1,200 Confederate dollars to purchase one U.S. gold dollar.

Chapter Three

THE LIFE OF A SLAVE

As they rode out of their night camp and again turned to the east, John swung around in his saddle and watched as the buzzards began their lazy circles overhead. He was always fascinated by the way they could find an upward wind current and drift for hours without flapping a wing. He knew the buzzards would prefer to feast on the horse, but would go for the braves first because the skin wasn't so tough and they could get at their meal with less effort. He felt a pang of sorrow for a brief moment; he'd been on battlefields and witnessed what the bodies of the dead looked like after a buzzard feast. But then remembered the plan had been for him and Joshua to be the feast, not to just watch it from a safe distance.

There were no more Comanche's to interrupt their progress, so by time for sunset two days later, they were just to the west of the Trinity River in east-central Texas, although that first day of travel after nearly finishing the bottle of sour mash had been hard on their aching heads. It seemed that day each step the horses had taken had been a reminder of just how hard they had hit that bottle the night before. But as many equally foolish men through time had done, they silently endured the punishment. The days had been uneventful and travel smooth; while they saw but a few other riders, all were white and seemed no more anxious to make any social contact than were John and Joshua. John found himself wondering if some of those other riders might not be Confederate deserters trying hard not to draw any attention. Not many were just walking and for good reason…this was certainly not good country to be afoot, what with the Comanche roaming further and further south of the Nations and the Red River. A man had best be good friends with his horse; for a man afoot in Indian country is a man who may not live to see another day. That's why horse stealing is a hanging crime. You steal a man's horse and you likely condemn him to death, much the same as two of the Roberts' brothers had condemned Mrs. Wagner to death when they stole her team up on the Red River and left her pregnant and alone; and for that two of the three brothers had died by their hand. Late in the afternoon John slowed the pace to let the horses blow and Joshua pulled along side, obviously wanting to talk. "You know John; to most folks who see us on this trail, this just ain't any way a natural partnership…a white man and a black man armed, well-mounted and riding side-by-side; that don't happen in this country."

With that, John abruptly pulled up the gray mare and turned in the saddle with a serious face and began to intently study Joshua. Finally John blurted out, "My God Joshua, you're right…you are black! I never noticed that before. In all this time, why in the hell didn't you think to tell me? As your friend, that's something I should have been told!"

"Don't make fun, John, I'm serious. In all the days we've been on the trail together, how many white men have you seen riding side-by-side with a black man…none, that's how many! Let alone sharing a meal, a camp fire and a bottle."

"Perhaps those folks didn't start out like you and me. There was a moment standing in the middle of Friel's saloon in Texarkana that I knew my mouth had led me far beyond my capability and I was likely gonna die right there. My only choice was out of that group I was facin', who I was gonna take with me? Then I looked up in that bar-mirror and saw you standing there behind me with my scattergun pointed at the group of men around the poker table. I didn't see no black man in that mirror…hell; I wouldn't have cared if you were green, at a time like that, color was just not the point. I saw a brave man I didn't even know, who had stuck his nose into the middle of a mess I had created and was likely gonna save me from gettin' my white ass shot full of holes! A man's color don't much matter at those moments, and if it don't matter then…then it shouldn't matter at no other time…if you're gonna share my fights; you sure as hell should share my fire and my meal and my bottle. With that said, now get your black ass back behind me where you belong and let's be on our way." And though trying hard to look serious, with that outburst, John's entire face started with a huge grin and then he roared with his own humor.

"You've been a good friend…for a white man, you gave me a side-arm and taught me to shoot, and you ask me to go along on this trip. Sometime I'd like to tell you what life's been like for me and my people, just so's you'd know…so's you'd have some understanding of this thing."

"We're gonna stop in a couple of hours and make a camp on the Trinity River, they'll be time for some talkin' then."

Then John went back to the thoughts Joshua had interrupted… namely, the good and the worrisome of how his life was about to change. As the young men rode on in silence, John returned his focus to his life with Sarah and Matt and all of the responsibility that he was about to take on. He loved Sarah, he was as sure of that as any not-yet 20 year old man ever is, and he did find the thought of his being together with her very exciting. Matt was a great kid and John looked forward to teaching him the things his Pa and grandfather had taught him…things that meant survival on the frontier. And, bringing them along to Texas and starting a new life was exactly what he had wanted ever since he had left the farm in Iowa. But…he had very much enjoyed this carefree life for the last couple of years; oh sure, for 13 months of it a lot of people had been trying to kill him, but he had only been responsible for himself. If he screwed-up, only he paid the price.….if he screwed-up in the future both Sarah and Matt might also have to help pay his price. One thing for sure, Sarah would want a home so she could sink a tap root for she and her son. John would have to quit staring at the western horizon and wondering what the hell was over that next hill, at least he'd have to quit doing it where Sarah could see him. But it did also occur to him that he might be having these thoughts kind of damn late in the process…before he wrote to her in January to ask her to come with him to Texas just might have been a better time to have figure this all out.

They came up on the Trinity about where the crude map had predicted they would. They found a good site near a spring, and while Joshua set up camp, John used the remaining light to ride up and down the river's bank. He wanted to mark on his map a good, safe place to cross with a wagon on the return trip. By the time he found what he was looking for, made the notes on the map, and returned to the camp site, Joshua had unpacked for the night and started a fire. "You know Joshua, I don't think we're likely to have any more Indian trouble this far to the east in Texas, but I'd be just as hard pressed to welcome into our camp some of those we've seen on the road the last few days. My Ma would likely say that's not the Christian spirit and I guess she'd be correct in that, but then she's not seen some of the trail-trash we have either. I think we need to continue sleeping out of the fire light, and probably one of us needs to keep a watch, and then trade-off."

When, by shortly after dark they were fed, the camp cleaned up, and the horses picketed, the men settled down with a couple of John's cigars and a near empty bottle of sour mash. As the passed the bottle back and forth, John looked at Joshua and said, "Okay this would be a good time, so tell me your story."

"Much of what I'm gonna tell you was told to me by my mother and to her by my grandmother who were slaves before me. You see, this slavery thing has been going on in the United States since about 1620 when the first Africans were brought to Virginia by the Dutch. The constitution of the Carolina Colony in the late 1600's authorized slavery and defined slaves as being property, much like in your United States Constitution. The European white planters were even given 50 acres of farming land for every male slave they brought into the Carolinas. The slavery system in America replaced the indentured servitude system that was so popular in Europe. For my people, the shameful thing is that most of those who would become slaves were first captured and sold to white slavers by other black Africans. They say because of bad conditions on the slave ships, as many as a third of the slaves died on the ships bringing them from Africa. But in spite of those losses, there were about 250,000 black slaves in America by 1750. The law was; *a slave in one state is a slave in all states.* So, when Thomas Jefferson decided to free his slaves, he put them on a ship and sent them back to Africa, rather than try to colonize them in America".

"Well, that's interesting old history, but what's it all got to do with you?"

"Well, I'm getting to that. There was a law, first in Virginia, then all over the South that a child took on the status of the mother. If the mother was slave, even if the father was white, the child was still slave. At the age of 14, my grandmother was raped by her white owner and the child of that rape was my mother but my mother was still a slave because her mother was a slave. So my mother's father, who would later become my grandfather, wound up being her owner. Then when he died the eventual ownership of her passed to her half-brothers and half-sisters. How strange is that; being a slave owned by your father and your half-brothers? The same white owner later came down to the quarters to have my mother when she was about 15, but he was getting on in years and she got away and hid. Eventually my mother was married to a slave on the plantation and he became my father and for a short while, helped her raise me. It had not been her choice to marry, but they were gonna be bred by the owner anyway, just like he'd bred his animals, so some old black man pronounced them as husband and wife first. Didn't mean much however, as soon as my mother was carrying me, her husband, my father, was caused to breed with another slave; then later after I was born, on he was sold off. Slaves, especially strong male slaves were valuable for the work they could do; I heard of one being traded for 5000 pounds of tobacco. I was taken from my mother and sold when I was about 6 or 7, and then a short while later was sold again to Mr. Alexander Clayton, Miss Savannah's daddy. He took me to Vicksburg, Mississippi. Because I was one-quarter white and fairer in color, Mr. Clayton decided to make me a house-boy. I was more fortunate than most at that time; they was good to me…hardly ever beat me, and I even picked up a little readin' from Miss Savannah. We kinda grew-up together and I never gave 'em any trouble, so when Mr. Clayton decided to get Miss Savannah out of Vicksburg before the big battle was to come there, he offered me my freedom to go with her and protect her, and help her to get Mr. Wagner, her husband out of that Confederate prison. What I was doin' in Texarkana was looking for her horses that got stole. You found the team before I did so I just decided to follow you thinkin' after you got 'em, I'd just steal 'em back from you. When I looked in the doors of that saloon, you had already started your move standing in the middle of that bar room…I must say, for an intelligent white man, it was a mighty stupid move. I didn't really want to mix in, all of you being white I thought hell just let those white people shoot it out with each other. But I figured that after they killed you, and they was surely gonna kill you, I'd still be alone trying to get Miss Savannah's horses back, and that likely wasn't gonna work out too well. So helping you kind of became the better of the poor choices I had. I must say, you are about the fastest white man with a gun I ever seed. That man at the bar made the first move goin' for his gun and you drew and shot him dead center before his gun even cleared. But the absolute best part for me was the look on that barkeeps face when you served that drink of his best, under-the-counter whiskey to me before we left. I figured we'd just grab up that team and high-tail it out of there, but no, you had to get all noble and go tell your story to the marshal and see he'd lock that last Roberts brother in jail. I was mighty proud though when you gave me that man's gun and then invited me to ride double with you. I figured then that you was gonna be alright and I'd go with you just about anyplace you wanted to go!"

"How come you slaves were always so dossal...how come you never rose up in a revolt?"

"Oh, it was tried, but every time we just got much the worst of it. In 1831, when my mother was about eleven years old in Virginia, a slave named Nat Turner collected about 70 free and enslaved blacks and started a rebellion against the white owners. Over the next few weeks they killed 57 white men, women and children; mostly hacked them to death with axes. The result was over 100 blacks were killed by the local army and Turner was captured and hanged. Following that, the treatment of blacks became much worse. There was a new law that no black could be taught to read or write. A new law that required white men to wear guns on Sunday to church cause the rebellion had started on a Sunday. In the end it was a setback for the cause of freedom for blacks. The Quakers had started freeing their slaves up north and there were already many free blacks in Virginia... there was even talk in Virginia of starting an emancipation program; but all of that ending with Nat Turner. Now I recon'we're looking to Mr. Lincoln to do for us what we couldn't do for ourselves."

"Livin' in Virginia, did you ever see the ocean...that's something I always wanted to do, but never made it?"

"I did when I was a small boy. I got taken to the ocean to help clean the master's fish."

"What's it like? I've heard tell its dark and always moving and will kill you if'n you get careless."

"It's so big! It's hard for a body to imagine anything so big. It dark and violent during a storm, then can be bluish-green and calm at other times, and the tides' always coming or goin'. It's never just still. You otta' go and see it someday John, you'd be impressed."

"I always figured to, but now with Sarah and Matt to be responsible for, I don't suppose that'll ever happen. Say, how come I've never heard your last name Joshua?"

"Slaves were never given last names like white folks. If a black ever did become free, he most often just took the last name of his last owner."

"Well, you're a free man…you need a new last name."

"I thought about that, but my last owner was Mr. Clayton and I figured that maybe Miss Savannah wouldn't like me using her daddy's name, especially us traveling together and all."

"What was the name of your first owner in Virginia; he could be a good candidate?"

"Horace Green; his family name was Green."

"That works fine. You could be Joshua Green. Now you got two names just like ever body else!"

"You know John, there's lots of ways the slaves in America have contributed to the culture…it's just not in the things you'd expect."

"Like what ways?"

"Most whites go to church and at sometime they all sing that hymn, *Amazing Grace*. Well the man who wrote the words to that was Captain John Newton, and he was for many years the Captain of a slaver; a ship that brought us Blacks to America. They say he was repentant for being a slaver and wrote those words seeking forgiveness. But, what most people don't know is that the music his words are set to is a slave chant that he heard coming up from the ship's hole during the crossings. Also if you ever get to Savannah in Georgia you'll see many of the white folks have painted a bluish-green color around the door and window frames of their houses. White folks think it will keep out the evil spirits; but that first came from the slaves who would, and still do paint that color around the doors to their quarters to keep out the spirits. It's called *Haint Blue* and it represents water, 'cause the evil spirits can't pass over water.

Having sufficient Black culture for one evening, John took the first watch and as Joshua moved out of the circle of the firelight, then settled in his ripped up bed roll, he kept runnin' his new name over in his mind; *Joshua Green...Joshua Green.* He liked the sound of that, and he liked bein' like ever body else. *John was a good man...first he gave him a gun and now he'd given him a name...made him just like white folks!*

John found a likely spot to see the land approach to their camp and settled down to watch and think. He thought Joshua was like a blind man that could suddenly see...everything excited him. John never thought much about his family name, he'd always had one, but to Joshua this was a big event...to finally have two names. It was good being with Joshua, made John appreciate so much more many of the things he had always taken for granted...maybe he needed to appreciate his family more...might even go back to see them, once this damn war was over. He'd take Sarah and Matt and be proud to show 'em where he grew up. Life was good for he and Joshua, and getting' better all the time.

Little could John imagine what surprises the trail would hold in store for them, and only a few days hence!

Author's Notes...

Ironically, it was a ruling by the Supreme Court of the United States which would assure that a civil war would ultimately be necessary to settle once and for all the issue of slavery in this nation. That case was Dred Scott-v-Standford – 1857. The name had been misspelled by a Clerk of the Court, and should have read, "Sanford".

Dred Scott was a slave from the state of Missouri that had been taken for awhile by his owner to live in the free states of Illinois and then Minnesota. Upon their return to Missouri years later, Scott was by law returned to his original status as a slave. The basis of the case was to determine if a slave, once free, could be returned to slave status simply by being moved from one sovereign state to another.

By a 7 to 2 ruling, with the Chief Justice, Roger B. Taney writing for the majority, the Court decreed the following: The right to hold slaves was a property right and Congress could not interfere with a man's right to hold property and as such, it could not prohibit slavery in the new territories; especially since no word in the Constitution conveys such special rights to the Congress. This ruling made the Missouri Compromise of 1820 unconstitutional and with it the agreement to divide the new territories into free and slave.

However, the Chief Justice could not leave the ruling there and went on to write that, *"Dred Scott a Negro of slave origins could not be a citizen of the United States. He and all people like him were simply ineligible. The Founding Fathers had only been thinking of white men in framing the Constitution. There is general agreement that Negros are beings of an inferior order and altogether unfit to associate with the white race, either in social or political relations; and so far inferior that they had no rights which the white man is bound to respect."*

All-in-all the Dred Scott decision did the reputation of the Supreme Court of the United States profound and lasting harm! Many years later, Chief Justice Charles Evans Hughes remarked that it was a case in which the Court suffered from a self-inflicted wound and characterized the ruling as a, *"public calamity and a monumental indiscretion."* The Courts prestige suffered immensely and Chief Justice Felix Frankfurter once remarked, *"That after the Civil War, Justices of the Supreme Court never mentioned the Dred Scott case any more than a family in which a son had been hanged mentioned ropes and scaffolds."*

The Chief Justice's assertion that Scott and all men like him neither were, or could ever be, citizens was eventually "reversed" a few years later by the bloodiest war in the history of this nation; in fact, a war that cost more in blood than all of the nation's other wars, before or since, **combined!**

Chapter Four

THE RATTLER

John took great delight in waking Joshua the next morning. It reminded him of his travels with Glenn a few months earlier as he tapped the sole of Joshua's foot with some authority using his pointed boot and announcing, "Good morning, Mr. Green, I'm here to inform you that you're burnin' daylight!" Truth was, it wouldn't be light for two more hours, but John's attitude was; *if I'm up, you need to be up also.*

They breakfasted quickly, cleared their camp and put their reluctant horses into the cool, fast running stream known as the Trinity River. John's gray mare shows her dislike of stepping into water where the water ran dark and the bottom was not obvious. When she finally agreed to leave the bank, she leaped from the bank into the river getting John quite wet in the process, and then to show her attitude, side-stepped to the opposite bank with her ears laid back. Her actions reminded John of his earlier intent to give her the name,

Rebel. What other name could so well fit one of God's creatures clad all in gray and so obstinate and bull-headed, and further so intent on showing displeasure in any situation where she was not in full agreement? But the sun came up bright and its warmth quickly dried his clothes and John's focus was diverted to finding the north-heading trail that would take them well clear of the town of Tyler and the Confederate prisoner-of-war compound known as Camp Ford. Camp Ford was the largest Confederate prison camp west of the Mississippi River, and his one visit there would be sufficient to last for this lifetime. As he rode on he suddenly remembered the Union prisoner he had met briefly there, Private Martin Kutcher of the Iowa 19th. John had written a brief note to his parents. *Wonder if the letter ever got there…wonder if Martin lasted through the winter of '62?*

John found the trail he was seeking, made his marks on his map and then they put their horses into a steady gallop, walking them for but 10 minutes out of every hour. It proved to be an uneventful day of hard riding that likely covered at least 30 to 35 miles. By the evening of the second day at that pace, the men were camped on the banks of the Sulphur River, just north of Bryans Mill. As John observed for Joshua, "One more day like this will put us in Texarkana and at the saloon of our favorite bar-keep sampling some of his good, under-the-counter special blend!"

Joshua had tired of the steady diet of John servin' broiled bacon and week old biscuits and with the remaining light, decided to take the scattergun and see what he could scare up for dinner. He had heard some quail calling just back in the edge of the near-by timber, and thought them a good choice. In anticipation, John had pulled a large supply of fire wood up from the river bank and carved a spit from some green willows; he wanted to be ready for whatever success Joshua enjoyed. John had finished his self-imposed, get-ready chores and settled back into his upturned saddle with a cigar when he heard Joshua scream out and then the scattergun fire. John jumped to his feet, sacrificed a nearly fresh cigar into the fire and started running in the direction of the shotgun's blast. Joshua screamed out a second time, "He bit me, that son-of-a-bitch rattler, he bit me!"

John heard the hollering and altered his direction slightly just as he saw Joshua charging toward him on a dead run, waving the scattergun over his head and calling out, but making no sensible sounds. As he started to run past John, John reached out, spun him around by his arm and threw him to the ground, setting astraddle of his chest. "Now stop that! If you want to die of that snake bite, just keep your heart pumping like mad and that venom will spread throughout your body. When it reaches your heart, you're done. Now you lay here and lay quiet, I want to see the snake to see what kind it is…hell, it may not even be poisonous."

"It's over there just to the right of that oak tree John, at least what's left of it. But I can tell you it's a rattler, I heard him sound-off that dry rattle, but too late."

"But first we've gotta stop whatever went in you from spreading." John pulled off Joshua's bandana from around his neck, twirled it into the shape of a small rope, and then tied it tightly around Joshua's upper leg near the groin. He put a stick through the knot and twisted it tightly against his leg. "Here you hold this tight just like that and don't loosen it till I tell you to…it'll stop, or at least slow, the venom from spreading through your body. We can't stop the spread completely, but we sure as hell can slow it down and even that will improve your chances."

John eased off of Joshua slowly just to be certain he was going to stay put and hold the stick tight. He saw the remains of the snake before he got up on it. It was a rattler alright, and though there wasn't much left of it, it had been a big one…as he reassembled the many pieces with his eye he guessed maybe five foot anyway and as big around as his wrist. He heard Joshua call out again, but this time with less panic, "John am I gonna die?"

"You are a mighty lucky man; first you got hit by a big adult snake, not a young one and second, you are with a man who has seen snake bite treated by a Doctor. My brother Matthew was bit by a water moccasin on the very day we had the Doctor to our house for supper.

And, I watched what he did. Now you're just gonna lay right there and do what I say while I take care of this."

"But what's so damn lucky about being bit by a big snake?"

"A young snake has no sense of proportion. When they strike they'll give you every damn drop of venom they have stored. But a mature snake will just inject a measured shot keeping some back, just in case he has to hit you again. Trust me, yours was a big snake!"

"Now I do hate to cut up these new pants that Miss Lucinda gave us, but I've got to get at that wound." With his Bowie knife, John cut up the outside seam of the pant leg and opened it up. The pair of holes was just above the boot top. Again you're mighty fortunate; the strike is above the top of the boot. You must be livin' right 'cause if he had bit through the boot, we'd have to throw the boot away. That venom would be in the leather and just keep seeping into your skin every time you wore 'em, 'sides, he probably would have broke off a fang in your leg trying to withdraw. With his knife still in hand, John punctured the skin and drew a large X through each of the bite puncture marks. As the blood poured through it quickly went from bright red to a thick dark red, milky mess. John continued to squeeze the two wounds as long any of the discoloration showed.

"Damn John, you could have told me you were gonna do that…that hurts like hell!"

"Just shut-up and keep a turn on the stick. You can know that regardless of how this all turns out, I'm not gonna send you a bill, even though I know you're a rich Black man and you got money to pay for my services." When the flow turned brighter red again, John bent forward, put his mouth over the wound and sucked the liquid into his mouth; then spit it aside and did the same to the other wound he had made.

"Damn, I never seed no white man do that before."

"Well, that's what the Doctor did with my brother."

"You never did say; did your brother happen to live through this treatment?"

"Yes and so will you. You can ease off on that stick now for a few minutes while I go back to camp and get some whiskey."

Joshua smiled weakly, "This is a hell of a time to stop for a drink, John!"

"It's not just for me." A few minutes later John returned carrying the sour mash bottle in one hand and dragging Joshua's saddle with his other. "I'm gonna move our camp up here; it's easier than trying to drag you down to the camp, 'sides, I don't want you up and moving around much. Okay tighten up on the bandana again…just like I had it before." John turned the saddle over, lifted Joshua's head and shoulders and made him as comfortable as a man who'd just been hit by a five foot rattler and then had his leg opened up with a Bowie knife was likely to be. Joshua watched as John took a mouthful of the sour mash, swirled it around and the spit it out.

"That seems like a waste of mighty fine whiskey to just spit it out."

"Well its no more waste that this." With that John tipped up the bottle and poured a generous amount over Joshua' open wounds.

"My god John but that hurts! You're sure as hell not a painless Doctor. Does that whiskey do any real good?"

"As I told Glenn when I poured whiskey on his gunshot wounds, I'm Irish, and the Irish rightly believe that whatever whiskey wont' cure, well there just ain't no cure for. Besides, even if it don't help, we know it won't do no harm, after all, Glenn lived. You should find some comfort in that. The Irish even rub whiskey on the gums of teething babies to sooth 'em. But just so you know, I'd a damn sight rather be drinking it than pouring it on you."

"How about a drink of that for me, it'll likely also do some good on the inside too?"

"No not for a few hours. Whiskey just speeds up your heart beat, and that'll just serve to pump the venom around faster. So, no my friend…no whiskey for you, but as your friend and traveling companion, I'll be pleased to drink your share for you and run the risk with my heart."

"You've always been honest with me, so tell me the truth now, am I gonna live through this?"

"Joshua I won't lie to you, you're gonna hurt like hell, every joint in your body will be on fire. You're gonna sweat and chill and have some damn bad nightmares; there may be times you'll wish to die but, yes, you'll live. I'll see to it! Now I'm gonna go bring the rest of our camp and the horses up here. You lay there quiet and when I come back we'll loosen the stick for a little while."

John set up their camp and then had the broiled bacon and week old biscuits that had started all of this. Joshua would sleep quiet for a spell, then thrash and moan till John would have to physically hold him down. He kept the bandana tight on the leg, but when he thought an hour would have passed, he would loosen it for awhile. He wished he had the Doctor's watch, would have made the timing much easier. He remembered the Doctor had cautioned them to loosen the bandanna every hour and let the blood flow some, or risk losing the leg. During the night John kept the fire built up so he would have plenty of light to tend Joshua. *The hell with whoever might see It, I'm in a foul mood and whoever comes in this here camp best come expecting some bad trouble.* He brought up cool water from the Sulphur River to bathe Joshua's face when the fever raged, then piled on the blankets when the chills came. Just before daylight, Joshua's fever broke and he began to sleep quietly. John took off the bandana, then lay down close to his friend so he would hear him if he called out; then he too slept for the first time that night.

They both burnt some daylight the next morning. Joshua was exhausted from his fitful sleep and John was exhausted from nearly no sleep. When John finally woke up, Joshua was not in his bedroll. John rolled over in a panic, but saw him just behind a distant tree relieving himself. As he turned and saw John, Joshua smiled and added, "I guess you did know what you were doing, although damn if I ever really thought so. But here I am hurting like hell in ever joint like you said, but at least able to greet a new day. Thank you, John. In my entire life, no one and especially no white man, ever put himself out like that so to save my life! In truth, I doubt any white man ever put himself out so to save any black he didn't own"

"Well if I had let you die, and a couple of times last night the thought did occur to me, I would have had to dig a damn big hole to put you in, and I was just too tired to be diggin'. We're gonna just lay over today, let the horses graze and rest up…we've been working 'em hard. Besides, a days rest wouldn't hurt me either."

"What you truly mean is that I need the rest for another day. It's just gonna make you another day late getting to your lady."

"That okay, she don't know for certain I'm comin' anyway. Besides we're gonna go make a social call on Mr. Friel next and we need to be well rested for that visit. In another day your system'll be ready for some of his good under-the-counter whiskey and you just know how pleased he's gonna be to see us!"

And, rest up they did…both men and horses! But then, all would be needing it before long.

Author's Notes…

Far to the east in Richmond, Virginia, the Confederate Congress is meeting to approve a controversial tax measure which will place an eight percent tax on all agriculture products grown in the South in the prior year 1862. In addition, there was a ten percent tax placed on the profits made from the purchase or sale of most food, clothing and iron products. At the same time, a gradual income tax is instituted. It is estimated that in 1863, $62 million would be collected from these measures, even though most southerners consider it a confiscatory measure.

On that day in 1863, Confederate General Thomas "Stonewall" Jackson died in Chancellorsville, Virginia, of gunshot wounds accidentally inflicted by his own men. So important was he to General Lee and the southern cause, that his death would be seen as a pivotal point in the war.

Chapter Five

THE FORK IN THE TRAIL

It was just after sun set of the second day as the two riders, one a former Union Corporal and one a former slave, approached the Texas side of the frontier town of Texarkana. John had thought to arrive at the German's saloon for their much anticipated "social call" a day earlier, but neither he nor Joshua were ready to depart the camp until late in the day, which then necessitated another night on the trail. The coal-oil lanterns on the building fronts were slowly being lit in this rowdy town of mostly false front stores and saloons that lined the main approach to the town. To give it the look of a town, the false store fronts had been hastily built from green wood and the boards were now warped and showing gaps. Occasionally a bar woman could be heard to beckon from a lighted window or bat-wing doorway as the two rode past and a sleeping dog might raise his head for a quick look. Most of the saloons and a few of the stores were actually just big tents which had bleached white in the sun, most with dirt floors, but someone had thought that with the wood fronts they would look like real businesses. John imagined there was a part of the town that most thru-travelers never got to see where the more stable of the citizens lived and traded, but it was safely set apart from what greeted them on this arrival. They passed the livery stable where John had located the team of matched Appaloosas belonging to Miss Savannah; the ones that had been stolen by the Roberts brothers. The stable was dark now, but the men had no mind to stop anyway. John knew to turn left up the hill at the edge of town to find the German's. It stood alone outside of town, which judging from the look and the smell of the place, was just as it should be.

They reigned up at the tie-rail in front and stepped down. The lantern light was already spilling out of the top half of bat-wing doors and the single front window. As John checked the loads in his Colt, Joshua ask, "You want I should carry the scattergun in?"

"No, that makes it look like were coming in unfriendly. Besides its unlikely there is anyone in there any faster with a side-arm than the two of us. Hold-on a minute and let me take a quick look through the window to see just what's going on."

"Seems pretty quiet; there's five rough lookin' cowboys playing poker at the table where you shot brother Garth Roberts. In fact, I believe that dark stain is a part of brother Garth still showin' on the wall behind 'em. And, there are two drinkers standing at the bar being served by Friel. There's a table off to the right of the door away from the window...we'll go sit over there with our backs to the wall where we can see the room. It's likely no one will know us, especially with my fine new hat, and we'll just leave it that way, if'n they'll let us. It's probable no one will come serve us, and if they don't, I'll go to the bar to get our drinks, you just keep a watch on the room."

"John, it's just also possible that they'll be some shootin' once we get in there; I'll try not to let you down."

"Joshua, sometimes the shootin' is the least of it. Any man can shoot a gun and with some practice he can draw fast and shoot accurate.

But what counts is how that man stands up when somebody's shootin' back at him. I've seen you there and I'll have you to stand with me anytime!"

John went through the door first as Friel and the two at the bar looked up, but paid no further mind. Then Joshua followed, and everyone in the place froze with his entry and watched to see what Friel might do with a black man in his place. The two young men found their chairs and sat down to watch the room. As John thought, no one came to offer any service. He leaned over the Joshua and said, "Looks like we have to get our own. You stay here and watch my back." The poker game had beckoned again and the five went back to their card game, but one of the players kept grabbing sly looks at John from under his hat. Friel moved down the bar to stand in front of John, "We don't serve his kind in here; in fact I don't even allow his kind in here except as swampers."

"We've ridden a fir piece and ain't looking for no trouble 'sides, you ain't gonna be serving him, I am. Now, if you'll be so kind as to pour me a couple of drinks, we'll wet our thirst and be on our way. And, not that swill from the back bar, I want ours from the bottle you keep under the bar."

"How'd you know about that?"

"I was in here once before and saw you serve from it. So that's where I want mine from. Also, I seem to recall a scattergun from under the bar, so kindly let your hands just come up with the good whiskey and nothing else."

Friel put the two glasses on the bar in front of John and brought up his good whiskey from under the bar. As he was pouring the second glass, he stopped and looked intently at John. "I've seen you before! You're that cowboy that shot two of the Roberts brothers in here and took Gene to the Marshal for horse thieving; no, you shot one and that black bastard over yonder shot the other. I'm surprised you're both still alive; you likely heard that Gene escaped from the prison wagon on the way to Huntsville prison. Killed a guard he did, broke his neck. He swore he'd hunt you down and kill you both and I figured he would have done that by now."

"Since I got out of the war, and beings I don't come in this place ever' day, none other than a few Comanche's have even tried to kill me lately."

"This is Texas boy, and if a man swears to kill you, you'd do well to believe 'em. Now you two have your drink and get out of here, I don't want no trouble in here from the likes of you."

John dropped a coin on the bar, picked up the two glasses and remarked, "No, I can see why you'd want to preserve these pleasant surroundings." As he turned to return to their table, John noticed that there now were only four men playing poker at the far table and the door in the wall next to the table was standing open. He made a show of handing a glass to Joshua so Friel couldn't miss it, "You best enjoy this one as I truly believe were going to be cut off from any more of the German's good whiskey."

"While you were at the bar, one of the players went out that side door. I think we best have our drink and ease out of here...less there's someone waiting outside in the dark."

"Well we've already paid the price, so let's enjoy our whiskey first. We'll go out like we came in; we'll walk together toward the door with you watching the poker players and I'll watch them at the bar. You go through the bat-wing quickly, then turn to the left and flatten against the wall in a dark shadow. I'll follow you and turn to the right. We'll let our eyes adjust 'fore we start movin' to the horses."

They drained the last of their very-good from under-the-bar whiskey, made a show of turning the glasses upside down on the table, and stood to start their slow "dance" toward the door. All eyes in the room were now on the two. John was slightly in front of Joshua and facing to the left to watch those at the bar, Joshua came up on John's right, his eyes on those remaining at the poker table and on the yawing open door in the wall. John was about to point out to Joshua the old blood stain on the floor by the bar where Clint Roberts had died and bled-out during their last visit; when Joshua pushed John hard to his left. John stumbled and tried to keep from falling where the evidence of Clint's stain remained; a hand gun flashed from the dark, yawing doorway. John drew his Colt and fired two quick shots spaced into the dark opening, then Joshua's falling body crashed into him and they both went down. John rolled over and came to his knees, his Colt sweeping the room, but no one had moved, especially not Joshua. John shouted, "Damn it Joshua, get off of my legs!" But when he looked, John knew the Joshua would no longer be moving under his own power. The large caliber slug had hit him in the high center of the chest and gone clean through and exited his back. John had seen too many men shot like that to have to wonder if Joshua was going to get up…he was not! The small amount of blood told the story; Joshua had been dead before he hit the floor. By his act of pushing John down, this dear friend had taken dead center the bullet intended for John, and it had killed him. John rolled over to get free and ran to the doorway in the back wall with the Colt still in his hand. He found a small blood trail leading toward the dark store room, and then likely out the rear door. He made his choice to return to Joshua, he was not going to find anyone out there in the dark, and just might get himself shot in ambush for his carelessness.

The two drinkers from the bar were now crowded around the fallen body, prodding it with their boot toe. Enraged John shouted, "Leave him be you sons-of-bitches!"

Friel responded, "Drag that black ass out of here; he's bleeding on my floor!"

John looked the three men straight in the eye, "You heard me, you so much as touch him and I'll kill the bunch of you where you stand. He's my friend and I'll take care of him with no help from the likes of you." John holstered the Colt, then with his two arms free, got Joshua up on his left shoulder, redrew the .44 and started for the door. Joshua's hat had fallen. One of the drinkers from the bar stomped it twice, then kicked it under the bat-wing doors and into the darken street. Quietly and with purpose John said, "Any one takes a shot at us when I get out there and I'll return with the scattergun and kill you all."

John looked into the dark street and seeing no movement, shouldered his load through the door and down to the waiting horses; thinking to himself, this *ain't over, not by a damn site it ain't over. When a sodbuster from Iowa makes you a promise like that, you best believe him!* With considerable care and effort, John draped the body of Joshua over his saddle and tied him in place. As he started to mount, he saw a small spade propped against the side of the saloon and picked it up and tied it off behind his saddle, then picking up Joshua's hat, he slapped the dust off on his pants leg. Collecting the reins, John mounted the gray mare and put his back to the German's, but he knew in his heart it was not for the last time. Just as John started to ride away, Friel stuck his ugly face over the bat-wing door and shouted, "Now you see what I mean Boy, when someone from Texas says he's gonna kill you, you best believe him!"

"Since you claim to be a friend of Gene Roberts, as that friend, you should tell him that he's no longer the hunter…he has now made himself the hunted! I'll find him and when I do I'm gonna take great delight in killing him. I'll be that noise he'll hear by his campfire in the night, but when he turns around no one will be there. Then one time he'll turn around and it'll be me, and when it is, I'm gonna kill 'em. You be certain he knows that, I'm coming for 'em!"

John deliberately rode straight through town on the rutted main street past lazy dogs lying on the porches; he wanted as many people as were out and about to see the procession trail through the border station and into Arkansas. His first thought had been to trail the body on to Sarah's and bury Joshua in a quiet location on the farm. But then realizing that he was still more than two days of hard riding away, he knew in spite of his feelings, the body could not stay out of the ground in this weather that long; besides, he wasn't quite ready to leave the Texarkana area just yet. As he cleared the last of the buildings of the wild frontier town, a faded white frame church with a small cemetery in the back came up on the right. The irony occurred to John to bury this black friend who had taken a bullet meant for him, in the cemetery of a white-folks church. The inappropriateness got the better of him and he dismounted and led the horses around to the grave yard. He found a cold lantern by the front door that he took along. Locating an empty grave site, he began the hard work of opening the grave. Even with the ground damp from the spring rains, it proved to be long and hard work, but he considered it a last labor of love for this true friend. Finally with the moon on the downward arc, John was satisfied and eased Joshua's body into the hole he had opened. With misty eyes, John gently arranged the body in the bottom of the grave, put Joshua's hat over his face, pulled his .44 and placed it in his right hand... that was the way he died and that was the way he should journey on. John crawled back up on top and extinguished the lantern...he didn't want to see down into the grave during the filling process. The more he shoveled, the more his eyes ran; and by the time he finished filling the grave, he wept openly, but quietly. John reached back into his upbringing for the right words to say over a man who had so willingly died in his place. Something a Union Chaplin had said once from Saint John came back to him; *"Greater love hath no man than this, that a man lay down his life for his friends"* (John 15:13). He then recalled the Psalms his mother had insisted her boys must learn as she taught then to read from the Bible, and began to speak it softly into the still Arkansas night:

"The Lord is my Shepherd; I shall not want.
He maketh me to lie down in green pastures; he leadeth me besides the
still waters.
He restoreth my soul: he leadeth me in the paths of righteousness for his
names sake.
Yea, though I walk through the valley of the shadow of death, I will fear
no evil;
For thou art with me; thy rod and thy staff they comfort me."

John's voice caught and would work no longer and he slumped to his knees in the soft clay of his friend's grave and with head bowed and eyes wet, he bid his heart to finish:

"Thou preparest a table before me in the presents of mine enemies;

Thou aniontest my head with oil; my cup runneth over.
Surely goodness and mercy shall follow me all of the days of my life;
And I will dwell in the house of the Lord for ever."

Some minutes later John rose, he could not recall in his thirteen months of war that he had ever cried over a single one of the thousands of deaths around him. Not that he wasn't moved to do so, but was always afraid that if he started crying for one, with the dead comin' so fast, he would never be able to quit. He looked at the last of the moon sitting on the western horizon and said his last, *"God I recon when it comes to You, a man's color don't make no never mind, I don't know much about this man's life before a few months ago, but what he did this night surely must have made him worthy of Your consideration. If he can't make it with You, I recon none of us likely will."*

His grieving finished, John threw the shovel into the weeds and out of sight, put the lantern back where he had found it, tied Joshua's bay horse off at the hitching rail, then mounted and turned the gray mare's head back toward his unfinished business in Texarkana.

He knew that he did not want his return to town announced or even noted, so he left the road and moved down into a small stream bed. He stopped to refresh himself, watered the big gray mare, filled his canteen and moved on toward the town ahead. After skirting the now darkened town, he left the stream bed and dismounted in a long-needle pine grove. Using his Bowie knife, he cut a four foot long live pine branch about as big around as his wrist. He then cut a large V in the tree's trunk and when the pine sap started to run, dripped it over the end of his branch. Satisfied, John remounted and staying with the shadows, began to work his way up toward the back of the German's saloon.

There was a lighted lantern hanging on a nail by the rear entrance, which he quickly extinguished. When his eyes again adjusted to the black night, he dismounted and moved to try the rear door...it was locked, just as he had expected. But just as he had done before on a Union raiding party, he wedged the blade of the big Bowie knife between the door and the frame and hit the handle a sharp blow with the palm of his hand…and, as it had before, the door swung open. John stepped quickly into the darken back room and pushed the door closed. He waited, frozen, not breathing, to see if there was anyone in the darkness. He knew that often swampers might be allowed to sleep in the back of saloons, and he didn't want any innocent victims for what he had come to do. Satisfied that he was alone and with his eyes adjusted, John moved silently through the room and found the door from which Joshua had been shot and killed. After a short study of the bar room, and again finding no one, he moved inside. John methodically moved around the room on his salvage mission. He picked up four bottles of the cheap, rot-gut whiskey from behind the bar and, while moving around the bar room, with two in each hand, splashed it on the furniture, the draw drapes, and anything else that would burn with some 'encouragement'; and then the same for the back room. Next John stuffed his pockets with those thin cigars he liked and selected three bottles of the under-the-bar; good stuff and set them all by the back door.

Finally ready to do the mission that had brought him back to Friel's, John struck a match from his pocket and held it next to the pitch covered pine branch, until the flame caught. As soon as he had it burning briskly, he started around the room touching the flame to everything he passed. When he reached the door to the back room he looked back at a room in full blaze and smiled at the success of his efforts. John quickly made a similar tour around the back storage room and because of the contents, it even caught more quickly. In passing, he saw a now full tin of cigars and tucked that under his arm. At the door he turned, tossed his torch back into the corner of the room and picking up his bottles of the under-the-bar good whiskey, exited and closed the back door behind him…his mother had always scolded him for going though doors and leaving them standing open.

John loaded his loot into his saddle bags, mounted the now fire-spooked gray mare and rode to the stream bed by the way he had come. He stopped just inside the tree line, and before descending into the stream, looked back at his handy work. The entire building was now fully engulfed in flames and the flames were now dancing over the dry pine shingles of the roof. He sat there on the mare watching, mesmerized as the roof began to sag into the building. He could hear the small explosions as the capped bottles exploded and see the small burst of flames as the alcohol hit the flames. It occurred to him that an Irishman should feeling badly from watching good whiskey being destroyed; but he satisfied himself with the knowledge that at Friel's there was damn little so called good whiskey! He lit one of his scavenged cigars and watched in satisfaction for a few more minutes; just long enough to witness the walls begin falling into the infernal. He was quite pleased with his work and knew Joshua would have been pleased also. That place had been such an assault on the senses of sight and smell and a body's civility that John thought the citizens of Texarkana might be pleased as well. They could think of it as Joshua's contribution to their small town's renewal program!

Author's Notes:

The Generals of the Vicksburg Campaign:

Confederate Lieutenant-General John C. Pemberton would become the man that history would blame for the loss of Vicksburg for the Confederacy. A loss that many would argue was more devastating to The Cause than the defeat of Robert E. Lee at Gettysburg. President Jefferson Davis called Vicksburg "The nail head that holds the South's two halves together".

Pemberton, an 1837 graduate of the U.S. Military Academy at West Point saw action in the Second Seminole War and was decorated for bravery in the Mexican War. Although born and raised in Pennsylvania, it was his marriage to a Virginia woman that would decide his choice of which side to support in the Civil War. He was in peacetime one of the most effective administrators in the military; and when the Civil War broke out, resigned and offered his services to his wife's home state of Virginia.

In spite of his obvious skills in administration and military politics, he was ordered to perhaps the most difficult command in the South;

the defense of Vicksburg. The city was the last major obstacle to Union commerce and military shipping on the Mississippi River. For several months during the winter of 1862/63, he enjoyed remarkable success defeating various attempts by Union General Grant to take Vicksburg. His orders from President Davis were not give up the river city, "even for a single day!" However, his immediate superior, General Joseph E. Johnston, ordered Pemberton to move out of the city's defenses, join with his forces and under Johnston's command, attack and defeat Grant before he could mount a serious threat to Vicksburg.

Torn by the conflicting orders coming from his superior and from his President, he did nothing while Grant's Union forces swept inland, scoring a series of quick victories. Pemberton belatedly made one frontal assault on Grant at Champion's Hill and was soundly defeated. Following yet another serious defeat at the Big Black Bear River bridges, Pemberton would retreat behind the city's defenses where his army and the citizens would endure a 47 day bombardment and siege before surrendering unconditionally. Pemberton became the pariah of the South and was accused by his immediate superior, General Johnston of causing the Confederate disaster by disobeying a direct order from a superior officer.

Pemberton would serve the Confederacy for the remainder of the war as a Lieutenant-Colonel of artillery in Virginia and South Carolina. After the war he settled on a farm near Warrington, Virginia, but his reputation would never recover.

Union Major-General Ulysses Simpson Grant arrived to take overall command of the Vicksburg campaign in October, 1862, with his military reputation in tatters. He had been relieved of command twice in the past year, and both times following victories. He reported to and was relieved by his superior, General Henry Hallack who was very jealous of the attention Grant had been receiving in the northern press. It finally took a personal intervention by President Lincoln for Grant to be restored, but even then Hallack placed him in a minor role. Grant needed a decisive victory at Vicksburg and Lincoln also needed that victory to relieve the pressures he was receiving to open the Mississippi River to northern commerce and the movement of military supplies and men.

After two failed attacks by Major-General Sherman from the northeast of the city, the cries again went out for Grant's removal. Grant then attempted five separate "experiments" to alter the course of the Mississippi River so that shipping could by-pass the Confederate guns of Vicksburg, which from its heights commanded all river traffic. He would then devise and execute a plan so daring in its concept that it would be studied into modern times by Cadets at the Military Academy at West Point. He would separate his army from its supply lines, march around Vicksburg on the west side of the river in Louisiana, through swamps and bayous that often required the building of corduroy roads for passage and cross back to the Mississippi side on boats that had run down river under the guns on the cliffs. Through his surprise movements Grant would win four decisive battles in five days and daringly drive his army between the armies of Johnston and Pemberton to prevent their linking up. Grant turned his forces to the east, crushed Johnston's forces, captured Jackson and looted it for supplies and destroyed everything in his path, including the railroads to Vicksburg.

Knowing the opportunity for any new supplies or reinforcements was now lost, Pemberton started a retreat back toward the city's defenses. Twice Grant's advancing forces caught up and both times delivered punishing defeats to the Confederates. What followed for Vicksburg was a 47 day siege and steady bombardment, from both land and water, until Pemberton's unconditional surrender on July 4, 1863.

On July 8, 1863, the Confederate forces at Port Hudson, Louisiana also surrendered unconditionally. This last Confederate stronghold on the river allowed the Union to open the flow of commerce to the Gulf and to cut the Confederacy in two.

Grant's reputation was now fully restored and he would shortly be promoted by President Lincoln as the Commanding General of the entire Union army, in which capacity General Hallack would now report to Grant. For his exploits during the American Civil War and especially at the Vicksburg Campaign, he would be described by the British historian, J.F.C. Fuller as *"....the greatest general of any age. We must go back to the campaigns of Napoleon to find equally brilliant results accomplished in the same space of time with such a small loss."* After the war, Ulysses Simpson Grant would go on to be twice elected as the 18th President of the United States…but his entire career would be under a name other than his baptized name of Hiram Ulysses, the one given him by his parents!

Chapter Six

THE REUNION

The moon was completely gone now and the dark of night had truly set in. John came up out of the stream bed on the Arkansas side of the border with Texas and again found the road he had taken with Joshua's body. He had seen no other riders going in either direction; many had seen him leave with the body, none had seen him return again without it, nor leave again just following the fire. He was somewhat relieved to again find the church and see the bay horse still standing where he had tied him. Seemed unlikely that anyone would be brave enough, or stupid enough, to steal a horse in the dark of the night, tied to a hitching post in the middle of a cemetery; but you could just never tell about some folks; besides the bay did carry a very nice rig, especially with that new Henry rim-fire in the scabbard. The two horses nickered their exchange of greetings as he rode up. John scooped up the reins, spoke to quiet the Bay and turned to leave, then paused to look back toward the grave, and though he could not even see it in the dark, he spoke a promise into the quiet night, "I'll be back my friend, you rest in peace."

John got up on the road that headed east toward the ford at the Red River. He was struck by the fact that the last two previous times he had been on this road, he had been with Joshua both times. The first was after that first shoot-out at Friel's and they were riding double on the gray mare, leading the stolen Appaloosa team back to the camp on the Red where Miss Savannah and Glenn waited. Then the following day John and Joshua returned with the others 'cause Miss Savannah had insisted that they had to again tell their story to the Marshal at Texarkana. Likely she had made a good decision since they never became wanted over the shooting; hard to tell how this one might yet play out. He had one more 'visit' to make in this area, and then he wished to be forever finished with Texarkana, but he knew he was only startin' with Gene Roberts.

Not feeling tired, John rode on deep in to the night and just before dawn made a cold camp on the north side of the river, just south of the crossing; about where he and Glenn had first met Miss Savannah. That would also be where she had held them at gun point thinking they might be the ones who had taken her horses. Made John smile to think on it; Sarah and Miss Savannah were the only two young, women he had ever known in the entire state of Arkansas, and each had held a gun on him the first time they saw him. *These southern women folk were just not very friendly toward Yankees!* He stripped the tack from the two horses and hobbled them in the good grass near the river. As for himself, he quieted for the moment the noise in his belly with some cold water and beef jerky. He upended his saddle and tried to get some sleep, but his mind insisted on just replaying over and over the events of the night. Finally John had a couple of pulls from the bottle of the under-the-counter good stuff, lit a cigar and laid back to watch the stars.

He couldn't help but blame himself for what had happened; it had, after all, been his idea to stop and twist Friel's tail a bit. If he had just not suggested they do that, well…. The idea that Joshua has sacrificed his own life for John's was more than he could wrap his mind around. After what Joshua's early life had been like, he should have just plain been filled with hatred for white men...any white man, and yet he stepped in front of that gun without a moment to even think about whether it was something he wanted to do, or not. Where do those kinds of unselfish men come from? Sometime later while John contemplated his own questions, exhaustion took its toll over him. When he awoke the sun was well up on its morning journey. John started a small fire to get some coffee water boiling while he saw to the horses and got them ready for the road. With his coffee, broiled bacon and stale biscuits finished, John cleaned up his camp, mounted and pointed the gray toward Camden.

He just did not wish the exposure that riding down Washington Street in Camden would bring, so John decided he would ease to the north and ford the Ouachita River above the Poison Springs about where he and Glenn had crossed months before. He knew there was a detachment of Confederates billeted at Fort Southerland in Camden to guard the Bradley Ferry crossing and there was always the outside chance he might encounter Simcox, the tax collector. After shoving his .44 Colt in Simcox groin when he put his hands on Sarah that day, it was just possible that there next meeting might not go so well. When he and Sarah returned west with the wagon, it would be necessary for them to cross on the ferry and that would take them straight through the commercial area of Camden...but that would be a problem for another day. Just a few miles shy of returning back to the Bradley Ferry Road, John found a free-running spring and made what he planned to be his last night of camp...at least the last one heading east. Tomorrow by mid-day he would arrive at the Graham farm and step out of the saddle and step into his new life. Every time he thought about that he would feel an involuntary chill run the length of his back, how was it that just the thought of Sarah could make the hair stand up on the back of his neck and his arms? John certainly hoped he was ready for this a big step and since he was still heading the gray mare east, he took that as a sign that he had decided that he was!

He was up and moving while the stars could still be seen in the western sky, *guess it's just possible I'm getting some excited about being there!* It was nearing late-morning when he passed the lane to the Purcell place; he thought he saw Jackson Purcell out working his yearling calves. John had a notion to stop and jaw a bit with he and Kathryn, but felt more urgent about getting to Sarah's. Besides they would be back to visit soon with their news. John continued to reach back and pull food items out of his saddlebag and wash it down with water from his canteen; all of this without pausing to rest. He rode past the point where the Confederate patrol under the command of Lieutenant Samuel Hicks had stopped him to explain the new Confederate conscription policy. *I wonder if that Private's nose ever healed where I laid him out with the barrel of the Spencer. That surely did feel fine, at least to me.*

* * * * *

"Jackson, I was beginning to wonder if you were ever going to come in and eat this noon meal, or if I was gonna haft to throw it to the pigs."

"Katie, the strangest thing, I was out there working the calves and I seen this rider go by on the road. And, damned if I didn't think it was that nice Yankee Corporal, John something that was up at the Graham place some months ago. Only thing, he was riding a horse that looked a lot like that gray mare of his, but he was leading a bay and if John was coming back to Mrs. Graham's he wouldn't be bringing another horse with him; there's four or five up to her place now. What do you make of that Ma?"

"Jackson, you've seen that Yankee boy ride past our place about six or seven times in the last six months, do you suppose it's just you a wishin' he'd come back? You had it all set in your mind that he was gonna marry with Sarah and fix up that farm so's you and he could sit out under our cottonwoods and drink your sour mash and smoke his cigars."

"I suppose your right; he wouldn't just ride past with out stoppin' to say 'Howdy' to me. He was just such a damn fine man and that Sarah was 'bout entitled to one of those in her life. For sure John Henry

Graham wasn't worth killin', why the way he hit that sweet woman, if she had any relatives worth warm spit, they'd have killed him long before the Yankee's did him in up there on White Mountain. No, you're likely correct, it's just me wantin' something real nice for that woman and her son and even if he was a Yankee, I think he'd fit that bill. Now Katie, how's it come you set this cold meal down before a workin' man at his own table?"

* * * * *

John made the last bend in the road and pulled up to look the place over. What he saw made his heart sink. Sarah in her letter said it was runnin' down, but he wasn't prepared for the sight before him. Most of the windows in the house were boarded up, with just little slits to see and get some light through. Significant siding was off of the side of the barn he could see, the gates were standing open, and not that it mattered as major sections of the pasture fence were down. The spring house he had worked so hard on had again fallen into the spring. 'Bout the only thing he could see working was the windmill, and it was still pumpin'…that was good, he could at least have a bath, and he was beginning to notice the need of one!

As they turned up the lane to the house the gray mare began to snort and prance, just like she knew where she was…and was very ready to be there. The bay horse just followed along like he'd been doing for the last four days. As John reined up and started to get down, he thought he saw the barrels of a double barrel scattergun ease through the slats covering the kitchen window. In the belief the person on the other end of the double barrel was Sarah; John continued to dismount, then turned toward the window and took off his new cowboy hat. The gun barrel disappeared and he heard the clear female squeal as the summer-kitchen door burst back on its hinges and the blond woman with the most beautiful green eyes John had ever known ran across the door-yard and jumped the last four feet to land in his arms. He had intended to speak a greeting to her but there seemed to be a sweet mouth plastered to his and two arms around his neck that would not have allowed him to back off…had he even been so inclined…which he was not! That kiss continued until both lost all breath. The last time John had kissed Sarah was that early morning he and Glenn had mounted and rode away. That had been a good enough kiss that John could still feel it after six months, but it couldn't hold a candle to this greeting.

"I don't know how John, but I've felt you close for the last two days and when I got up this morning I put on this old pale blue dress you liked so well, 'cause I just knew you were gonna be here soon".

"There must be something about that blue dress Sarah, 'cause both times when I've come callin', you were wearing that dress, and both times you've pointed that scattergun at me; but then neither time have I minded!"

With that Sarah jumped into his arms again and they did it all over again. "I'm sorry John, maybe that's too much kissing too soon."

"There just ain't no such thing as too much kissin' with you Sarah!"

"There isn't too much kissing with you," Sarah corrected.

"Yeah, that's the way I feel too Sarah, there ain't no such thing as too much kissin' with you **either!**"

At that moment Matt, followed closely by a large, black, mixed parentage pup came bounding through the summer-kitchen door, slamming it back as though to once again test the hinges. "John, John you've come back…you gonna stay this time…where's Glenn… how come it is you got two horses…you got a new hat, John…John, momma thinks there's a soldier livin' in our barn…I think Duke members you…you member Duke?"

"Wait, wait, there's a soldier livin' in the barn?"

"I think so John, I've been afraid to go check."

"I'll go take care of that right now; he is after all occupying my bedroom."

"I well…I thought maybe you would stay in the house. It would be a true comfort for Matt and me. I could likely sleep through the night for the first time in six months."

"I just don't feel right about that Sarah in front of Matt and us not being married and all."

"Not with me silly! I was thinking in the summer-kitchen where Glenn stayed. John, I have been so full of fear since all of these people took to the road and just took over this farm. We've barricaded ourselves in the house like we're under siege, only coming out late at night for our necessary things."

"You needn't be fearful any more and yes, I will sleep in the summer-kitchen, but first I'm gonna clear out the barn. That's where I go for my cigar and bath, besides these horses have gotta get some feed and some rest. They've come a long ways."

"Please be careful John I have no idea how many may be in there. Is there anything I can do to help you?"

"You can hand me the scattergun, that's always a good equalizer of numbers. Yes there is something you can do. I'd like you to stand out here in the door-yard where you can be seen from the barn. If they're anything like me they won't be able to not look at that blue dress and the pretty woman wearing it, that'll give me a chance to move around to the back of the cow shed and go in that way."

"Matt, let go of John's leg. He's gonna go up to the barn and we'll wait here in the door-yard."

"You be careful," Matt warned. "Momma says there's some bad men in there!"

As he walked around to the far side of the barn, John loosened the rawhide loop from the hammer of his Colt and broke the scattergun to check the brass loads. It appeared to him that someone had used the horse trough and his shaving mirror since he was last here…

damn it that makes me mad! Who'd these damn renegades think they are to be using my things? He lifted up the wooden hold-close latch and eased the cow-shed door open slightly with the scattergun barrel. *Good, the hinges didn't give him away.* He stepped quickly through the opening and aside out of the back lighting.

A man in the tattered rags of what once had been a butternut uniform was standing at the half-door appreciating the blue dress as Sarah stood in the door-yard. A second man, same colored uniform, was curled-up asleep in his bed roll; his dirty bare feet sticking out from under his blanket. For a brief moment, soldier-to-soldier, John's feelings went out to them and their circumstances. *There but for the goodness of Sarah, stand I.* Sarah; yes, that's why he was here in this barn at this moment!

The sound of the scattergun's hammers being cocked back were deafening in the dark, quiet of the barn. Both renegades jumped as if already shot and swept their eyes frantically through out the dark spaces till they located John; and with John the double-barrels pointed at them.

"That pretty straw-haired lady you've been a watching so intently owns this farm and she ask me to ask you gentlemen to please move on. Now I've not got her upbringing and manners, so I'm just gonna tell ya' to very carefully gather your belongings. If there's a gun in any of those piles you might want to let me know about that, and now would be a mighty good time. You see I've rode a long ways and I'm a mite jumpy today and if either of you comes up with one or does anything that surprises me, well he get's to stay here while the other one will travel on alone. We clear on what's gonna happen here? Don't stare Gentlemen; just nod your head if you understand."

"Mister, I've got an old smoothbore pistol under that blanket."

"Pick it up with just two fingers of your left hand, open the hammer and blow out the igniter cup. Then you can stick it under your belt. But do it easy like!"

"You there in the bed roll, get your boots and put 'em on, you're goin' for a walk."

"I ain't got no boots Mister."

"How long you been walkin' around like that?"

"Just since the frost went out. I'm kind a getting' used to it now. When I was a sleepin' some body stole 'em."

"Which side?"

"Sorry to say, my own."

The surprised men made quick work of gathering their few belongings; all the time watching John as he gave them directions by waving the barrel of the scattergun. John really would not take offense if the two thought him just a little bit crazy.

The three walked slowly down Sarah's lane to the road...the two ahead stealing side-ways glances at the house looking for the straw-haired woman in the pale blue dress; and the one with the scattergun coming along behind. At the road the renegades turned left; toward the west. "If you should decide to try to slip around and come back, know that I'll be watching and well, next time you're gonna be the cause of me diggin' a hole out behind the barn." With those words of parting and a wave of the gun barrel, he watched them trudge out of sight.

John scooped up the ground-tied reins of the two horses and started for the barn. Almost two hours later, bathed, shaved and the horses tended, he returned to the house; stopping to rip the barrier boards off the kitchen windows before he entered to drop his bed-roll on Glenn's cot on the summer-kitchen. He turned to see that he wasn't the only one who had bathed and cleaned up, but thankfully, she had put his favorite pale blue dress back on. *My God but that's a handsome woman!* Sarah had her color of straw hair combed out and laying on her shoulders and when she looked at him with the most beautiful green eyes he had ever seen, his heart just slammed against his chest wall like it needed to escape. And, today she was not even pointing a scattergun at him. *What's that smell; it's kind of like Ma's lilacs in full bloom.* "Sarah, I have so much to tell you, after supper could I put Matt to bed then let's you and me sit on the bench and talk like we did before?"

Later sitting alone on the bench, Sarah was startled and jumped when the screen door shut; her mind was off in Texas in a life she was trying very hard to imagine, yet as hard as she tried, it just wouldn't come to her. She knew it would be alright though because she would be there with John.

"I'm sorry to have startled you just now. As tired as that boy was he just couldn't go to sleep until all of his questions were answered. He's been thinkin' about this trip a whole lot. I believe Duke was asleep before Matt."

"He's so excited and happy that you're here John, but I guess that pretty much describes each of us. We are both gonna be on your heels everywhere you go for the next few days, till we're satisfied you won't be slipping off again without us. Come, sit here and let's watch the evening arrive, I've missed doing that and I've especially missed doing that with you. We had some wonderful conversations on this old bench; I think we need to be taking it along to Texas with us. Please, sit; I'll get us some coffee."

They didn't speak for awhile; they just held hands and enjoyed the peace of the coming night and the pure joy of just being together. Then the flood gates began to open on what had accumulated on John's mind and in his heart and he started to talk about the trip he and Glenn made after leaving Sarah's. He told her about meeting Savannah Wagner and her newly freed slave, Joshua; about his going into the German's saloon lookin' for the men who had stole her team of Appaloosas; and how when he bit off more than he could chew, Joshua had appeared with John's scattergun and covered his back; how they broke Savannah's husband Lewis, a Union Naval Captain, out of the largest Confederate prisoner-of-war compound west of the Mississippi River; Sarah's beautiful green eyes had teared-up when he told her how Lewis had died in Savannah's arms a few days later; And then she laughed when John told about being afraid that he would have to deliver her baby in the back of the wagon before he could arrive at the McCord ranch; how proud he was to be the Godfather of Michael Glenn Wagner and how he thought Savannah and Glenn would soon marry, but how Glenn just didn't know it yet; and finally he described the McCord's and their big, rambling, adobe ranch house and how excited and thankful they were that Sarah and Matt were coming.

"Sarah, I need to tell you how Joshua and I became friends and how I got Joshua killed, that would be how come I'm trailing a horse with an empty saddle behind me. But first, I need to speak about what's in my heart about you…before it just plain explodes! I'm for very sure not much in the way of a proper candidate for a husband for you Sarah. The only thing I own in this world is the gray mare I rode in on, and as you know, I stole her at Pittsburg Landing. And worse, I've no reasonable prospects ahead of me. I know as the oldest son, the homestead in Iowa would be mine when the folks are gone, but I'd likely be arrested by the army if'n I tried to go claim it. But I do believe as does Mr. McCord that we have a reasonable chance to round us up a herd of wild cattle in the southern breaks of Texas, drive them into New Mexico Territory and sell them for Yankee gold. There's said to be over 5 million maverick longhorns runnin' wild in Texas. If we can pull that off, we'll have plenty of money for the McCord's to save their ranch after the South loses this war, and you and me we'll have a start for a ranch of our own…I know it's a wild idea, but I believe we can make it work."

"I've never done this before and I'm not knowing the right words to be said; but as poor as I am Sarah, I'm rich in my love for you. I promise you that I'll love you ever day of your life and more than that, I promise you that you'll know you are loved ever day of your life. I will never lay a hand on you in anger and I promise that no one will ever hurt you again and live to see the following sunset. And, just as I'll be a good husband to you, I'll be a good father to Matt and you and me we'll raise him up to be a good man and to know to love his country and do his duty when called on, and perhaps we'll even give him some brothers and sisters. What I'm trying to say is to ask you proper to marry with me and be Mrs. John Kelley and come to Texas and you and me we'll start a new life together!"

John continued to try to speak some more, but as his heart just continued to push the words out of his mouth it turned to babble. Sarah just gently put her fingers over his mouth and bid him to stop. "I was always told a person shouldn't over sell; when you've got an item sold, just quit and be quiet. John, I just died inside when you rode away six months ago to take Glenn home and I promised myself that if you ever came back up my lane, I would be yours regardless of the terms or conditions. I love you more than I've ever loved anyone and I just cannot imagine any life that does not have you and me together. So yes John Kelley, I'll marry you and feel that rich or poor I've made a wonderful bargain, and my promise to you is there will never be a **night** in your life that you don't know how much you are loved! So when can we do this?"

"I promised Mrs. McCord that we would come back and have the wedding at their place, besides they're about all the family I've got since this war started."

The most important issue settled, John then went on to tell Sarah of his deep friendship for Joshua and how he got him killed when Joshua stepped in front of a bullet meant for John. Before he could finish John begin to let out all of the grief and tears that he had forced down during his trail ride here. Sarah held him, gently rocking their bodies together, and spoke softly to him as he cried it out. She began to understand that Joshua had become the symbol of all the thousands of dead and dying this gentle young man had witnessed, and helped to caused over the last 13 months of the war. She would likely never know what all that had been, what all John had stored away, what it had been like to kill or be killed for days and months on end, without let up. She would help him forget and to fill the void it left with her love for him.

Finally the sobbing had stopped and she just continued to hold him until he was ready to sit up. "There now, I don't have to ever do that again. Tell me, how come it is woman; if you really love me so much, that I'm sitting here with a cup of cold coffee?"

Author's Notes...

Morgan's Raid was a highly publicized invasion of four northern states by fast-moving Confederate cavalry under the command of Confederate Brig. General John Hunt Morgan. The raid jumped off on June 11, 1863, and while called by the name of its commander in the Union States, in the Confederacy it became known as **"The Great Raid of 1863"**. After leaving Sparta, Tennessee, and for the next 46 days General Morgan and his 2400 handpicked Confederate cavalrymen, supported by a battery of light artillery would bring terror and destruction to parts of Tennessee, Kentucky, Indiana and Ohio before their final capture on July 26 near West Point, Ohio.

Morgan's commander, General Braxton Bragg had approved the raid into Kentucky and Tennessee to take some pressure off of his forces, but he had specifically forbid the crossing of the Ohio River and the subsequent invasion of Indiana; an order which Morgan disobeyed, when on July 8 his forces captured two steamboats at Brandenburg, Kentucky, and made the crossing. They continued north across Indiana and on July 13 entered Ohio near Harrison. On July 26, 1863 the Confederate raider with 364 men was cornered and defeated by Union Brig. General James Shackelford at Salineville, Ohio. Morgan and his remaining officers were taken to the Ohio State Penitentiary in Columbus rather than a prisoner-of-war camp; however, the General and six of his officers made a daring escape by tunnel on November 27; only two of the officers were later recaptured. His enlisted men were taken to Camp Douglas outside Chicago, later described as "Eighty Acres of Hell". A compound with one of the highest per capita death rates of any prisoner-of-war camp during the Civil War...on either side!

During his successful raid, Morgan's units captured and then paroled about 6000 Union soldiers, destroyed 34 bridges, disrupted railroads in more than 60 locations, diverted more than ten thousand Union troops from other duties, and seized and destroyed tens of thousands of dollars worth of supplies and food. In Ohio alone, 2500 horses were stolen, and 4374 homes and business raided at a cost to the Ohio taxpayers of nearly $600,000 in damages and $200,000 in militia wages.

The distraction provided by Morgan and his raiders allowed Confederate General Braxton Bragg's forces to execute an orderly retreat to the south without being molested by flanking forces. Morgan would be killed less than a year later in Tennessee while trying to surrender.

Chapter Seven

THE MESSENGER

The five Mexican Vaqueros came up out of the valley of the Middle Concho River east of San Angelo. They were returning from Coahuila in Mexico with 31 head of fine mustang horses of somewhat unclear ownership. The mustangs had also been returning from Mexico, as the herd had been stolen just three weeks before in Texas and driven over the Rio to the south. Initially those thieves thought to sell their new-found herd to the Mexican Emperor Maximilian. But since he had been *installed* by the powers of Europe as the new Emperor of Mexico, he seemed more likely to just take most of the horses he wanted rather than pay gold for them. The next possible *customer* was thought to be the revolutionary leader Benito Juarez. But while the revolution did need horses, it lacked the means to buy them and instead just appealed to the citizen's patriotism for donations. The five men who currently had possession of the herd had left Mexico with 33 head in somewhat of a haste, rather than remain and discuss the various ownership issues with the men who were at the time also laying claim to the herd. One of the mustangs had stepped into a prairie dog hole and broke his front leg and had to be destroyed, and one who obviously had preferred life in Mexico, left the herd during the night crossing of the Rio Grande River and did not returned. But 31 head was more than enough for the cattle drive according to Mr. McCord. Mr. McCord had sent them to Mexico looking to buy about 20 head, but this herd had proved to be a much better deal; besides what little gold Mr. McCord could muster to give them would not have purchased much in the way of trail-worthy horse flesh.

The five men were brothers, just not all to each other. Pedro Alverez was not the oldest of the group, but was considered by the other four to be in charge since he had been with the McCord brand the longest. His brother Juan was the older by a year and considered the best judge of horse flesh. Pedro believed Juan could talk to horses and that he understands them when they talked back. He had seen his brother tame the wildest of horses by just talking quietly to them... horses that would have killed any man that tried to come into their corral. Pedro was glad Juan had agreed to come on this little trip to Mexico, because he, Pedro, really hated horses. As a younger man he had been bit, kicked at and thrown; many times each. To him a horse was one of the dumbest beasts God had ever created. They had that huge and powerful body topped with a brain so small a man could hold it in his one hand. Yet in this country to be without a horse was to be soon dead.

The other three men riding the flank and drag were Pedro and Juan's cousins. After they had listened to Pedro, they decided that trying to drive a herd of wild cows, through Union army lines for no pay except for the prospect of shares at the successful end of the trail, just might be a good thing. The fact that the three were wanted for reasons involving various questionable ownership claims on both sides of the Rio had been helpful in their decision process. They also had been most helpful in locating a mustang herd that might meet the need of their cousins. In fact they themselves had been eyeing this very same herd to sell to yet a third possible customer, the Confederate army. But they decided to yield to their older cousins for the prospect of some Yankee gold down the line, rather than settle for worthless Confederate paper, and all of the alternatives in Mexico seemed quite poor.

Riding the point, Pedro had been the first one to top the ridge out of the river valley. As he always did before leaving the tree cover, he stopped just inside of the tree line to study the open land ahead. After riding under the dark canopy of the fully leafed cottonwoods, the brightness of what lay ahead blinded him. There was another smaller grove of cottonwood trees a few hundred yards ahead, which usually meant more water, but which also would provide cover to whatever, or whoever might be out there. Pedro looked with his practiced eyes both right and left of the cottonwood grove. He saw a dark shape in the grass, which might be just a rock outcropping…but then, might not be either. He waited for the sun blindness to clear and again studied the dark shape, which he noted had not moved. He wanted time to be certain, so he turned in the saddle and held up his hand for the other four to bunch the herd and hold them. A horse, especially one on the trail, is an eating machine and as soon as the riders quit pushing them, the herd immediately stopped in the lush grass, content to do what they had wanted to do all along. Again Pedro looked at the dark shape and this time he decided it was a dead animal of medium size and now he saw the buzzards that had arrived for their meal. As his sight cleared further he began to detect other shapes, this time colored in dark gray, scattered randomly in the grass. He believed them to be sheep…sheep at rest. But sheep would not lie down in the hot noon-day sun to rest when a few yards away they could find cool shade and likely water. He turned back again and called to Juan, "Hold the herd here while I check this out, but keep a watch for my signal."

As Pedro rode out of the tree line he reached back and pulled the new Henry rifle that Mr. McCord had insisted the men bring along. The Henry was still rare in this country and as such quite expensive. Pedro's biggest concern had been that his cousins would try to sell or trade the ones they were carrying. Pedro had promised them uncomfortable and severe consequences should they violate Mr. McCord's trust in them. Pedro chambered a shell and then eased the hammer closed while he was riding. As he approached the closest "outcropping" he could see some white and then realized it was a dead sheep dog. The animal had lain in the sun for some hours and been torn at by the buzzards, so though Pedro could tell it had once been a dog, that was about all. As he rode up the birds backed off a few feet, but as soon as he moved on, they returned for dinner…*not all of God's creatures were beautiful; in fact these were downright ugly!* The first gray bundle was actually a dead ewe and her young lamb. The ewe had been shot at close range and her lamb horse-stomped. *Now who in the hell would do such a mean evil thing?* From his vantage point, Pedro could now see about 25 to30 such bundles; none were moving. As his eyes swept toward the stand of cottonwoods, he saw a man standing, tied to a tree, his head was down and like everything else in view, he was not moving either. This time Pedro eased the hammer full back and cocked as he pointed the horse toward the man and spurred him forward.

Pedro dismounted at the edge of the tree's shade; ground tied the horse and moved cautiously toward the man. He was Mexican, that much Pedro could tell, but he had been severely beaten; probably pistol whipped, and then his clothes torn and hundreds of knife cuts slashed over his face and upper body. He had lost considerable blood and was still bleeding, but the way he hung in his bindings, Pedro thought perhaps he was already dead. He grabbed the canteen from the saddle and approached the man, or what was left of him. As he pulled his head up to look at the face, Pedro's lung full of air left him; the man was Manuel, his youngest brother. He called out to Juan and waved him to come over as he cut the bindings and laid the man down. He bathed his brother's cut face and touched the canteen to his lips, the man's eyes fluttered and then opened, at first not recognizing the face of his brother…then with the recognition, attempted to smile. Pedro held his brother in his arms and spoke softly to him as he tried to clean up his cuts and keep the flies out of the wounds.

"What has happened here, my brother…who did this evil thing to you?"

Manuel eyes opened again and as he tried to speak his voice cracked. When Pedro bent his ear close he heard, "There were three men I never see before. They came hours ago and shoot my dog and my sheep, then the leader he whipped me and cut me and tied me to this tree. He said don't worry spick, your Brother is not far away and he will arrive before you die."

"Why did they do this if you did not even know them?"

"I am on my way to sell my sheep to get money to pay the loan Mr. McCord gives to our mother. When McCord do that, I tell him it is my debt and I will pay him back. That's what I am doing, not because Mr. McCord says time to pay, he says nothing; like loan does not even happen. I do this because I said I do this." Manuel sips again from the offered canteen, and then continues, "These men who come, the leader says he hate John Kelley and will first kill all who love John Kelley and then kill all who Kelley loves, and then he will kill John Kelley. He says I should tell you that "the friends of my enemy are also my enemy". I say I do not know this John Kelley and he says that is okay because I am his messenger and I must tell my brother that he is Eugene Roberts and what he said to me. Then he cuts me some more and they go away. Do you know this John Kelley my brother?"

"Yes, I know John Kelley. He was staying at the McCord ranch, but now he goes to fetch his woman in Arkansas. He is a good man, he saved Mr. Andrew's life, and I do not understand how he could be the cause of this."

"This man Roberts, he says Mr. Kelley kills his two brothers and tries to kill him, but he gets away and already he kills the black man Kelley rides with and soon he will kill all who try to help him. You must warn them quickly, Pedro. This is a very bad man!"

His message and his warning delivered, Manuel lay back in his big brother's arms as if to sleep, but an hour or so later, he just stopped breathing. Two of the cousins stayed with the herd and the other three men dug a grave in the shade of the cottonwood grove. In it they put their dear brother and his dog…the two had spent their lives at hard work together and now they could spend eternity resting together. Over it they placed a simple wooden cross. The sheep they lassoed and pulled into a pile; then set the pile on fire. They agreed that their brother's message was important and Pedro should break off from the herd and ride hard to the McCord's' to tell what had happened here. Juan and his cousins would bring in the horse herd. The Messenger had done as he was told; now it would fall to the rest of them…the Hunter and the Hunted.

Author's Notes…

Colonel Benjamin H. Grierson would lead one of the most successful cavalry diversionary exploits of the entire Civil War. Prior to the war he had traveled the country from area to area starting high school bands; and even had written a campaign song for Lincoln's 1860 run for the presidency. Wanting to do his part for the war, Grierson had volunteered as a private in the infantry; he wanted no part of anything to do with horses. He had nearly died from having been kicked in the face by a horse as a child. Thus it was that in May, 1862, he would be commissioned as a Major in the Illinois 6th Cavalry.

His raid through the length of the state of Mississippi was launched from LaGrange, Tennessee on April 17, 1863, for the purpose of diverting attention and Confederate forces from the defense of Vicksburg. The raid would take 16 days of constant movement spreading a wide range of destruction through the state. In his memoirs, General Grant would describe is as, "One of the most brilliant cavalry exploits of the entire war." However, initially it was left to General Sherman to convince Grant that it was possible for a fast moving force to operate cut off from communications and all lines of supply; a tactic that Sherman himself would use very successfully in his later "March to the Sea". Grierson left LaGrange with 1700 men armed with the new Colt repeating rifles, six 2-pounder cannon, a compass and a pocket map of the state of Mississippi.

Before the column again surfaced in Baton Rouge, Louisiana, the raid covered over 600 miles in 16 days, virtually without rest and with the men limited to one meal per day. They were credited with 100 Confederate soldiers killed or wounded, the destruction of 50 miles of railroad track and telegraph lines on the south's two main rail lines, the capture and destruction of 3000 arms, thousands of dollars in supplies, property, and rolling stock, and the capture of over 1000 head of horses and mules. They tied up all of Confederate General Pemberton's cavalry, over one-third of his infantry and two regiments of artillery for most of that critical 16-day period.

Promoted to Colonel, Grieson would continue to serve the Union cause with distinction throughout the war, moving up to command of a cavalry corps. He would remain in the regular army following the Civil War, battling Indians as a Colonel in command of the 10th US Cavalry (this is the unit that Custer rejected when it was first offered him because it was a colored unit; Custer then selected instead the 7th Cavalry. We now know how Custer's decision worked out). Grierson retired as a Brigadier General in 1890.

The "Hollywood version" of Grierson's Raid was popularized in the movie, **"Horse Soldiers"**, with John Wayne in the starring role.

Chapter Eight

THE RETURN TO TEXAS

When John awoke he couldn't believe how well he had slept, especially for being inside and up off the ground...well, after he finally got to sleep that is. Sarah had come on to the summer-kitchen to kiss him good night and that would have been disturbing enough; but then when she stood in the doorway to talk with him and was back lighted by the lantern in the kitchen, well that image just 'reset' John's sleep clock and suddenly he wasn't tired in the least. *That is one mighty handsome woman and I am so blessed to have her in my life!* Duke finally found John on the cot just after first light and licked the hand that was draped over the side until he was let out. John set the coffee and then went to the barn to start his day and to tend to his horses.

The first task he set himself that day was to rebuild the fence around the barn pasture so he could turn his horses out in the deep grass and could bring the two yearling calves and the three remaining horses that had belong to the renegades, up closer to the house. Sarah had certainly done the correct thing getting them out of sight from the roadway, given the kind of traffic that was comin' past, but now it was time for them to reclaim the farm! Next he went to work greasing the wheels on Sarah's farm wagon and making certain it was going to be road-worthy…that wagon was just a little on the light side and awful small for the trip they had ahead, especially if Sarah wished to take many things along to her new home; but that was what he had to work with and it would make do. He was anxious for them to go to see the Purcell's and that would be a fair test of his team and wagon.

Each evening was spent with them having their coffee together on the bench by the summer-kitchen door, holding hands…John was getting right good at managing a mug of hot coffee with only one hand available, if something had to go it was gonna be the coffee, not the hand! Sarah was filled with questions about Texas, the McCord's, about getting married and starting their life together and this wild-cow hunt and the cattle drive to follow seeking Yankee gold. John shared all he could, but there were many unanswered questions for him too…but one thing he knew; they'd be finding those answers together and that's what, for him, made it worthwhile…more and more he knew he wanted no life that did not include Sarah and Matt. That's what this had always been about; he just didn't know who the life partner in that plan was to be. They each had tried to share their excitement for the future with Matt, but for the six year old, as long as he and John and his momma were going to be together; and he could take Duke along, his world was already complete.

On the fourth day, John hitched his young team to the too-light wagon, saddled Mr. McCord's bay horse that needed some exercise, and with his 'new family', went to call-on the Purcell's. John thought it best if Sarah and sometimes Matt did the driving as they were going to have to do most of driving the team to Texas; he was going to have two yearling calves and two other horses to tend on the road. He felt responsible to take Mr. McCord's horse home that Joshua had been riding, and the way John figured when you owned a bull calf and a heifer calf, well you were on your way to becoming a cattle rancher, and that's what he intended to be…just stay out of the way and let nature take its course. And, he responded to Matt, "Yes, Duke could go to the Purcell's with them and visit his mother one last time."

John was surprised at the large number of ragged Confederate soldiers still on the road, all heading west…many with bad lookin' wounds and limping; many wounded and likely more that a few deserting…all looked sadly under clothed and all were underfed. They were mostly polite and stepped aside as the wagon approached, but all stopped and looked Sarah over as she drove by. It did occur to John that perhaps at least some of their 'manners' might be coming from the 16-shot Henry rifle he had pulled and carried over the saddle in front of him. All at the Purcell's, including Duke's mother, seemed very happy to see them. The day did not get very much older before Jackson, with a nod of his head, directed John out to the chairs in the shade of the cottonwoods. There John told his good Confederate friend about their plans to go to Texas and start their lives together. When the subject of their marriage came up, Jackson excused himself and returned shortly with a clay jug of his sour-mash whiskey; John produced cigars and the two good friends began to drink to everything they could think of that deserved their good wishes; that of course excluded anything related to the war or its politics. Shortly after the drinking started, Jackson gave John two additional Black- Angus calves as a wedding present; now making two horses and four calves John had to try to get to Texas. Mr. Purcell said it was no problem with the calves; they would just put heifer halters on them and after a couple of days of draggin', those calves would walk on to Texas just as nice as you please.

While they were drinking to being able to teach the calves to lead, having run out of things related to marriage and Texas to drink to, Purcell took note of Sarah's spring-board wagon. "Now that's what I otta have, that big Studebaker wagon of mine is just too large and too heavy for Ma and me to just go to Camden in…we just don't need anything like that! You know John that Studebaker of mine would be just the thing for the goin' to Texas in. I've got an Osnaburg top in the barn that would keep all of ya' and Sarah's things nice and dry…yes Sir that would be just the thing."

"I know what a Studebaker wagon is; they're made up there in Indiana by those brothers. We used a lot of them back when I was in the army. But what's an Osnaburg top?"

"It's a waterproof sheeting goes over the wagon. They were first used on the Studebakers to keep folks and their things out of the weather on the Oregon Trail back in '37."

"Damn that would make a nice rig for our traveling alright, but that lightweight team of mine could never drag that heavy schooner all the way to Texas."

"Tell ya' what; we can just make us a trade; how many head of horses you got up at Sarah's anyway?"

"Well I've got five, but I couldn't trade my gray mare, we've been through way too much together, 'sides I stole her and you wouldn't want to be trading for a stole horse. The bay horse I rode over here on belongs to Mr. McCord. My friend Joshua was riding him when he was killed in Texarkana, so I'm honor bound to take that bay back home, course originally he was stole from the army too.. That leaves three; these two and another just like 'em. And you know from my tellin' you before that their ownership might be questioned also, they were rode in by the renegades, but none rode out again. So you're warned that I'd be tradin' horses that I can't prove any ownership on."

"Well from what you told me, that ownership issue likely as not won't ever be raised by the former owners anyway, since you and young Mr. McCord planted them up behind Sarah's barn."

"Please; I'd just as soon every one in the county didn't know about that plantin'!"

"Well then let's do each other a favor; we'll trade wagons and horses. I've got a big, good lookin' team of black, eight year old mares and I'll just trade you the whole lot; team, wagon and top for your three horses and Miss Sarah's spring-wagon. And consider you were doing me a favor."

"I haft to tell ya' Jackson, if I hadn't been drinking your sour-mash and you hadn't been smoking my cigars, and we hadn't already done one fair deal with the calves, I would no more horse-trade with you than I'd fly off of your barn. I think normally you'd just skin this ol' Yankee farm boy from Iowa, but with your affection for Miss Sarah, I'd just likely trust you enough to be inclined to do this deal. But that spring-wagon belongs to Sarah and I best go talk to her first. Being the perfect host you are, you might want to replenish the sour-mash clay-jug while I go have that talk; and be back directly."

"Sarah allows that would be fine with her as she could then be taking more along. She mentioned the *armoire* her mother gave her; pray tell me what's an *armoire?*"

"It a big piece of furniture that's like a closet to hang a person's clothes in. But I've seen the one of Miss Sarah's, it knocks down to lay flat and what's left is a wooden trunk to store in. I'd think you would make her mighty happy if you were to take that along and I'll come up and help you take it down when I come to fetch the other horse you owe me. Besides as you are about to learn from experience, it pays big rewards to have your woman happy with you!"

"Well then, I guess we've got a deal. Let's go see about some harness for my new team and gettin' the top for the Studebaker."

Just before dark when the three and Duke started home in the big Studebaker pulled by a fine looking pair of black mares, each with a bald face; it was agreed that John would also ride with them in the wagon. Sarah's stated reasoning was just in case she had any trouble with the new team; the true reason had more to do with John being able to sit a horse after he and Jackson Purcell had spent much of the day too close to the clay jug. They also had the two new Black Angus heifer calves haltered to the back; and as Mr. Purcell had suggested they would, they were dragged most of the way home, balling all the time. The bay horse was also tied to the back, but he kept walking as far up beside the wagon as the lead rope would allow. John thought he was perhaps ashamed to be seen walking in the company of those bawling calves.

Over the next few days, John would grease yet another set of wagon wheels, wet down the Osnaburg top and stretch it tight on the wagon frame and build a false bottom in the wagon as a place to hide their "valuables" and the other weapons they would be taking along. Sarah and Matt thought the funniest thing they had ever seen was John trying to wrestle down the first two calves and get them haltered. He finally won the battle, but both clothes and body washing had to follow as those calves each drug him through a big mud puddle besides the creek. In a few days the Purcell's drove their new spring-wagon and team up to help load out the Studebaker and close up the farm. It was clear that this last step was the most difficult for Sarah; trying to make decisions as to what to take to her new life and what to leave behind in the house. She had the hollow feeling that she would never see the place again, and while that also meant she could leave some very bad memories behind of her life with John Henry, it was still the place she knew best and had made a home for she and Matt ever since John Henry left them for The War…the war he did not come back from.

Before dawn on the 14th of May, 1863, Sarah and Matthew Graham, definitely of the "Southern Persuasion", were seen in the company of a Mr. John Michael Kelley, late of the Iowa 14th Regiment of Grant's Army of The Frontier as they stepped up into a Studebaker schooner with a tight, white Osnaburg top and started down the lane to a western-heading wagon road. They were but ten yards into their trip when John hollered for Sarah to stop as he dismounted and ran back to the summer-kitchen door. He returned to the wagon with the old bench where he and Sarah had enjoyed so much coffee and conversation…in fact, where he had proposed marriage to Sarah and she had accepted! That piece of furniture simply had to go to their new home, even if something else had to come off the load! Sarah turned her head away so John could not see the tears his sentiment had brought forth.

* * * * *

It was already light far to the east in Washington City as the 16th President of The United States sat in a quiet corner of his office with his writing desk perched on his knees. He looked back from his office window and took up the pen and started a note to his latest appointed General who, like the two before him, had failed to lead the mighty Army of The Potomac to prosecute the War. "My Dear General Hooker", it started; then went on, "Some of your troops and Division Commanders are not giving you their entire confidence, as Sir, neither is your Commander."

One month later, on June 15, Lee's smaller Army of Northern Virginia is already pressing northward into Pennsylvania and moving around Hooker's 122,000 man army. General Hooker will wire the President; that the Southern invasion is something that, "it is not in my power to prevent." On June 27, President Lincoln finally removed General Hooker from command and replaced him with General George Meade; this but three days before the start of the great campaign at Gettysburg.

* * * * *

John was less than comfortable as the team and his tethered animals stepped off of the Bradley ferry onto the streets of Camden, Arkansas; in fact he was mighty uncomfortable. But they were left with little choice; he knew most of the trails north of Camden that crossed the Ouachita River and none of them would permit passage of their Studebaker schooner. Besides, Sarah feared she might owe the storekeeper at the Emporium some money for butter or cream that she had not been able to deliver and wished to settle up; and too they would need some supplies for their trip. John's other concern, besides the fact there were Confederate troops stationed in Camden, was that the Emporium was directly across Washington Street from the Tax Collector's office. That was the office where he had jammed his .44 Colt into the groin of Mr. Simcox, the Ouachita County Tax Collector, when that bastard had come around the counter and put his hands on Sarah during their last trip here together. He had seen himself as God's gift to widows, especially those widows who owed back taxes and had little money with which to pay them. He had a scheme all worked out that would involve 'trading favors for favors'. John had with some physical force and great satisfaction quickly settled the issue; besides Sarah had the money to pay, thanks to the four renegades that were now buried up behind her barn. He decided he would stay with the rig and the animals while Sarah went inside. She had suggested that she would buy John a new pair of boots; his current ones showing much wear. But he had firmly declined with, "I have soaked these leather boots and walked them dry many times till they just fit me real fine, I've no need for others nor time to fit 'em. But I sure would admire to have a tin of those yeller peaches."

As it turned out, John's concern was all for not as it seems that the Tax Collector had left his position as County Tax Collector in somewhat of a rush. This had occurred when a Confederate soldier long thought dead on the battlefield had returned to learn of Mr. Simcox's "tax payment" plan for his 'widow'. It made John sorry not to have witnessed that 'discussion' and the hasty departure of Simcox! So with that departure, John and Sarah's Camden visit proved to be uneventful.

They arrived at the ford for the Red River late in the day and exhausted, with Sarah and the animals all just wanting to rest and wait to cross in the morning. But John was adamant that they would cross yet that evening. "There's been rain up stream some. If we wait to cross in the morning and the river swells over night, I could be puttin' all of you in danger and that I'll not do. No, we'll cross now then camp." And, cross they did! But first, John and the gray mare made a number of trips back 'n forth to check the condition of the bottom. Satisfied, he motioned Sarah forward with the request, "Stop in the middle for about five minutes, I want those wheels to soak and swell against the iron rims. Then after a time, pull forward just enough for the other half of the wheels to soak; besides it'll give the animals a chance to water." They had a quick meal, cleaned up and went to bed, Sarah and Matt in the Studebaker and John, as he always did, on his upturned saddle just out of the fire light…the Henry and a cup of Sarah's coffee close at hand.

Just before the dawn, John awoke as usual, but this time to the noise of the roaring of water. He moved to the bank of the Red to see that yesterday's quiet stream had risen about two feet over night and watched as the strong current was sweeping piles of dead tree limbs and debris ahead of it. John didn't mention the change in the strength of the river, but he saw Sarah take note of it as they were getting ready to leave. The four calves seemed to be getting the idea and this morning decided to be led, as opposed to being drug. The best part of this morning so far was Sarah's good morning kiss, John missed trailing with Joshua, but Sarah's morning greeting certainly was much the better…a fella could get use to that!

Just before reaching Texarkana, John led them off the main road and pulled up before a country church and its next-door cemetery. He dismounted fished around under the false bottom on the wagon and withdrawing a board; he said he would be back shortly. Sarah knew from the story John had told her on his arrival that this was where he had buried his friend Joshua. While John secured the cedar board at the head of Joshua's grave, Sarah and Matt picked a bunch of Black-eyed Susan's from along the roadway and joined John at the grave site. He had mounted a marker that he had hand-carved, and with Mr. Purcell's help, had painted in the white letters:

Joshua Green
1841 – 1863
RIP

"That's mighty nice John; is that what you've been doing up in the barn for the last few days?"

"Yes; I promised Joshua I would be back and mark his grave. He has no kin that I know of so I guess it don't matter to anyone but me; now then I've kept my promise to the man who gave his life for mine. He and I had just picked his new last name the day before he died, so I guess this now makes it his." As John look back at his handy work, he was pleased that the letters in the name "Green" had come out just a little the larger.

On the way out of the other side of town, John pulled up and pointed out to Sarah the burned-out pile of rubble that once had been Friel's saloon. "That's Joshua's other marker. I gave him that one too."

John spent a part of his days riding in the wagon with Sarah and Matt. It gave him the chance to relieve Sarah of all of the driving and it gave him the chance to be close to her. The wagon seat was generously wide, but he did notice that when the three of them rode the seat, Sarah's hip and thigh were always pressed tightly against his...not at all an unpleasant experience. When he did ride the mare to give her some exercise, John had taken to riding double with Matt. Matt was always full of questions and it gave the "boys" a chance to bond. The sight always brought a smile to Sarah's face and that for John was also not an unpleasant experience either...*that is one mighty good lookin' woman.* On one such ride Matt began to question John about the war and wondering what it was like. Finally John said of his army life, "There's a lot of just waiting around, followed by some very long walks through strange country to another place to wait around. There's standing in line and there's getting' real dirty crawling through the brush. Ever once in awhile there's a lot of shootin' with you tryin' to kill people you don't even know but that look a lot like you...and there's them shootin' back and tryin' to kill you. If'n you're lucky, it don't last too long and you don't get shot. The rest of it is just bad food and boredom and a good thing to stay away from."

The next two days were uneventful on the trail. The animals had become nicely trail broke and Sarah was doing a fine job driving the team of black mares, even Matt drove a little when he wasn't riding up behind John on the gray mare. On the plains west of Tyler, they decide to call it an early day; to give John a chance to check the grease on the Studebaker's hubs after their many river crossings, and to try to find some of the quail that he had heard calling all afternoon. After the camp had been set up and a fire started, John took his double-barreled scattergun and walked up into the timber. Remembering Joshua's experience with the rattler, he spent much of his time looking at the ground before he stepped. He likely missed seeing a few birds because of that, but still returned with four nice quail. And, as his grandfather had always cautioned him, he let them fly a bit so when he shot the birds were not all shot to hell. He remembered that as a youngster, the first rabbit he had brought home for supper; and the pile of buckshot on his grandfather's plate after he ate the first piece. Then Grandpa's instructions to the young hunter, "Next time boy, you might let him run a little 'fore you shoot".

The sun was still well up as John and Sarah took their coffee to the summer-kitchen bench that John had brought out and set up by the fire each evening. As they were talking, John noticed Duke raise his head and then heard the low growl develop. As he started to turn, he saw the horses also reacting to something, or someone. Their heads had popped up and their ears came to a full point. John immediately sent Sarah and Matt into the wagon and picked up his Henry and chambered a shell. Horses and dogs were much too good of a sentry to ignore; they heard and smelled things long before a human could, especially when the breeze was in the right direction. With Duke at his side, he stepped away from the wagon and into the tree line and settled down to wait. Shortly, a single rider crested the hill about 500 yards up their back trail. He clearly had seen their camp and was riding toward it at a slow loop. About 50 yards out the rider stopped and hailed the camp. John studied the single rider through his spy-glass; he didn't look to give cause for concern…just the usual caution with a stranger on the open trail, providing of course he wasn't the advanced rider for a larger group to follow. John returned the hail and invited him into the camp but with the warning to keep his hands visible.

As the rider came closer, John's first mystery was solved. He could see something black on part of the stranger's face, but couldn't see it well enough to identify. Now he saw, it was a black eye patch covering the left eye, with a black band around his head to hold it in place. The man stopped his horse and waited for the invitation to get down. "Where you from and where you headed out here?"

"Well, I've been trying to get into this war, but neither side it seems will have me cause I'm short one eye. I keep trying to explain that's the eye I close when I shoot anyway, so I don't really need it, but that didn't help. As for where I'm going, I don't rightly know, I'm kind of following this horse and at the moment he's headed west, but I'm hopeful that I'll recognize the place I'm seeking when I ride up to it."

"We're just having our coffee and you're welcome to light and have some with us. We've finished dinner, but my...er...wife will fix you a plate if you haven't eaten in a spell."

"I'd much welcome both of those. I wonder if I might strip the rig from my horse and let 'em rest a spell?"

John offered out his hand with the greeting, "My name's John Kelley and this here is Sarah and Matt. You are?"

The stranger looked at Sarah and swept off his hat turning loose a flock of reddish hair. "I'm Bernard Tierney, my middle name's Craig so most folks just call me BC. Kelley is it, now that sound's Irish?"

"In deed it 'tis, Orange-Irish! My Grandfather came from Ireland in the hole of a leaky ship he stole aboard and went to Iowa to homestead. And you Mr. Tierney?"

"Well sir, your grandfather and I likely left the mother-country from the same place. You can only leave by sea and so most that leave come out through the city we Irish call Cobh, that's Gaelic, but since the English took over our country they won't allow Gaelic to be spoken. For awhile we were forced to call the city Cove, but then they decided to rename it for their Queen Victoria and make us call it Queenstown. So that's how it's known now."

"That's terrible to make you give up your country's language."

"Well, one day we'll drive their bloody army out just like you folks did and then we'll rename it as it should be called; Cobh!" Now me, I'd be a follower of the Church of Rome and I was raised in Limerick, Ireland. My mother and my two sisters work in the Tait Company factory there for Mr. Peter Tait himself, sewing uniforms for the Confederate army. That's how I became interested in coming to America and being in this war; but no one side would have me."

(BC's prophecy of an independent Ireland did not come to pass until the proclamation of The Republic of Ireland on April 18, 1949.)

"Confederate uniforms are made in Ireland?"

"Deed some are. Mr. Tait started the company in '52 sewing uniforms for the British Army in the Crimean War. Now he sends his uniforms to the Army of Northern Virginia and the Army of Tennessee."

"Well, far as I know, I've not put any holes in any of your mother's uniforms. But if'n I have, it was truly done a purpose."

The longer the two men talked the more they revealed and the friendlier they became. Finally when John thought it impolite to welcome a fellow Irishman, even one of the Pope's people, without a cigar and a taste of good whiskey, Sarah bid her goodnights and she and Matt left the fire to the men.

"Mr. Tier...BC, since you're not having to be someplace in a hurry, maybe you'd care to ride along with us. Miss Sarah, no she's not my wife just yet; we're going to the Hill Country in western Texas to a friend's ranch for Sarah and me to be married. But first, we're all going wild-cow huntin' down in mid-Texas to build us a herd of unbranded maverick cattle. They're just runnin' wild and we're gonna catch a thousand or so head of 'em and drive 'em to the Union forts in New Mexico Territory or on to the Colorado mines for Yankee gold. How's that sound to you?"

"You've gotta be Irish alright. No one but an Irishman could concoct a wild idea like that one and then expect others to just throw in with ya'. Didn't hear you mention pay; and besides what do you, a farm boy know about rounded up and driving wild cattle?"

"They'll be no pay cause there's no money with which to pay any of us. We're doing this for trail-meals, cartridges and shares at the end, so you'd have to come that way too. As for wild cattle, I don't know a damn thing about either roundin' up or drivin', but we'd be going with some good people who do. I just figure to keep my eyes open, my mouth shut and pay attention and learn. You could consider tryin' the same."

Two days later, the four pulled up to water the stock and themselves at Marshall's Ford on the Llano River. Again, John saw recent tracks made by about a dozen Indian ponies. He pointed them out to BC, but he'd already noted them. John was becoming more comfortable that he'd found a good man to join their next adventure. That first morning as they were saddling their horses, BC had looked at John's rig and noted, "That's one of those new Henry rim-fire, 16-shot rifles isn't it? There's not many of those around; in fact the only other one I've seen was being carried by Yankee Colonel named John Thomas Wilder of the 17th Indiana Lightening Brigade. He had bought new Spencer .56's for each of his troops and a Henry .44 for himself…all out of his own pocket."

"I know of the Colonel, he fought with us at Pittsburg Landing under General Don Carlos Burell."

In the late afternoon one of the Vaqueros that rode for the '*A-L*'brand had spotted the wagon and the two riders and had ridden hard to alert the McCord household. By the time John, Sarah, BC Tierney, Matt and his dog, and the collection of led horses and yearling calves arrived at the sprawling adobe home, all the residents were gathered for the welcome. The look of astonishment was obvious on their faces when they noted that John, who had left with a black man, had returned with a white one…with reddish hair at that! Well into the late afternoon there were introductions, handshakes, and lots of huggin'. As welcome as they made BC feel, there was great sadness over the death of Joshua and even more admiration as well when John told the story of why and how he had died.

BC was made comfortable in the bunkhouse and warned about the near-colorless liquid that the Vaqueros would be passin' around in fruit-jars. Sarah and the women went off to another part of the house to start making plans for not just one, but now two weddings…seems John's observations about Glenn and Savannah Wagner had been correct. Angus, Glenn and John retired to their favorite location around the fire pit, even with out a fire; it was their favorite spot… and with it always came cigars and now some of John's under-the-counter whiskey, unintentionally furnished by Mr. Friel.

When all the story telling was finished, Angus ask John about Mr. Tierney and if he would be up to the task ahead.

After some deep thought, John responded, "At first, I think he hung around and rode with us cause of Sarah's iron-skillet biscuits and my whiskey. But later when I told him of our plans and we shook hands, I looked into the face of the man. There was pride and courage there and it told me that if trouble comes, this man would stand. That was good enough for me, so I invited him to throw in."

"He'll likely be tested along with us and any who ride with us." Then Angus told John about Manuel's painful death and the threats delivered by Eugene Roberts; how he now had the house guarded at all times and any who rode from there always rode in pairs; never alone.

"When he shot Joshua like a damn coward from ambush, I had the message delivered to Roberts that he would now become the hunted, no longer just the hunter; perhaps it's time for me to go find him and settle this for all time!"

Author's Notes...

The **Missouri Compromise of 1820** was but one of many acts that attempted to avoid a war between the states over the issue of slavery by proposing to define how slave-verses-free status would be applied in the new western territories of the Louisiana Purchase. At the same time both sides felt the need to maintain the balance of slave states and free states in the congress of the United States. That issue had been become somewhat less complicated in December, 1819, with the admission of Alabama with a constitution which recognized slavery; that action had again brought balance between slave and free. It was then agreed in the congress that since Missouri had applied for admission as a slave state, Maine would be admitted as a free state...the balance continued; however, this agreement left open the question of what to do with the new territories as they applied for statehood.

Congress then adopted an amendment by Representative Jesse B. Thomas of Illinois which excluded slavery from the new territory north of the parallel 36 degrees-30 minutes (the southern boundary of Missouri) except within the limits of the proposed state of Missouri. U. S. Senator Daniel Webster endorsed the Compromise as a means of preserving the Union and delivered an impassioned three hour speech to the Senate to achieve a favorable vote. This compromise would stand until 1857 when the U.S. Supreme Court by a 7 to 2 vote, ruled it unconstitutional.

(Note on the following map of the young United States and the territories at the time of the Compromise of 1820.)

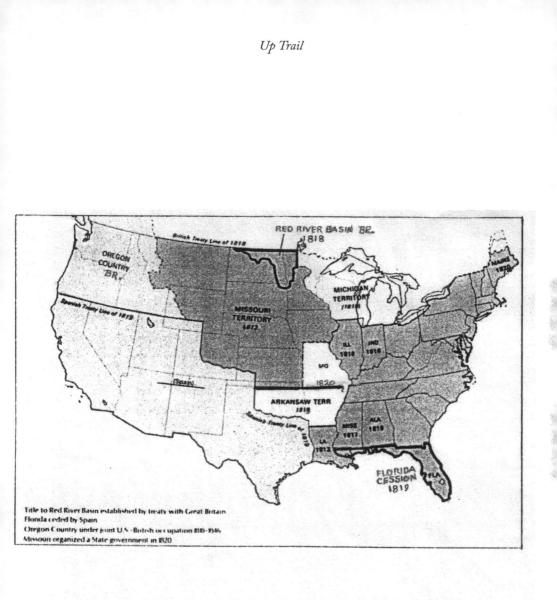

THE LINE OF THE MISSOURI COMPROMISE OF 1820

Chapter Nine

'THE HUNTER' BECOMES 'THE HUNTED'

John stretched out to his full over six-foot length on his bed, hands clasped behind his head and smiling toward the dark ceiling of his room. It did not matter that all of him from of his ankles down was at that moment hanging out over the end of his bed. He was comfortable and he was happy; as happy as he could remember being at least since he had left his ma and pa and the homestead. It just didn't matter that this bed was considerable too short for his frame, when he slept in it he slept on his side and was a good fit. When he slept on the ground, he slept on his back and, well there was nothing to hang over when he slept on the ground.

Since he, Sarah and Matt had arrived at the McCord's, and now with Glenn and Savannah planning their wedding also, John thought this must be about as good as life can get! They were going to have to find a suitable man for Suzanne, but the man strong enough for that match just may not have been invented yet. He would have to be someone with an excess of patience, and yet great firmness, and the wisdom to know which to apply, and when. Perhaps BC the Irishman they had met on the trail? They'd all have to watch and see if he measured up to the size of that task; she was a beauty but she would surely be a handful. When John and Glenn had first started on the trail to Texas, John had at times let his imagination wonder about Suzanne, but after he met Sarah, faded blue dress, scattergun and all, his entire world had changed.

With the arrival of the horse herd from Mexico, the plans for the wild-cow hunt and the drive into New Mexico territory for Union gold were coming together. It all made John feel Joshua's absence more deeply. The two of them had planned to make this drive together and maybe start ranches beside each other, spending their lives being neighbors and helping each other. The trail of his thoughts now re-focused on Joshua and the selfless sacrifice he'd made to save John's life. He was so deep in thought that when his ears first registered the high-pitched scream that split the quiet of his night, his mind being elsewhere he could not identify it. Now there it was again…almost human, and yet not quite human. Now certain he had really heard this primal noise, John pulled on his sail-cloth trousers, stepped into his boots and pulled them on, pulled the Colt from the holster draped around the bed-post and stuck it behind his belt, all as he headed for the door. He wasn't certain in which direction to head, and then he saw the Vaqueros carrying pitch torches and running toward the fenced pasture close-by the barn. As he ran up to the circle of cowboys, they parted slowly and he saw his gray mare thrashing on the ground. She continued her screaming until she saw John, and then became quiet as if waiting for him to help her. As he walked up, she followed his movements with her big black eyes. As more light came into the circle it illuminated the mare and the problem; she had what looked to be the handle of a pitch fork coming out of her chest with the tines buried so deep in her that they were no longer visible. Large rivers of dark colored blood were running from her open mouth and nose and squirting from around the pitch fork in her chest, as though under pressure.

As he watched dumbstruck, John felt a hand clamp firmly on his shoulder; he turned and looked into Glenn's face. "Who could do this? What mean, sick son-of-a bitch could do this?" But, he knew the answer, though unspoken.

"We'll speak of this later; right now she's got to be put down. You walk away and I'll do it for you, and for the mare; I'll end her suffering."

"No! She and I, we've been over too many tough trails together. This is my job, I owe her." John pulled the .44 from his belt and held it down close to his right leg where she wouldn't see it as he approached her. He knelt down, put his hand on her bloody muzzle and spoke softly to her. Then he stood and walked around her head; she tried to follow him with her eyes, but John cupped his hand around her eye like a blinder. She pawed the ground trying to move her body around with him, to stay close to him, to just be able to see him. Her ear sensed the close presence of the big Colt and twitched like she was shooing a fly. The night's stillness was interrupted by the report of the big Colt and then again by the echo that was returned from the nearby hills to the small circle of the *A-L* residents gathered there.

Even though he knew it was coming and thought himself set, Angus' body jumped at the report of the .44. He saw the mare's fore legs thrash as she tried to move with John; then with the noise, she relaxed and was still. The shoulders of the young man standing at the mare's head holding the now smoking .44 slumped and shook slightly as his body sobbed. Then he straightened, drew up to his full height, and when John turned his face to the light of the torches, Angus knew he had never seen such rage on a face before. This young man had put on the mask of the hunter...a killer; maybe it had been hidden there just below the surface since Joshua was killed; but it was certainly there now. Angus said a silent prayer for the young man before him and also prayed that for however long he might be allowed to live on this earth; no one with such a look would ever come lookin' for a McCord.

"Mr. McCord, I'll be needin' the loan of a horse, if you please."

"Sure boy, but you can't go do this thing alone. Let me send Pedro along. If Roberts did this thing, there's bound to be 3 maybe 4 ridin' with 'em."

"Pedro's welcome long as he don't get in my way. If'n there's 3, 4, I don't care how many; I'll just intend to kill 'em all and leave God to sort 'em out."

Then Pedro walked up to the group and announced to Angus, "Mr. McCord I'll be leavin' you for awhile to go find these killers of my brother, they've now got to be close by. None of us are safe here, nor ever will be again as long as he's allowed to live. At this moment we've got guards riding in pairs around this ranch and yet this happens just a few feet from the house."

"John's determined to go run 'em to ground, if'n you're going', I'd like the two of you to go together. Can you get a horse ready for John?"

"I told you, I don't need anyone to go baby-sit me. That son-of-a-bitch has killed Joshua and now my mare. He's made this personal between him and me and I intend for it to be settled now before it involves Sarah, or some of your family!"

"John I respect that, but you don't know the country you'll be riding over, Pedro does. Most folks between here and the Rio will be Mexican and you not only don't speak their language, you don't even speak our brand of English very well. Who's more likely to be able to get the help and the information you'll be needin', you or Pedro? Besides, you simply can't go before it get's light. Hell boy use your head, you must know better than that to have lived for 13 months while people shot at you. He's likely waiting out there for you to go chargin' off into the darkness."

"Alright, it's me and Pedro, now how about the horse?"

"Mr. John, I will have my brother Juan get you a horse from the mustang herd. Did you see anything you'd fancy?"

"We're not gonna do this 'Mr.' crap! This is the same conversation I had with Joshua…its Pedro and John, or you don't go. Now I haven't got the time or inclination to try to rough break a wild mustang, I need something that's reliable and trail-ready. But if'n I did, I'd try that dun mare with the black mane and tail, she looks to be strong enough for the trail."

"You may talk funny, but you've got a good eye for horse flesh; she would 'ave been my choice. As for breaking 'em, no need; my brother, he talks to horses. By the time you are ready and its light enough to be safe, the mare will be ready also."

John knew that the next person he must talk to would be Sarah, and when he turned from Pedro, there she stood; waiting. Her hair was down loose on her shoulders and kind of combed out, all straw colored and catching the light from the torches. She had a long robe or maybe it was a blanket around her and clutched tightly in front. John's first thought that did not include his gray mare was to wonder what she might have on under that blanket and suddenly he could think of nothing else beyond what that might be…or might not be. She was never more beautiful that he knew for certain, and as he moved toward her the most beautiful green eyes he had ever seen were filled with tears and locked on his. He wrapped her in his arms and suddenly realized they were both inside that blanket and he never knew just how that happened…nor cared!

"Oh John, I am so sorry about the mare, I know what she meant to you and what the two of you had been through together. But please John, don't do anything foolish, I've waited and searched all of my life for you and I could not bear it if I were to lose you now. Why can't you wait for the Lord to deliver this enemy to you? He will put this enemy in front of you."

"I will be careful Sarah, but when you think on it you'll know this is something I have to do…for me and for us. We'll never be free to live our lives as long as this evil is allowed to walk the same earth with us. I aim to fix it so's he never a threat to us again. Besides, perhaps the Lord has just now put this evil man before me. As my pa would tell us boys, 'it's always good to ride around trouble when you can, but they'll always be just some trouble you can't ride around'. You focus on getting' our weddin' planned, just don't you dare start without me!"

"John it just seems like every time we get close, something happens and you leave me again."

"You well know why I left you in Arkansas; I had made a pledge to get Glenn home and that I had to do. Yes, he released me from that promise, but it wasn't his to release. Sarah, it seems for the last five years of my life I've always wished to be someplace where I was not; then I met you and since the moment I first looked into those green eyes, I've only wished to be where you are. I'm gonna go and get this done, then we can begin our life together."

"But John there is not enough of you, there's only you and Pedro, and Roberts could well have four or five men waiting out there in the dark for you!"

"What Roberts don't yet know, but will soon learn, only one of us Kelley's can be quite a few, when we're mad; and I'm mad as hell!" Then they kissed goodbye.

Angus, Pedro, Glenn and John hunkered down in the dust and by the light of a lantern, started working up their trail plan by drawing maps in the dust. Every time one disagreed with the others, he would swipe out the dust map the other had made and start his own plan. It was finally agreed that if Roberts had remained close by watching and waiting to see if he was to be followed, it would likely be to the south or southeast; there were more towns in that direction and it was an easier trail to Mexico if'n he decided to head there for things to cool off. So, John and Pedro would leave just before first light and ride west from the ranch into the Blanco River canyon for cover. Then follow that to the southwest and swing around east and head for the first town of any size, San Angelo. That would possibly put them between Roberts and the Rio, if they were headed to Mexico and not in any hurry, or if the gang got there first and were ahead them, at least allow them to cut their trail and then follow on. Pedro knew a lot of people around San Angelo and, if he checked, likely had lots of relatives that would be sympathetic to what had happened to his brother, Manuel. If Roberts had gone that way, someone would have seen 'em and if that someone was Mexican, he would tell Pedro.

John did not understand any of it, but had to admit Pedro had been correct about the "conversation" between the dun mare and his brother Juan; she behaved just like she had been trail-worthy all of her young life. Could be augured that her manners were better than the gray mare's, but John did not want to make that comparison, least not now. The two men, with three horses, left an hour before there was any light on the ground; John had to ride close and rely on Pedro's knowledge of the terrain. They decided to take one horse as a pack animal because Lucinda had packed enough food for a small army in the field; and it would give the men another horse to ride should anything happen to a mount. About the time the first light appeared in the east, the men entered Blanco Canyon and disappeared from sight. They agreed that even if Roberts had waited to see if he was to be followed, he would be too nervous to wait long after first light.

The sun was well into its journey to the western horizon when the men came up out of the canyon formed by the Blanco River, and being careful not to get silhouetted against the bright sky, began to move south for the Johnston Draw which would eventually carry them back toward the east and the Middle Concho River. It was a wild, rugged and mostly uninhabited country, very unlike any John had ever seen. Pedro had cautioned to be on the lookout for Indians, for this was the home range of the eastern Muscalero Apache, a tribe of fierce fighters that roamed throughout the southwest. Best get used to it as most of this up-coming cattle drive would be on their hunting grounds. The Muscalero could catch wild cattle to feed the tribe whenever they needed, but wouldn't as long as they could steal 'em from someone who had already rounded 'em up! John was excited with all of the wild, maverick cattle they saw running the breaks. As soon as this business was out of the way, they'd be back for the wild-cow hunt, and there appeared to be plenty to hunt! Pedro said they would bring the horse herd and the wagons down and start the trail drive from here; then working west into the desert and on to the Pecos River. Then they'd be following the river north to the Yankee forts of the New Mexico Territory. John thought that certainly sounded easy…how difficult could that be?

They stopped well before dark each day. Pedro wanted to build a small cook fire and then have it extinguished before it was dark enough to be seen. After dark, they would climb the highest rise in the area, and with John's spyglass look for careless camp fires. John liked traveling with Pedro and hearing the stories of his growing up in this country and learning from his knowledge of their surroundings. After their scouting for fires and before one of them hit the bed roll, they would share a drink, usually Pedro had tequila and John the sour mash, they had traded drinks, but each decided to stay with what he had become accustomed to; and John would bring out a couple of the German's good cigars. Pedro was more than a little interested in how John had acquired so many good cigars. When they were packed and ready to mount up the next morning, Pedro watched John and then commented, "You're much like an Indian the way you clean up a camp before you go. An Indian can stay all night and cook a meal and the next day one would have to look close to see even wood ashes. You leave a camp that same way, you part Indian?"

"No, but growing up my best friend was and he taught me the respect the Indian has for Mother Earth and wouldn't camp with me till I did the same. Just a habit I never got over."

They worked their way down the wilds of the Middle Concho which Pedro said would eventually lead them to the frontier town of San Angelo. This was clearly sheep country and on this second day, Pedro had twice stopped to visit with the Mexican sheepherders they encountered. None had any news that proved useful, but then perhaps no news was good news; since there was no report of the Roberts gang being spotted it likely meant they were still somewhere ahead of them. John was fascinated watching the way the sheep dogs worked at keeping the sheep moving, yet at a pace that allowed them to graze. With the dogs constantly moving around the flock, it was as if they knew where every animal was at any given minute. Pedro told John this was what his brother, Manuel, was doing when Roberts and his men jumped him and killed him and the flock, and how he had ridden up on the scene a short time later, just before Manuel died. Then they took a short side trip so Pedro could visit his brother's grave.

John was standing off a respectful distance, holding the reins of the three horses, hat in hand while Pedro spoke a quiet prayer over his brother's grave. Something flashed in the corner of John's eye and distracted his attention; he looked to his left in time to see the sun reflect briefly off of something metallic. His months of army training and war experience shouted "gun" in his head and he hollered a warning to Pedro and then dove between the horses. The pack horse screamed and fell into him…then he heard the report come echoing over the plains they had just crossed. John jumped up and pulled violently at the two saddled horses and the three ran into the grove of cottonwood trees where Pedro was crouched low behind a tree.

"Did you see that John, what the hell was it?"

"Someone on that rise out there about 500 yards just shot at us. Think he likely killed the pack horse. Hell of a shot from that distance must be a Sharps, likely a sniper's rifle which was good in a way because they are only a single-shot weapon. We'll just hunker down here for a bit, see what he intends cause I expect he's waitin' to kill us if we move out of this cover."

"Was he shooting at you or the horse?"

"I believe it was me. I just saw the sun reflect off something and dove between the horses. Sides, the horse likely never did anything to 'em, but I sure as hell have."

"I'm pleased it was the horse not you; I just don't want the job of going back and telling Miss Sarah!"

John pulled his spy glass, telescoped it out and began to study the rise. "If'n it's a Sharps, they are a .52 caliber; a long barrel weapon with a big projectile. They're used by Union Army Sharpshooters known as 'Berdan's Sharpshooters'. You gotta be a good man to use one, but used proper, it'll kill out to a thousand yards. I'd say our shooter knows how to use his."

"You figure it's this Roberts fellow?"

"Likely not him, but someone he's got riding with him; unless that is you got some husband mad at you over something I don't need to know about!"

"We got good cover for us and the horses here, let's just sit awhile and make some coffee and get acquainted. If they decide to try to rout us out we'll see 'em far off and kill 'em out there in the open."

About the time the sun was going behind the western hills, John could no longer see anything on the ridge through his glass, so he ventured out of the tree cover and took their supplies off the dead pack horse. They divided up the things they most needed and hung the rest high in a cottonwood tree, cinched up their saddles and rode to the east along the Middle Concho toward San Angelo. When they hit the Mexican village at the edge of town, Pedro began to ask everyone he met for any information about Roberts and those riding with him. At last a late arriving sheepherder came in from the south that had seen a man fitting Roberts's description and the three men he had riding with him. They were heading south toward the village of Ben Flickin, about five miles down the Concho River. While Pedro was collecting information, John rode up the street a piece to check out the settlement. From what he could see, San Angelo was a typical rowdy frontier town of mostly saloons, prostitutes and gamblers. Was said that the founder, Bart. DeWitt had named the settlement after his sister-in-law, a nun in San Antonio. Based on what he saw, John didn't imagine the nun would be terribly pleased having this place named after her. Two hours later, after a hot meal and fresh coffee, the two "hunters" rode south along the river. They weren't gonna try to get there in the dark, just get close and ride up in the early morning. As they were settlin' in, each with his own bottle and one of John's cigars, Pedro ask, "John we've both been done much evil by this Roberts, how we gonna decide who gets to kill him?"

"My friend, sober he's likely fast with a gun, you fast enough to take him face-to-face?"

"I don't know. From what Joshua had said, I'm not near as fast as he thought you to be."

"Well we both want him dead. I know Roberts; we've starred each other down before. How bout I take Roberts and you can have all them who are ridin' with 'em with my blessings." It wasn't a question. That decided, they put out their fire and both got a little sleep. John was already up before the eastern sky was even streaked with the new day. He tapped the sole of Pedro's boot and announced, "Come on; you're burnin' daylight! Its dawning clear and as my Sergeant was known to say, it is gonna be a good day for someone to die, so let's go help 'em along."

They decided to ride around Ben Flickin and come in from the south; not that it was gonna take long. Mostly the village was just a stage stop for the San Antonio and El Paso mail route. The entire town consisted of a low building made of logs and green lumber that served as the saloon, the only place to eat and the only place to sleep if you felt the need to be in-doors. Out back were log corrals for the teams to be exchanged on the stage and in front a hitching post with three horses standing easy swishing flies. John observed, "This sure as hell ain't much of a town, yet it has a name."

"In Texas we call anything a town where people stop for any reason; a stage stop, a store, a saloon or even a good river crossing. I heard tell of a whiskey salesman broke a wheel on his wagon so he started just selling whiskey by the side of the road out of the back of his broke wagon; and people named it and it became a town."

"That has the sound of a story the locals would tell a Yankee; many bite on it?"

"Can't rightly say as you being the only Yankee I know."

"It would appear that those we hunt just might be in the stage stop drinking up some early morning courage. I've never know anyone to be made faster, smarter, or more accurate by drinking whiskey so early in the morning, so what say we ease up there on that rise and sit a spell in the shade and have a first-of-the-day cigar? Another thing my Sergeant was very found of saying; don't **never, never** interrupt your enemy while he's in the act of making a mistake!"

"Your Sergeant must have been a good man to know."

"He was a tough as nails son-of-a-bitch that kept me alive for thirteen months while many others out there were trying to kill me. It does get right difficult not to like a man that does that for a body!"

"Only three horses at the hitchin' rail; what do you suppose happened to the fourth rider?"

"Don't rightly know, but if we wait a spell he may ride up. I'd just as soon have them all four in front of me and accounted for when we go through the door."

It was a pleasant morning for that time of year in south Texas; bright morning sky, gentle breeze and not too hot nor too humid. John observed out loud again that he thought it a good day to die, but Pedro was not certain just who John might be applying that to and was afraid to ask. They finished their cigars stood and stretched, checked their hand guns for the fourth time, cinched up the saddles and rode slowly down off the rise toward the stage stop. They each noticed that the fourth horse had still not arrived, but neither thought any comment necessary.

"Bein' in the war John you've had a lot more experience than me, do you feel it when it gets this close? Dry mouth so, you want to spit, but can't? Something crawling in your stomach? Short of air?"

"Yeah, I feel it. If you don't feel nothin', there's not much point in doing the thing."

They tied their horses to the top rail of the corral; John wanted them off to the side and more or less out of sight. Pedro decided he would carry John's scattergun along with a holstered hand gun. He told John, "There's many faster than me with a hand gun, but few faster than me when I'm holding a scattergun."

"We'll go through the door quietly so's not to stir up a fuss, you move to the left and stand by the back wall till your sight accepts the dark room. I'll ease the bat-wing doors closed and step to the right and we'll wait together. If'n they don't take any note of us, just wait for my move. I'm going to take the Henry with a chambered round, but the hammer down and leave it standing by the door, just in case either of us needs it or if anyone gets past us. Okay my Mexican friend, you weren't satisfied till you bought in to this, so let's you 'n me go among 'em!"

Each man went quietly through the bat-wings and to his assigned position along the back wall. John eased the doors closed, and both waited. The three men were standing straight in front of them leaning on what passed for a bar and if they heard the two enter, took no note. John smiled that there was no bar mirror. The only other person in the big, open room was a bartender off to the right down at the end of the bar polishing whiskey glasses with the tail of his long-ago white apron. As soon as he could see clearly, John nodded to Pedro and the two stepped into the middle of the room. Still those at the bar paid no mind, but the bartender straightened and starred at the new arrivals. John looked him in the eyes, patted his holster and shook his head. The bartender put both hands on top of the bar, palms down and in plain sight, but did not move. When he reached the center of the room, John stopped and called out to the three at the bar, "We've come to collect a few scores with you three bastards, now if you'll just turn around slowly, we'll be settlin' up accounts."

Roberts was in the middle of the three and turned quickly as did the one on his right, and both pulled open the duster they were wearing and eased their right hand close to their tied down holster. The third man was slow to react like he'd had his nose in the sauce for a spell, but eventually figured out someone was speaking to him and also turned to face the two. "Hello U-gene, I know you must be tired of chasing me around Texas, so I come to make it a bit easier for you. This here is the brother of the sheepherder you and your men cut up and tied to a tree to die, and he kind of wanted to come along to meet you also. Now we can do this only one of two ways; you can drop your guns and surrender and we'll march you down to the Sheriff, or you can make your play when ever you are ready."

"You've live a charmed life kid; I had you dead to rights in Texarkana, then that damn darkey stepped in front of you. You killed my two brothers and I recon' this is as good a day for you to pay for that as any. I'm getting' tired of just killin' your friends and your horses!" The other two each took a side step away from Roberts and squared themselves, ready. Roberts pulled his duster further back out of the way of his draw and looked at John with a smile that became more like a sneer. "You other two kill the Spick brother, this damned Yankee is all mine." Robert's right hand moved to his holster and had just started the upward motion when the Colt .44 roared, once, then a second time. On top of the second noise was that of the scattergun. John had deliberately gut-shot Roberts, but just as deliberately had put his second shot into the upper chest of the one on his right; he died on the way to the floor. Pedro was either excited or filled with revenge; at the first sound of the .44, he had fired both barrels of the scatter gun into the man ten feet on his front. It was going to take someone considerable time and effort to just clean him up from all of the places his pieces now rested. John moved to Roberts and kicked away the hand gun he had dropped and then looked down, almost satisfied at the dark blood bubbling from his lower gut and out of his mouth. "Roberts, I recon this will end here between us when you've finish bleeding out; I just want you to know that man you killed in Texarkana was a damn good man and a damn good friend. Also, that gray mare was a good friend, so if there was any way I could cause you to die twice, I would do that. Since that can't happen, gut shootin' you was the best I could come up with."

"Kill me you son-of-a-bitch, get it over with." While the two men had a drink of good whiskey down the bar; Roberts breathed his last and it was finally ended!

"I was kind of lookin' for the fourth man," John said to the bartender.

"He rode south some time ago, likely clear to Ciudad Acuna by now. Thought since they didn't kill either one of you, his talents might be more appreciated by the Emperor down in Mexico. Besides, they're paying in gold and Roberts had 'bout run out".

John held up his half filled glass toward Pedro, "Here's to a day's work done my new friend!" With that they drank, broke the glasses against the back bar and walked into the bright sun toward their waiting horses, then in unison stopped in mid-stride and returned back through the bat-wing doors.

Author's Notes...

The Wilmot Proviso: During the early days of his presidency, when ask by a reporter what he had accomplished as a member during his single term in The House of Representatives, Abraham Lincoln answered that in his two years in Congress he had voted in favor of the Wilmot Proviso 46 times.

The Proviso was first introduced in the U.S. House as a rider to a $2 million appropriations bill intended for the negotiations to finally resolve the Mexican War. The Proviso was authored by David

Wilmot, a Democratic congressman from Pennsylvania, and was first introduced on August 8, 1846. Its purpose was to prevent the introduction of slavery in any territory acquired from Mexico. It was defeated; as it would be for the next 45 times a vote was taken. The $2 million bill would be again introduced, only this time as a $3 million bill and the Proviso would also be expanded in its scope to, "exclude slavery in any territory now on the continent of America or which shall hereafter be acquired." To dissuade the members, Representative Stephen Douglas of Illinois reintroduced the Missouri Compromise with the line of separation between free and slave extended to the west coast; this modification was also defeated and the $3 million bill was then passed with out further tinkering. When in 1848 the Treaty of Guadalupe Hidalgo finally ending the war with Mexico was submitted to the Senate for approval, the Proviso was again attached…and again defeated.

Many historians believe it was the inability of the Wilmot Proviso to ever receive a favorable vote that made it the initial event on the long slide through the 1850's into secession and eventually the Civil War.

Chapter Ten

THE WILD – COW HUNT

It was quite late in the day when John and Pedro finally departed San Angelo and headed west. It was actually too late in the day to expect to make much progress on the trail toward the McCord ranch, but both men had just plain had it with San Angelo and everything associated with it. They were most anxious to return to the people they loved and missed, and who it was hoped, loved and missed them. They had delayed leaving Ben Flickin to help clean up the mess in the stage depot; the mess they had made with Eugene Roberts and the two who rode with him. The most challenging clean up job was finding all of the pieces of the renegade that had taken both barrels of the scattergun from Pedro. But as John had pointed out as tough as that was, it is much preferred to be the 'cleaner' rather than the 'cleanee'!

The men had a meal with the stage depot keeper and his part-Indian woman, a few drinks of the good whiskey; they tied the remains of the three renegades over their saddles and took the bodies to the marshal in San Angelo. Pedro, lacking complete and absolute faith in the Anglo justice system, would have preferred to dump the three unceremoniously in a hole behind the corral. That would have been done to them, and ride on to the ranch but John insisted that there were murders to be resolved; not just Joshua and Manuel, but the guard on the prison wagon as well. Turned out to be a profitable decision as the three brought a total of $350 in bounty, paid in the local coin of Mexican gold. John and Pedro divided the reward; Pedro thought it not right to be paid for killin', but John convenience him it was honest got and besides he now had the money to pay off his mother's loan from Mr. McCord. Besides they had some needed gold for supplies for the wild-cow hunt and cattle drive.

About dusk, and still in sight of San Angelo, they made camp and for the first time, while enjoying their after-meal cigars, begin to talk about the shoot-out. "Joshua always told tales in the bunkhouse about how fast you were with a gun, but I thought that was the tequila talking. But you rightfully are about the fastest white-man I ever saw. You shot each of those two, exactly where you wanted to shoot them and before either got a shot off. I'd heard tell that Mr. Colt's .44 would sometimes fire two cylinders at a time and your shots were so close together, I plain thought that was what had happened"

"Well, they had been drinkin' for a spell and that likely didn't help their cause much. I had faced Roberts before in Texarkana when he had been drinkin' and he didn't seem like much then when face-to-face, he seemed to do much better shootin' from behind cover. So, I just gut-shot him quick cause the other looked like the shootist to me. I had no idea that they had a price on their head, though now that I think on it, it seems reasonable. I just didn't want anyone makin' up a story about what had happened after we had moved on. Besides, it was a mess of our makin', so's it was ours to dispose of. Let's move this on to something more pleasant...Pedro you ever had a wife?"

"I never really had time to do a proper marriage. I was a young kid when I met Mr. McCord shortly after the war for Texas independence and threw in with him to raise cotton and kill Indians. We were always too busy with one or the other for me to do much courtin'. Years ago I had me a real sweet, tiny little Mexican *senorita* down on the Rio; but when I saw her a few years later she had a passel of kids and a butt that appeared to be at least two ax-handles across; so I just tipped my *sombrero* and rode on, never been back and never saw another woman I really wanted for more than a night. That can be a real hill to climb in a marriage! You fixin' to marry up with Miss Sarah?"

"Just can't wait! She's the reason Joshua and I went back to Arkansas; to fetch her. When we get our gold from this cattle drive I figure to marry her and we'll start our own place close to the McCord ranch. I've got me those four Black Angus calves to start a herd of mixed breed beef cattle that should do well after the war. Any way, that's my plan…first time in my life I had me a plan beyond tomorrow. Guess the love of a good woman will do that for a man."

"You mentioned 'after the war' and you've seen some good part of it; how do you figure it'll turn out?"

"I've been trying to impress on the McCord's that by my way of thinkin', there is not any way the Confederates can win this war, and perhaps the South can't even survive after it's over. I know that's a likely too broad statement, but even though the South has most of the smartest generals, unless they can get either France or England into the war on their side, or the folks up north just plain get tired of the dollar cost and the deaths, the Union will just eventually wear the South down to the point they either can't fight, or won't. The North has a nearly inexhaustible supply of men and equipment, yet when the South looses a man or a gun, there's no way to replace 'em. Makes no difference if the North wears 'em down or just plain whips 'em, ever which way it is, the Union will have won, the CSA will be no more, and the slaves will be free…free to do what, no one has tried to say yet."

"What do you figures gonna happen after the North wins?"

"There will be hell to pay everywhere in the Confederate States. The Union will send in an occupying military army followed by an army of politicians, and just take over...that's the way it always is when you win. They'll throw out the Confederate money, throw out the governments, slap on taxes people can't pay and they'll wind up owning everything for pennies on the dollar. That's why we have to be successful with this cattle drive. We've got to store up some Yankee gold so's the McCord's can hold on to their life's work after the Union occupiers arrive. And, I don't know how much time we have before the South collapses...how they have held on clear into mid-1863 is a mystery...for sure Vicksburg is gonna be sieged into surrender which will open the Mississippi River for the Union and isolate Texas; they say General Lee's army is gonna invade the North again and the last time was a disaster for the Confederates. Lee's the best there is on either side on defense, but he does not have the forces or the supplies to go on offense, especially clean into Pennsylvania. No, this can't end well for the South!"

"John, you ever think much about which side's in the right?"

"Glenn and I used to have some heated discussions on that subject when I was bringing him home from the battlefield at Pittsburg Landing...don't know we ever settled it. He believes the South had every legal right to voluntarily separate from the United States and form a new nation...says that even the writings of James Madison when he framed the Constitution guaranteed that right. I don't know about that, but I think Mr. Lincoln mostly just wants the nation to stay together and figures now that the war is the only way he can make that happen. I'm not certain if I should care about that or not; Glenn says I should. I do think the slavery thing is wrong, but I wonder if cooler heads mighten have settled that is a more peaceful way. I mean you and Mr. McCord made this place here in Texas grow and prosper without slaves, why couldn't every one have done the same? But the thing not to loose sight of is that wars never determine who's right or wrong, only who gonna be left after."

117

"There were a few years we'd finish up the pickin' and figure we just about worked for a slave's wages…next to none at all! But I recon' the difference was we were free to decide to do it the next year or not do it…since we never had a better plan, we always did it one more year."

"I believe the money, the army, the agriculture, hell the entire economy of the South will be destroyed before this ends. That's why we gotta make this drive…we gotta get ourselves ready for what's certainly comin'."

The dun mare snorted and stomped her front foot, so John got up to go see what the bother was. Just flies he decided, and returned to his spot by the dying fire. "Your brother surely did pick me a good horse in that dun mare, and I'd a bet she would have been hell to trail break."

"Never seen it fail. He just has some strange connections to horses and them to him. He talks to them like most of us would talk to our children; he tells them to behave and they always do. How come you don't ever name your horses John? I know you never got around to naming that gray mare."

"I always intended to…was gonna call her *Rebel* or some name like that just to irritate Glenn, but that son-of-a-bitch Roberts ran her through with a four-tine pitch fork 'fore I got around to it. This dun reminds me of a sand storm, so I thought about calling her that."

"That would be *La tormenta de Arena,* and that too long for a horse; they're right stupid you know. Maybe shorten it to just *La tormenta.*"

"So what's that?"

"That's 'The Storm' in Spanish."

"You think that mare speaks Spanish? Hell, I don't even speak Spanish!"

"Well maybe she's smarter than you are; cept according to my cousins, she's likely been stole three or four times so she's spent more time south of the Rio, than north of it...so, yes...I figure she likely understands Spanish."

"Alright, *La tormenta* it is."

The sun was just ready to explode over the eastern horizon and announce a new day in central Texas. The men had finished their morning meal and coffee, and John was doing his usual clean-up routine around the camp. Twice from the corner of his eye he thought he had caught the dun with her ears erect and looking at the rise off to the west, but each time he looked to check, there was nothing there, and when he looked back at the mare she was eating again. Finally Pedro came back into the camp and paused in front of John, "If you look just past my right ear, I've seen a couple of riders coming over the ridge line and then quickly dropping back into the valleys. They are generally heading southeast, but each time they reappear they seem to be closer to our camp."

"I haven't seen them, but the mare has noted something a couple of times. You stay here and fuss with the gear, I'm gonna slip down in the ravine off to the right and see if I can work up behind them." John pulled the Henry and was out of sight before the pair of riders reappeared, then again disappeared below the ridge line...once more somewhat closer to the camp than before. Dropping down into the ravine, John ran in a crouched position trying to close the gap on the 'visitors'. He knew that most men you encounter on the frontier turned out to be friendly...but some did not and it was best to be cautious till you were certain which they were gonna be. John had advanced about 200 yards up the ravine when he was about to run out of cover. He stopped, worked on his belly up to the top of the ridge but when he stuck his head up for a reconnoiter he found he was looking into the muzzle of a hand gun; that unblinking black eye just inches from his forehead.

"Just lay the rifle down boy and ease up here where I can get a look at you."

The voice was harsh and menacing, yet familiar. John looked up into the face of Glenn with a crazy wide grin. "What the hell…"

"John too bad you can't see what you looked like peeking over that ridge and into my hand gun. You truly looked like a kid with his hand in the cookie jar."

"You crazy bastard, I was working up here to take a shot at you if need be. What the hell are you doin'?

"Pa sent Juan and me riding down here to find a box canyon to use as a holding pen for all those wild cattle we're gonna be rounding up, but we decided you two had been gone long enough and were likely hopelessly lost, so we were either gonna find you and see how this had all turned out, or perhaps take your bodies back to the ranch. We kind of promised Miss Sarah we check on you without Pa knowing we was takin' a side trip."

"How'd you know I'd come up for a look see right at that spot?"

"You need to be more careful Yankee. I've been over this country many times and you haven't. I knew you'd run out of ravine about there and I know you well enough to know you'd go that far thinking you were behind us, and then pop up for a look. I don't know Yankee, God must have been smiling on you to keep a dumb sodbuster like you alive this long."

"He certainly was that, cause He knew you weren't smart enough to get your shot-up ass home on your own with out someone along to wet-nurse you all the way. I don't think He cared about saving your sorry ass, but He felt sorry for your Ma and Pa. Come on, let's build up a fire and have some coffee."

Their coffee laced with a little good whiskey and handed out all around and each puffin' on one of John's cigars, Glenn said, "Alright, so admit it, Roberts got away while you and Pedro were chasing loose women!"

But before John could return the smart comment Pedro stepped in, "We caught up with Roberts and two of his men at the stage station in Ben Flickin after their sharpshooter shot our pack horse up by Manuel's grave site. There was a third rider but seems he decided to look for work on the south side of the Rio. Joshua had always told stories in the bunkhouse about how fast John had become with a hand gun, but he understated it. John let Roberts and one of his shootist make the first move, then he drew and gut-shot Roberts and chest-shot the other before either of them got a shot off."

"And little brother, what were you doing all this time while the men folks were having their shoot-out", ask Juan?

"Your little brother nearly blew the third man in half with both barrels of my scattergun from a distance of about ten feet; made for a hell of a clean up job, We took the bodies into San Angelo and collected a bounty of $350 in Mexican gold." said John. "Should be a help with the supplies we'll be needin'".

"Well Pa has decided our best cattle-huntin' will be along the Midland, Mustang and Johnson Draws in Midland and Upland Counties. That's close by the headwaters of the Middle Concho River. From there we'll head the herd to the west and north till we hit the Pecos River. I'm sorry John, you bein' a Yankee greenhorn you likely don't know where we're talking about."

"I'd say your Pa is absolutely correct. We rode down that way to try to get behind Roberts and saw lots of cattle back in the brush. What's he have you two scoutin' for, besides us?"

"We're lookin' for a four to five acre box canyon with a narrow neck and steep enough walls the cattle aren't goin' a walk out. Needs good water and good grass for the cattle cause we may be holdin' 'em for awhile. Pa's hopin' to start the drive with at least 15 hundred head. Juan thinks he knows a place to fill that bill and that's where we're going now that we were able to save the two of you. When you get to the ranch grab a couple days to rest up, then I think you should round up the remuda and bring them and the rest of the *Vaqueros* and the chuck-wagon down cause we're gonna be staying here and we'll likely start the drive from down here anyway."

It was decided that they would ride together to the west for a spell. John decided he wanted another night on the trail so he could shave and clean himself up before seeing Sarah. Besides he had someone else's blood all over one side of his sail-cloth pants and that had to come off before he returned to the civilized people. The three mounted and then waited while John again went through his clean-up routine of their camp area; finally cutting a small sapling with his Bowie knife and dragging it over and back the main camp area obliterating that they had ever been there.

Juan looked at his brother and asks, "He always do that?"

"Always!"

"He part Indian?"

"No, just Yankee gringo."

Satisfied, John threw the sapling aside, mounted and spoke to *La tormenta.*

"How come the Yankee gringo took a Mexican name for his horse?"

"He just decided it was the right one and after I saw him shoot, I sure wasn't going to tell him no."

Juan just shook his head and the other three fell in line behind him as he started west for the Middle Concho headwaters. By mid-afternoon they arrived at the springs that make up the start of the small river. John and Pedro would camp here one more night and start for the McCord's ranch at dawn. Juan and Glenn were anxious to look over the box canyons that Juan had seen; so they decided to use the rest of the day and ride on into the Breaks.

The men on the western frontier in 1863 never spoke much about their feelings for one another; it was in their nature to share their food, their camps and whiskey and often their fights. Many times when there were no fights to be shared, they would just fight each other, but only till a better one could be found. These four were no different, as they separated, two goin' west and two goin' mostly north, it was obvious the affection each held for the other, the two who were brothers by the blood they shared and the two who were brothers by the experiences they had shared. They shared their food and cigars, said their goodbyes and rode away not bothering to look back.

The pool of water below the springs was cold for the time of year, but having no choice; John stripped down to his red drawers and waded into the water to start scrubbing the dried blood from his sail-cloth pants. Pedro had tethered the horses and started a small cook fire before he took much notice of the sight in the water. He began to laugh and each time he looked at John the laugh got louder and more riotous, there hadn't been much that was funny in his life for awhile and when this sight finally arrived, he wasn't going to be able to waste it. John turned away from his companion partly in modesty, but that only made the circumstances worse when Pedro noted that two buttons were missing from the "trap-door" on the back of John's drawers.

John had washed his clothes and laid them out over a growth of sagebrush to dry, he had scrubbed himself and shaved his face. John felt, and looked almost human again. They cooked up most of the food they had remaining and after a big meal, settled with good whiskey and cigars, the men themselves settled in for their last night on this trail. "Pedro, before we get back to the ranch and jump into our next routine, I want you to know how much I appreciate all you've done to make this trip successful. I wasn't too keen on having you trail with me, but we succeeded because of the reports you were able to gather, and I'm likely alive because of your nerve with a gun in that stage depot. I had always heard that any man can learn to shoot a gun and with some practice, can get good at it. But what will always count most is will a man stand-up when someone is shooting back at him. I'll ride with you anytime my Mexican friend!"

"Thank you John. I wasn't too keen about dragging a gringo along till Mr. McCord told me I had to. But for a Yankee, you're a damn good man John Kelley and I'd go to hell and back with you and the way things have been around you lately, I may still get that chance!"

Even though they had only been gone but a few days, there was much celebrating when the two returned to the ranch and all the stories were told. John participated for only as long as he needed to be polite, but then he took Sarah's hand and they slipped off to hold their own more private "welcome home". It was agreed that the men should have a couple of days to rest and get their gear in shape, but on the third day the horse herd, the chuck wagon and the rest of the hands that would be working the drive, would leave for the Breaks and the wild-cow hunt. John promised Sarah that when he returned this next time they would be married for sure. She shook her head in agreement as her lower lip quivered slightly, then looked quickly away so John wouldn't see the moisture coming up in her eyes.

* * * * *

Wild-cow hunting was some of the hardest work John had ever done, and in his life on the homestead in Iowa, he had done some damn hard work. They were in the saddle from first light to the very last and even changed mounts with their noon meal to keep from breakin' their horses down. Most of the cows were found way back in the brush and brambles and almost defied removal. Once they could get them out in the open, at least they could get a couple of ropes on 'em and, if need be drag them to the canyon entrance. A few would actually herd, but most just put their tails up over their backs and charged down through the canyons…and those were the good ones; the bad ones would turn and charge the horses. They put down three horses the first few days from being gored. Once a Mexican longhorn on the charge hit a horse that was usually the end, if the horns didn't stick the animal, just the force of the blow would break 'em up. The difficult part was for the rider not to get gored at the same time. The canyon that Juan and Glenn had located was ideal; about four acres in size, with a narrow entrance, runnin' water and good belly-deep grass. Perhaps the best part was that there were already a couple of hundred head grazing in the canyon when the men found it...a couple of hundred head that they did not have to dig out of the brush.

By the third week they were working further and further away from the mouth of the box canyon, and at Mr. McCord's orders, they were now always working in pairs. There was not only the issue of just plain needin' help with a wild-cow, but they had been spotting Indian signs around as well. John was riding beside Mr. McCord as they prepared to drop down onto the broad flat plain before them. Seeing a few cows around, the men decided to move in opposite directions to come up behind the grazing cattle and try to drive them back toward the canyon. Just before they were to ride out of the draw, they stopped as they always did just inside the cover of the tree line. They rarely ever spotted any other riders, but you only got one chance to be careless in this country; Indians, renegades both white and Mexican, and Comancheros, all roamed west Texas at will and with little regard for the others. Two white men on tired horses presented too tempting a target. John was about to ride forward when he spotted some movement from the corner of his eye. Without speaking, he reached and put his hand on Angus' arm to hold him back. John reached into his saddle-bag and pulled out his fine, brass spy-glass. As he extended it Angus inquired, "That come from the same place as your fancy compass?"

"Same place, same conditions; but not the same owner."

"I 'spect Glenn don't cotton to that one either. What'd you see?"

"I thought I saw some movement over on that brown mesa. Yes, there they are...five, no six Indians ridin' in single file with their heads just popping up above that ridge-line."

"They'd be Muscalero Apache likely…and more probably people-huntin' than cow-huntin'. We'll just sit here a spell and let 'em pass. When we get our herd together and move 'em out of that canyon, we'll need to be very watchful…they'd like a herd they didn't have to round-up."

The two men rounded up eight steers off of the flat plain and had started pushing them back toward the box canyon when Angus hollered out to John, "Watch that black pool in front of you, if'n you get cows in that mess we'll just have to leave 'em."

John saw the pool of thick, black, bad smelling goop, it wasn't quite liquid, but it wasn't quite solid either; as he watched bubbles would form on the surface and burst giving off a foul smelling gas. He had seen similar pools during this round-up, but had no idea what it was; they certainly had nothin' like that in Iowa. "What is that stuff?"

"They call it pet-roleum and it's all over these parts of west Texas. They say there's even some water-well digger and his sons back east actually drilling to find this stuff. They boil it or somethin' and make coal oil for lamp-burnin' out of it, and I don't know what all. That's why this land in west Texas will never be worth a tinkers-damn; those pools of stuff just mess up good grazing land; cow gets in there it'll just gonna get sick and die. No sir, never be worth anything!"

By the start of the fourth week Angus decided it was time to take a tally and see just where they were. He announced again that he wanted to arrive at the Union forts with about fifteen-hundred head…where ever it was they were gonna be finding those forts; and assuming the soldiers there even were buying cattle. Other than not being certain where they were goin', or what they would find when they got there…they pretty much had this thing figured out!

On July 4, 1863, what would become know as the "McCord Cattle Drive" moved out from the safety of the box canyon in the Midland Break of west Texas with 1,694 head of wild steers led by a dun-colored, broken-horned Mexican Brahma and began pushing the herd northeast searching for the Pecos River valley in New Mexico

Territory. As a guide they had an ex-Union Corporal from Iowa holding a Confederate Officer's compass taken from a battlefield in Tennessee, and a crude map drawn by some drivers and shotgun riders for the Butterfield Stage Company after they having been bribed with a bottle of cheap whiskey. But the cowboys were so damn tired of chasing wild cattle through the brush and briers and getting gored or snake bit, that this new task already sounded much the better! It was just after dawn when the ropes fell over the posts that had held back the cattle in the canyon and the barrier fence came down…with a yell and some pushing, this desperate drive was underway. The cattle actually seemed reluctant to leave the grass and water of the canyon; made Glenn wonder what the cattle already knew that the drivers were yet to find out.

Author's Notes…

Far to the east, General Robert E. Lee's Confederate Army of Northern Virginia was in full retreat away from the battlefield at Gettysburg, Pennsylvania. Lee was thankful for the poor weather that had engulfed his remaining forces as it would make it difficult for General Meade's Army of The Potomac to follow. Lee knew that seriously challenged, he would have to surrender his army just to save the lives of his remaining forces; 28,063, or more than one-third of Lee's original force were now casualties, with 3,903 of those dead. The Army of The Potomac fared little better with 23,049 causalities, including 3155 dead. For the next four days Lee is allowed to retreat facing little more resistance than occasional skirmishes. Finally, after the strong urging of President Lincoln, General Meade began to move his army in pursuit, but arrives at the Potomac River just after Lee's successful crossing back into Virginia…yet another opportunity to measurable shorten the war is lost to timidity by the Union. Lee's Army of Northern Virginia would, however never recover from the losses of men and equipment at Gettysburg, yet they would doggedly carry on the fight against superior forces and superior armament for another 22 months.

On January 31, 1865, General Robert E. Lee would be named by President Davis as the Commander-In-Chief of all Confederate armies; however Lee's total focus would remain with his Army of Northern Virginia. When Lee finally surrendered to General Grant at Appomattox Court House on April 9, 1865; it would only be his army he would surrender as the South would continue to have over 100,000 men in the field and under arms.

On August 27, 1859, Edwin L. Drake drilled the first successful oil well at Titusville, Pennsylvania; with that the "oil rush" was on, delayed only by the outbreak of the Civil War.

Chapter Eleven

THE PALE MORNING

The evening before the barrier came down and the cattle were headed up-trail, Angus gathered his key partners; Glenn, John, BC, Pedro and Juan together to make the individual assignments for the drive. He wanted a final review and discussion over the crude, hand-drawn map. Angus expected each man to know what his assignment was and before they hit the trail to let out any of their bitching such an assignment might draw. He also wanted each man to have an understanding of where they were going and how he thought they would best get there; again, to deal with any disagreements now and only now. He did not expect to get any feed-back on either subject, but since this was to be his last democratic act for the duration of the drive, he felt it a necessary step. There were no disagreements offered! Each man understood they were working for shares and those shares would pay off only at the end of the drive…if you didn't finish; you would receive no pay-off, no discussion, no excuses, and no pay-off! Further, the pay-off amount each would receive would be determined by many factors; the market demand and the price per head, the number of cattle they could actually delivered to that market, their condition at delivery, and the number of drovers who survived to share at the end of trail. At this moment, none of those factors were within the complete control of the individuals who were starting this adventure! Such was the nature of the times and the business they were in. But the idea of them as Confederates selling wild cattle to the Union Army for their gold just was not an issue for any of them in these desperate times.

They gathered around the camp fire in the fading light of the day and looked over the crude map. John had the continuing nagging thought that it was a map that had been drawn by hard-drinking stagecoach drivers after having been bribed by some cheap whiskey, but decided, wisely, to keep that thought to his own counsel. Mr. McCord had made it quite clear that there would be no drinking until the meeting was over; John kind of felt Angus was directing his comments to him, but took no offense.

"I think that big, dark-dun, broken-horned Brahma will likely lead and the herd will just fall in behind him. He just seems to have become the boss ever since we put him in the canyon. Our main job will be to keep pushin' him in the direction we want him to go, and keep the rest of the herd moving behind him. Pedro and Juan and one of their cousins will take charge of the remuda. You can move them ahead or off to either side of the herd, and Cookie, I want your chuck with the horse herd."

Juan had already thought that through. "We'll keep 'em to the side, then if the herd should spook they won't be tramplin' and scatterin' our mounts. Sides the horses will move faster when they move and stop to eat more often than the cattle."

"I will lead, so keep the Braham movin' forward toward me. Glenn you and BC each take a side toward the front of the herd to keep them from spreading out and keep them following that bull. Then I want the other two of Pedro's cousins on each side on the back quarter and the three new men pushin' from behind. We've got a hell of a lot of cattle here for eight men to be drivin' so stay alert. When we stop for the night we'll break-up into two-man teams for night-watch, so every one gets some rest. We'll have no graze and no water till we get to the Pecos in New Mexico, maybe 5 to 6 days or more, so they'll have to be pushed until they smell water then you best get out of their way. Ever man is to pack as much water as he can and Cookie's to be certain the water-barrels on the chuck wagon are full."

John looked surprised that his name had not been mentioned for an assignment. "What about me, Mr. McCord...what'll you have me doin'?"

"You're gonna be our trail scout; you can read a map, you've got a compass, and you're good at survivin' on the trail alone; that's the three biggest qualifications. I want you not just leading the way, but finding the best trail possible for the cattle. You should be workin' about one or two day's ahead and leaving signs, and be damn alert for Indians...they may, or may not be a problem; but you'll likely know that soon enough! Now all you get up here where you can see and let's go over this map."

"We'll head northwest out of this Midland Draw, till we find the Monument Draw about here and follow it into New Mexico Territory, and stay with it to the headwaters. From there we'll pass north of the Antelope Range and north of the village of Eddy, and then turn somewhat north of west to the Pecos River at about the North Seven River junction. From the headwaters of the Monument to the Pecos River is about 70 miles, likely as many as 5 or 6 days, with not much grazing and no water. That'll be the toughest part of the drive for man and beast. At the Pecos we'll turn north and follow the river, likely crossing it many times. Even though most of the small rivers that feed into the Pecos are dry this time of year, the Pecos flows out of the mountains to the west and should have enough water for our needs. We're heading toward Fort Sumner about 120 miles away, but they'll be decent graze and water all the way. There will be a few Union forts and camps to the west of us along the Sacramento Mountains and many to the far west along the Rio Grande, but I'm told that we have to go to Fort Sumner to do any business with the Union Army; so that's where we be a goin'. John, you best sit here and draw you a copy of this map on this here paper so's we'll both have one; any questions?" There being none, the men were told to check their gear over, and then turn in.

The stubborn steers seemed not to want to leave the good grass and the abundant stream of the canyon. But once the broken-horn Brahma decided to move, the herd began to slowly fall in behind, two hours later the canyon was empty and the herd pointed northwest. John helped get the herd bunched and started, then moved well out in front and began looking for the easiest trail to the Monument Draw. Wasn't going to be much for him to do for a few days as a blind mule could find the Monument Draw; he'd just try to provide the best walking trail for the cattle. While he was riding along enjoying the country side of west Texas and thinking about the map he'd stayed up half the night drawing, the words, *"Gadseden Purchase"* came into mind and the discussion he had overheard between his pa and ma some years ago about it. Seems his pa had been contacted by something called the Border Commission about coming back to work for the Army Corps of Engineers and helping survey a new border between Mexico and the Territory of New Mexico. His pa had been a good surveyor during the Mexican War and could speak some Mexican and there was going to be lots of work as a result of this new territory. John wondered if he'd be passing through any of it. His pa had told them like everything in life, the timing had to be right, and as much as he needed the cash-money for the homestead, this timing was not right. He had a young family with two small boys and another one coming, and the homestead was his to run now as grandpa could no longer do the physical work, so he'd declined and stayed home.

They got the cattle to the headwaters of the Monument River with out any problems. Mr. McCord had decided they'd spend an extra day there to allow the cattle to graze and water their full as the next 70 miles had little of either. John gathered up an abundance of supplies and he and *La Tormenta* began the lonesome trail out ahead moving toward the Pecos River. It wasn't hard work as there was nothing much in this country to impede the herd's progress; no trees, no grass and no streams…he'd just try to keep them out of the country that was crosshatched with gullies and of course any box canyons where they would have to turn the almost 1700 head around and retreat. He and Mr. McCord had worked out the markers they would use to set the best trail for them to follow. It was more boring than John had thought it to be when Mr. McCord had given him the assignment, but he supposed that looking at the east end of a west-heading steer all day wouldn't be any better.

It was late afternoon of the fourth day out of Monument and John was looking for a place to camp. There truly was plenty of light left yet, but he didn't want to work too far ahead of the herd and he was likely three days out from them now. He topped a rise and then rode down a ways so's not be silhouetted against the skyline. He had not seen another human-being in the four days since he rode out of camp, but he had seen plenty of Indian signs a time or two, and besides he was by nature a careful man. In one wet-sand wallow he had seen where Indian riders had dug a four foot deep hole and waited for the bottom to fill with water. He tried it and got the same results, but the water that seeped in looked like something neither he nor his horse would drink until just before death! As he squinted against the afternoon sun, John saw a large flight of buzzards circling like they were impatiently waiting for their dinner to die. Having nothing better to do, he decided to go disturb their wait. He had a true hatred for buzzards; he could remember how they would sweep onto a battlefield before the dead could be removed and start their tearing at the bodies; often not waiting for the "meal's" final breath to start their feeding.

He rode around the circling and came in from the far side; if anyone was up there watching for the end of life he didn't want to be discovered before he was ready. As he came over the last rise he could see the form the buzzards were after. Already about six were on the ground and walking slowly up on the bundle. It clearly was not that of an animal, what he saw was covered over with some kind of a tattered old blanket. He pulled the Henry from the scabbard, chambered a shell, ground tied the dun and slowly walked up on the form on the ground. The buzzards parted as he approached, but wouldn't back-off very far. John used the Henry to prod the blanket pile and got a near-human sounding grunt in return. He prodded again...same grunt. Again with the Henry, he flipped off the blanket and would have dropped his teeth, had they been removable; before him curled in a fetal position was a young Indian woman, probably 16 or so, badly beaten and bound hand and foot with rawhide lashings. Her deer skin dress was mostly gone and it showed her skin to be lighter in color than he'd seen in most Indians, but with her jet-black hair, he was certain she was at least part Indian. John found himself hypnotized by the harsh whip marks on her back and legs; some already scarred and some fairly fresh. The brutality brought to his mind the damage done by green willow switches. There was such snap in them that every time they fell they broke the skin. The fresh cuts were swarming with flies and red ants almost as large. As she turned to look up at him John saw the large dark bruise on her cheek, likely made by a fist or a club. It stood out in sharp contrast on her pale skin. John's memory immediately replayed the savage beating Sarah had endured at the hands of the leader of the Confederate renegades as she refused to give up John and Glenn's location. As the rage built in John he felt his control diminish...not a good thing in this country. Then his memory switched scenes to the round he had fired on the run from his Spencer into the center of the chest of the leader of the renegades, as he had again raised his hand to strike Sarah. He could see in his mind that round leave the barrel of the Spencer and its flight into the man's chest. Never had killing a man felt so good, well killing Roberts was likely close!

He spoke to her and she opened her eyes briefly against the bright sun, and then started trying to crawl away from him, not doing well with her hands and feet tied. He spoke again trying to assure her that he meant her no harm...she'd already been harmed almost to the level that the buzzards would make short work of. He felt sorry for her but caution helped him to decided to try to understand the situation before he cut her bindings; he knelt and put his canteen to her lips...she gulped eagerly till he took it away and splashed a little on the cuts and bruises on her face. He pulled her into a sitting position and saw both a look of fear and of relief around her eyes.

"You speak any English?"

No response and realistically he had not expected one. "I said do you speak English?"

"I can speak a little that I learned from my father and in the mission school, but I speak more Mexican than English."

"Well we're stuck with English, that's my only choice. I'm gonna move you over there in the shade. Don't be frightened, I'm not gonna hurt you…someone else already did a damn good job of that."

Over the next two hours John learned that she was a slave of the Muscalero and they simply called her the Lakota Woman. When John said he thought that was the name of a tribe in the north, she said she was of the Lakota people and her Lakota name was *Pale Morning,* because of her light skin. She had a Canadian father who fur trapped every winter and spent his summers in the lodge of her mother, who was a Lakota of the Sioux seven councils. When the councils had split up and each gone its own way, she and her mother went west with the Saone council where her mother was killed and she was captured by the Cheyenne; to be presented as a wife for the Chief. Being a rebellious fighter, the Chief thought her not worth his while, besides she might try to kill him in some moment of passion, so she had been traded for two horses and an old muzzle-loader to the Muscalero to be their slave. When she repeatedly tried to escape, they beat her and eventually tiring of that, tied her and dumped her in the desert for the rattlers, the scorpions and the buzzards to finish off. And, John should know they were likely being watched now and would probably both be killed sometime well after dark, to which John replied to no one in particular, "Like some others, they just might find me damn hard to kill."

He did finally cut her bindings, but wasn't certain who he should fear the most, this young Indian woman or the braves who were watching and waiting for dark. He gave her his only other shirt to cover herself and a minimal amount of water to clean up with. They made a big show of setting up a camp like they expected to spend the night. John built a fire and Pale Morning fixed some of his bacon and coffee while he unsaddled the dun mare. He gathered firewood and dried brush, stacked it on a short slope directly above his fire pit, and tied it in place with the rawhide bindings. When Pale Morning questioned him, John told her, "This is a trick I saw my Sergeant pull on some Rebels one night when they had us pinned down. As soon as it gets good and dark, I'll re-saddle the horse and wet this rawhide and put the end in the fire. Then we'll quietly slip out of camp. As the rawhide slowly dries it'll start to burn through, when it gets weak enough it'll break and the wood and brush will slid down the little grade into our fire. That'll make it look like we're still in our camp and just building up the fire. They'll wait a couple of hours for the fire to burn back down fore they creep in; should give us a 3 or 4 hour head start. Not enough when we're ridin' double, but it's the best I can think of at the moment. We'll ride to the east headin' for the herd. When your 'friends' catch up in a few hours, we'll find a spot to make our stand."

"Do you think they'll follow?"

"There not gonna want to go back to the Chief and report that a snip of a woman out foxed 'em and gotta away. Might just be hard on their health."

They finished their meal and made the show of settling for the night. John poured a little water into his skillet for the mare to drink, then after dark he saddled her, they mounted and lit out for where the herd otta be. About two hours later they stopped to let the mare catch her breath. John was surprised to still be able to see the small glow from his fire in the dark of night and while he was watching, it flamed up and sparks journeyed into the night sky as the brush fell into the fire pit. Perhaps Sergeant Mullins had just saved his ass yet again!

They didn't talk much as they rode, not much left to say, besides talking just uses up your body's moisture in the desert. John figured out early-on that there was no use running the mare in this sand and sage brush. If those behind them truly wanted them, they were not going to get away anyway, and no need to kill the horse and put 'em afoot. Pale Morning was riding behind and her job was to watch the back trail for the arrival of their pursers. It was about mid-afternoon when she first saw them, riding hard toward them. John rode down into a small ravine, just deep enough to hide them from their sight. He and the young woman dismounted, he pulled the Henry and made certain the actions worked smoothly on both the rifle and the Colt on his hip. He ground-tied the mare; he supposed Pale Morning could have held the reins, but he didn't want to look up and see her riding hell bent for leather down the ravine on his only horse. It wasn't so much that he didn't trust her, it was just that John's experiences, not all of which had been good, had taught him to be a cautious man. He crawled up to the lip of the ravine, made himself a little wallow in the sand where he could see the back trail without being too exposed, and waited for the followers. The three topped the crest of a ravine about 400 yards away and halted, seemingly confused that they did not see their prey. There was no wind, so John corrected the Henry's adjustable sight for the needed elevation, drew a deep breath, let part of it out and squeezed the light trigger. Without waiting to see the outcome, he rolled to his left, chambered another cartridge, rolled back into his wallow, sighted and squeezed again. He repeated the process a third time, when he rolled back two were on the ground but the third had disappeared behind the sand brume; of the two on the ground, one was moving and one was not. *There's the reason a man should not stop on the top of a rise!* "Damn", he murmured. "I would like to have ended this here."

Leaving the girl in the ravine, he mounted and rode hard toward the two downed braves. The one not moving was chest shot and the other gut shot and would not have to wait long on this side of the great divide. While he was checking them, the third briefly topped a rise riding hard up their back trail, but before John could react, the brave disappeared again. Deciding with Pale Morning in tow he was in no position to pursue, John spoke softly to the nearest pony, caught-up the reins and returned to the spot where he left the girl. "Well two of your tormenters are dead and as hard as the third was riding that pony, he'll be afoot soon."

"Will not matter. When the pony drops, he'll stop and drink the blood and eat his fill of the meat and then run the rest of the way to their camp. *Senor, is este caballo por mi?*"

"What?"

"Sorry, is this horse for me?"

"Yes, mount up and let's get the hell out of here!"

With two horses, they were able to ride hard the balance of the day, until it was too dark to see the trail. They made a cold camp, shared their water with the horses, and at first light with a hard biscuit for each of them, were moving again. John believed he knew about where the herd should be and wanted to arrive there with his warning by mid-day. Sure enough, he spotted the dust plumb in the late morning…just where he thought. *Hell, this scouting stuff wasn't that difficult, he was a natural at it!*

Author's Notes…

The Village of Eddy: The small collection of weather-beaten shacks, a store, a stage stop, and a saloon in the southeast desert of the New Mexico Territory was not christened the Village of Eddy until September 15, 1888, and was not organized into a municipal Corporation until 1893. When the nearby mineral springs became known for their valuable medical qualities, the then town of Eddy changed its name to Carlsbad; that after the famous European spa Karlsbad, Bohemia (now the Czech Republic). On March 25, 1918, the Governor of New Mexico proclaimed Carlsbad to be a city. Today it thrives with a 27,000 population.

The Gadsden Purchase: Even though the Treaty of Guadalupe Hidalgo, signed on February 2, 1848, had formally ended the war between the United States and Mexico, tensions along the border between the two, and especially in the Mesilla Valley of present day Arizona and New Mexico flared for years, as both sides claimed ownership. With the troops of both sides again facing each other, President Franklin Pierce called upon the Ambassador to Mexico, James Gadsden to meet with Mexican President Antonio de Santa Anna to resolve the issue. The eventual purchase would include the lands south of the Gila River and west of the Rio Grande running west to the town of Yuma on the Colorado River. This would add 29,670 square miles to the southern New Mexico Territory and form the southern border of the United States as we know it today.

The purchase was strongly supported in the Pierce administration by the young Secretary of War, Jefferson Davis. Davis saw this as an opportunity to acquire the land necessary to support a southern route of a transcontinental railroad through Texas and linking Charleston, South Carolina with San Diego, California. The United States Senate reduced the purchase price to $10 million and reduced the original 45,000 square mile territory, excluding a piece of Baja California that would have supported a deep water port. The debate over the treaty became a sectional dispute over slavery and no further progress was made on the construction of a southern transcontinental railroad before the Civil War. The border survey was completed in 1855 by Major Emory and Lieutenant Michler.

Jefferson Davis, following his service as Secretary of War, would go on to become a United States Senator from the state of Mississippi. However, on January 21, 1861 he along with four other southern Senators would resign from the United States Senate.

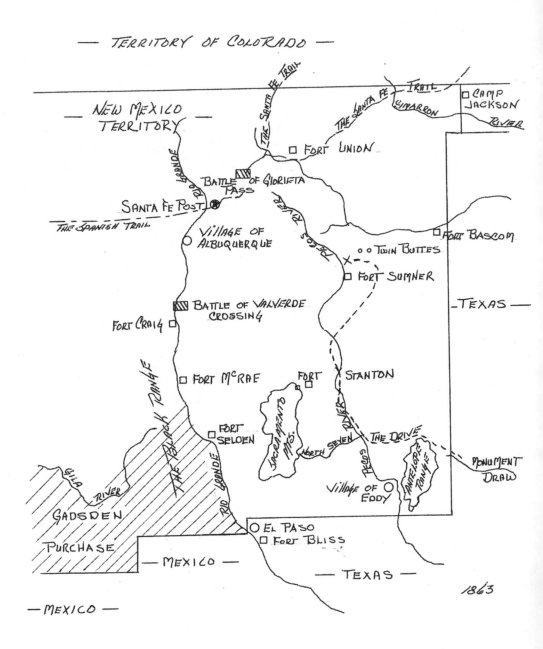

Chapter Twelve

THE PECOS THEN TURN NORTH

It was early evening, but still light and quite pleasant when Mr. McCord had bunched the herd for the night. There were still enough hours of light to move a few miles further, but he was concerned about John and here the herd had at least a little brown scrub grass that they could work on. He had not seen John or any trail sign left by John, for two days now and that was unlike his "trail scout". Fact, he thought at day light he would put Glenn up front as a guide for the busted-horn Brahma and he would ride ahead for awhile; anything ever happen to that boy, would be like losing one of his own…and Lucinda would likely never speak to him or sleep with him again in this lifetime. He had just unsaddled and turned his horse over to Pedro when two riders became visible over the far rise to the west.

Apparently all had been concerned about John because when he rode into camp it caused quite a stir…but then the stir could have been caused by the partially-dressed, part-Indian woman riding with him. All of the attention from the gathering men scared her and she moved her pony up close to John and he offered, "It's alright, these are the men I ride with." They dismounted and gave over their horses to Juan, then set for a rest and the offered hot meal.

Mr. McCord rightfully wanted to know, "What's that you got with you and why is she here?" Between bites of food John explained the buzzards, the story the young woman had told him, and then killing two of the braves in pursuit of her but with one getting away.

"I'm sorry Mr. McCord, but there was little I could do but bring her here; in her condition she'd die in a short while out there. The worse part is the one Indian gettin' away, if he lives, and Pale Morning says he will, then he'll likely return with friends and find us, so it's likely I've brought you a fight sometime within the next couple of days."

"Pale Morning?"

"So she tells me. She's part Lakota from the north and part white… Canada actually. She was captured as a young girl when her mother was killed and selected as a chief's wife, then later sold to the Muscalero as a slave. She apparently didn't cotton much to being a slave and got so rebellious that the Chief ordered her beat and dumped in the desert to either die or be eaten. That's when I came along and got involved."

"You gettin' involved does not surprise me a particle, you seem to do that with some regularity. So what now?"

"We can't just feed her and kick her out…she'll either die out there alone or perhaps worse get recaptured. I kinda figured she could ride along with us, maybe help Cookie for her keep. When we get someplace where she'd be safe we could turn her over to others."

Then Glenn started in, "So you two were together for two nights out in the desert and her without many clothes on her back? Sure that's a likely story; she sure does seem to cotton to you, my friend."

Angus could see the anger rising in John and thought to step in before it got out of hand and cost these two young men their friendship. "Glenn I'll have none of that gossip from you. You of all people should know John's an honorable man. Why if gossip like that ever found its way back to Sarah, it would break her heart…and it might just break your butt cause you're not so big I can't still wail the tar out of you, Boy! Do we understand each other, Boy?" To which Glenn nodded. "Don't just nod your head at me, I want to hear you speak that you and I have reached an understanding!"

"Yes Sir! We have reached an understanding."

"Good. Now John get on with your story."

"Well I don't figure we've heard the last of the Muscalero council on this matter. The chief ordered her dead and I've killed two of theirs, so I think in a day or two they'll be comin' for us. If Juan'll fix me up with a trail smart horse, I'll be going out at first light. I'll check the trail markers for the herd and scout ahead for the war party so's we'll have some warning. The Indian woman should be okay here."

John could just see a faint light in the east and figured it must be about time to get up and get his gear organized. As he was trying to talk himself into getting out of his bedroll, Juan appeared with a saddled horse for him. He was a rangy black gelding with a bald face and looked to be strong and trail worthy. "He will serve you well Mr. John; we've had a talk about what's expected."

"There's that damn 'Mr. John' again, but thanks Juan, give the dun mare some special care, she did well for us. I know the black will be good if you picked him out and gave him his marching orders." John gathered his gear, the Henry, plenty of cartridges, and some food and water. As he was about to step into the saddle Mr. McCord put his hand on his shoulder.

"Be careful out there boy, remember it's just like in the war, everyone you see'll want to kill you and if that should happen I'm faced with a cold bed for the rest of my life…not a pleasant thought! We'll be following up the trail you mark for us. What should we be doin' with the herd if'n we don't see you?"

"Just drive 'em till they smell the Pecos; they'll take it from there. Then you just turn 'em north."

At the first rise John stopped and looked back at the camp now up and ready to move out. He felt unusually lonely as he rode down the rise and off into the desert's fading darkness. The first trail marker he came to was still standing where he had set it, but the next two had both been moved to the south. Someone had relocated the trail markers and in doing so were deliberately pushing the herd south toward the foothills of the Antelope Range; Mexican bandits, Muscaleros, who? He moved the markers again to the north in their original positions, and then decided to drift a little south himself to see what might be out there.

At each wet-sand wallow he came across he found there had been considerable activity and many pony tracks. He judged there were about 50 in the party, but with so many tracks; it was difficult to be accurate. From the direction they were moving it was still possible they did not know exactly where the herd might be, so John decided to ride up their back trail for a ways and keep an eye on their movements. It was after dark when he finally saw the glow from their fires and knew exactly where they had stopped to camp. John felt it was a good omen since without even a trace of a moon; it was as dark as a well-diggers elbow on the desert. At least on the river the star-light seem to gather and be amplified, but not out here…it was just dark! Ground tying the big black, he moved forward quietly from scrub to scrub. It figured they would have the young men out guarding the pony herd, so he tried to move around and by-pass where he thought the horses to be. Finally he topped a small rise and had his first view of the camp. In his initial count he saw about 30 to 40, *good that is a little more manageable than the 50 of my first guess.* They were not heavily armed though each it appeared had a muzzle loader, and all had bows and lances. John wondered if the were skilled enough to load and fire those rifles three times a minute like he had trained his squad to do…doubtful! He smiled into the dark as he remembered the 'ramrod incident'; it was during the battle at Belmont, Missouri when the Confederates had attacked the squad's position in strength. One of his new volunteers became so excited that during the reloading process he failed to remove the ramrod before firing at the on-coming Rebs. The ramrod shot out of the barrel and like a spear, struck the charging soldier in the chest and brought him down. Might prove to be the only causality in this war to be taken down by a spear!

The Indians around the fire were heavily painted of face and body, as were the two horses he saw in the circle of the fire light, and from their dance they likely had been drinking something, probably some Tequila they had liberated from a Mexican village. John couldn't be certain, but to him a couple of the dancers looked to be Mexican. *Well, while you celebrate we'll go prepare a welcome for ya'; and all of this over a young woman who didn't even look to be Indian!*

John slowly belly crawled back the way he had come; when the black horse nickered a welcome from the dark, it scared the hell out of him. Hopefully none of the young guards had heard it. John spoke and touched the black's muzzle to quiet him, eased himself into the saddle and retreated into the cool desert night…if the desert floor was so damn cool at night, how come he was so wet with sweat?

As the night wore on toward dawn, man and horse were near exhaustion; they'd been at this now for a full day and a full night without rest. One of these days Juan was going to turn on him for going through his remuda so fast. He didn't know what the big black horse thought about that spurred him on at a time like this, but for John a stiff drink of sour-mash sounded good. The light was good in the east when John confirmed for himself that he had found what he was looking for and knew how they might use it; and then he moved on to find the herd. When he saw them, camp had been broken and the busted-horn Brahma was again out front and had 'em on the move. He swung in beside Mr. McCord and was just getting ready to report what he had seen, when Pale Morning ran up beside him with a plate of food, John was pretty certain all this attention from her was not a good thing, but he was hungry, so he thanked her and proceeded to eat whatever meal this was as he rode and reported. He told Mr. McCord that he thought they could expect an attack on the herd tomorrow just after sun-up, but not likely today given the heavy drinking and dancing last night.

"How many you figure?"

"Don't worry; they'll be plenty to go around…I think like upwards towards fifty."

He then told Mr. McCord of his plan to drive the cattle and horses into a big box canyon up ahead. Then deploy those with the Spencer rifles hidden just inside the canyon mouth and the five with the Henrys on the lip of the canyon walls. The canyon was deep enough that the herds could be moved well back from the opening, that way they would allow the Indian raiders to enter the canyon, then between the placement of the ones armed with a Spencer and those with a Henry, they would have them in a cross-fire. Was a little risky to allow then to get inside the canyon, but Colonel Joshua Lawrence Chamberlain had proven the value of holding the high ground at Gettysburg…proved it to those on both sides of that battle.

About mid-afternoon, John found the entrance to the box canyon and directed that first the chuck-wagon, then the remuda and finally the cattle be driven in. There was lots of grumbling that this was a crazy plan devised by a man with too little sleep, but under Mr. McCord's orders it went as planned. It was decided that the evening meal would be early and then the men would be deployed just after dark with directions to sleep in shifts. There was no need for out riders as the herd was not going anyplace, so every man was at his assigned location. John still didn't think they would attack until just after dawn, but everyone was in place, just in case.

He had been sleeping, exhaustion having taken control of his body, when he heard someone whisper, "Here they come." A loud noise likely would not have disturbed him, but that whisper brought him fully awake. He looked where BC was pointing and saw the dust boil that was rising. They were coming at a good clip just following the tracks. With almost 1,700 head of cattle, a chuck wagon, a horse remuda and drovers, hiding their trail was not even a consideration. John extended his brass spy-glass and drew the expected look of disapproval from Glenn that the spy-glass or the compass always brought, *what the hell was his problem?* He saw what looked to be about 50 riders, perhaps a few more, with out-riders leading the way. If they just kept coming he figured about a half hour before they were on them, and at that point John's first mistake at placement would be apparent…the sun would be full up in the east and shinning directly in the eyes of the five with the Henrys; nothing to be done about it now. He did repositioned BC and Pedro about a hundred yards further down the rim of the canyon, with he, Glenn and Mr. McCord staying toward the mouth…if nothing else, it would establish a better angle for a cross-fire. All around him rifles were clicking as the men checked again, for at least the fifth time, that their weapons were full loaded. On his signal, the men with the Spencers drifted back into the rocks and out of sight; there to remain until the raiders were well inside of the canyon entrance. On they came in full confidence that they had the cattle and the drovers trapped inside of a box canyon. John was reminded of a line from something his mother had read them, *"Into the valley of death rode the 500."* From Tennyson he thought…how pleased his mother would be to know that something she tried to expose him to actually taken root. There was going to be some killing here today, and if all went as he had planned, he and his friends were going to be doing most of it!

The four out-riders walked their mounts cautiously into the yawing mouth of the canyon and stopped just inside. The rest of the riders had stopped about 50 yards back outside. The out-riders could see the cattle plainly, just milling and stirring up dust. The herd was parched after three days without water or green grass and likely thought they could smell water, but it was clearly not in the closed end of this box canyon. The out-riders were apparently satisfied that they saw no threat and signaled the rest to come into the canyon.

All came, but at a slow walk. John watched through the dead leaves of the scrub that protected him from their sight…he was holding his breath that some one of their men didn't cough, or loosen a stone, or do something to give them away. They were all in the canyon now and moving abreast down on the cattle, their backs now to the hidden drovers. John stood, aimed and shot the one with the most feathers off of his mount. With that signal, all hell broke loose in the canyon. The riders wheeled their horses back toward the mouth of the canyon at about the same time as the five with the Spencers stood and cut loose. The five Spencers held nine shots each and the five Henrys held 16 each. In a very short while the dead and dying were piled so high that the riders who had led the way in, could not get over the mounds of bodies of men and horses to get away. There was one thing that no one on either side had thought through; with the first shots, the spooked 1700 head of cattle turned in unison and charged back down the canyon, through the remaining riders and out the mouth of the canyon. They were followed almost immediately by the 20 some head of horses. Just that quickly, those Indians who had not been shot were trampled under the charging cattle, as were at least some of their horses, the rest of their ponies turned and joined the remuda as it went past. As the dust began to settled, the canyon was empty of anything living except the chuck-wagon that came slowly toward the mouth through the dust and driving, to the best of cook's ability, around the dead and dying on the canyon floor. From his vantage point on the rim, John could see the stampeding cattle and horses turn slightly west as they ran toward the smell of the Pecos River.

Mr. McCord moved up to the rim so he could see the charging herd and thought aloud, "How the hell are we ever going to get these wild cattle back together again?"

"Shouldn't be a problem. Those that are able will likely run clean to the river, those that can't we'll pick up and drive to water. "Spect we'll find that busted-horn Brahma about half way. Unless they run themselves to death, we shouldn't lose too many head." John heard the firing of hand guns and knew the Mexicans were finishing the job on the canyon floor. He had no wish to watch that, and so set down in the shade of the dun mare and lit a cigar.

It took the rest of their daylight to ride down the trail left by the stampeding cattle and horses. The men spread out over a wide front and picked up and moved along those cattle that were straggling. The worst of it was when they would find a horse that had stepped in a Prairie Dog hole and broken a leg and had to be destroyed. Was strange how the men could shoot the Indians from ambush that were trying to kill them, but look so pained when they had to pull a trigger on a horse, maybe a horse they had ridden in the days before. Course in this country; to these drovers a friendly horse had much the greater value. By the time they had the Pecos in sight they had picked up about 150 head and killed three of their horses. The early arrivers had drank their fill and moved off to the green grass that the river supported. The cook and Pale Morning came on with the chuck-wagon, set their camp and cook fires, and as though it was a typical day on the trail, served the evening meal. Mr. McCord did put out two night-riders, but this herd was tired and finally had something to eat and drink…they were not going anywhere.

John sat casually, relaxed on the dun mare, one leg over the pommel horn and she with her two front feet in the narrow, shallow running Pecos River, *sure ain't the Mississippi,* he thought. There were a couple of times back there he wondered if they'd ever see this. He was taking in the crisp early morning air and the uncommonly bright blue sky and listening to the sage quail call, off to the west he could see the Sacramento mountain range jumping up out of the otherwise flat plain. He knew from the crudely sketched map that the Union Fort Stanton was between him and the mountains, but he couldn't see it. While he was lost in his thoughts, Mr. McCord rode up beside him, "Mr. McCord if you're accepting ideas for this fine day, I'd let this herd stay put at least till tomorrow…let everyone rest up, feed and drink and the men get their gear in shape. Later today I'll start working north up this river valley looking for the best trail and the safest river crossings; we should be at Fort Sumner in about three good days drive and then we can sell our cattle, pack up our gold and I can go home and get me married."

"Sounds like a good plan, Son, let's do 'er!"

According to the entry in Glenn's diary, the day was July 18, 1863.

Author's Notes...

Colonel Joshua Lawrence Chamberlain: Not all of the great leaders of the Civil War received their education and training from West Point, VMI or The Citadel; one of the great leaders came as a minister from Bowden College in Maine. Lawrence Chamberlain was a professor of rhetoric and oratory when he accepted a commission as a Lieutenant Colonel of the Maine Twentieth. While he saw considerable action at places like Antietam and Fredericksburg, it was his determination not to be routed for two days at Gettysburg for which he is remembered. The value of taking and holding the high ground was never more clearly demonstrated to both sides than during the critical last two days on Little Round Top. His men of the 20th of Maine occupied that vacant knoll at the extreme left end of the Union lines and would repulse attack after attack by the Arkansas Fifteenth. Finally running out of ammunition, the men from Maine fixed bayonets and charged down the hill breaking the final attempt by the Confederates to gain the high ground. It would not be overstated to conclude that Colonel Chamberlain's actions not only saved the Union positions and the Union supply park; they likely saved the battle of Gettysburg for the Union; which also very likely saved Washington DC from capture by Lee's forces attacking from the city's undefended north approaches; which most assuredly would have make impossible a Union victory in the war.

Chamberlain would receive the Congressional Medal of Honor for his actions those two days. He would go through the entire balance of the war, wounded six times, reaching the rank of Brigadier General with a brevet to Major General. He would be selected by General Grant to receive the surrender of General Lee's Army of Northern Virginia at Appomattox. After the war he would become Governor of the state of Maine and later President of Bowden College.

The Massachusetts 54th Regiment: Except for the 1st Rhode Island Regiment of black freedmen which fought briefly with General George Washington during the Revolutionary War, the all black 54th Massachusetts was the first all black unit of its kind authorized in the armed forces of the United States. It was authorized in March, 1863, by the governor of Massachusetts and took on life after the passage of the Emancipation Proclamation. Secretary of War, Edwin Stanton decreed however, only white officers would lead the "all colored" unit. The ranks were filled with free blacks from Massachusetts and Pennsylvania. Upon learning of the Union intent to recruit such a unit and place it in the field, Confederate President Jefferson Davis proclamation of December 23, 1862, put the black troops and their white officers under an automatic sentence of death should any such be captured.

The enlisted men of the 54th were paid $10 per month, $3 less than their white counterparts. A situation finally rectified by the U.S. Congress, but not until September, 28, 1864.

The regiment's first action occurred on July 16, 1863, in a skirmish with Confederate troops on James Island, South Carolina. They stopped a Confederate assault losing 42 killed. The 54th was selected to spearhead the July 18 assault on Fort Wagner, near Charleston, South Carolina. During this battle their commander; Colonel Shaw was killed along with 272 other casualties. Although the Union was not able to take and hold the fort, the 54th was widely acclaimed for bravery and valor which helped encourage the further enlistment and mobilization of Black troops. Decades later Sergeant William Harvey Carney would be awarded the Medal of Honor for the action at Fort Fischer; the first such award to an African-American.

Chapter Thirteen

THE DRIVE TURNS NORTH

John just so enjoyed this time of day, in part because he knew the long day in the saddle for this day at least, was almost over. The sun had been below the horizon for about a half hour. While there was still enough light to see the details of the ground clearly, the trees and the scrub had lost their color and turned to black silhouetted against the darkening orange sky. *La Tormenta* seemed to sense that she would soon get some graze and was stepping lively to get wherever it was that her rider intended for them to go. She splashed through the shallow waters of the Pecos for about the sixth time of that day as they had tested for solid footing for the crossings by the herd. John eased the mare part way up a shallow rise and into a stand of cottonwood trees where they would make their night camp.

By the time the mare was cared for and hobbled in the good grass, his fire built and the evening meal consumed, the night had arrived and John settled in with a cigar and his 'rationed' one drink of sour mash. It was not just a concern of running out of sour mash that prompted the ration. After the fight with the band of Muscalero, it drove home for him just how alone he was scouting out here and how he needed to be constantly at his most alert or die. Besides one good drink should be sufficient for any working cowhand; certainly would be if Mr. McCord were close by. This leg of the drive had gone well for John; he was gaining an understanding of the land and with that had sharpened his ability to evaluate what was before him and pick out the most likely trail for the cattle. The river crossings were not as easy with the shifting pockets of quick sand, but he and the mare worked both up and down stream at each potential crossing site before he marked it for Mr. McCord's lead. He figured he was now 3 to 4 days ahead of the herd and in the morning after he set the next marker, he would start back to join them. His food supply was running quite low and he just felt the need for conversation with someone beside a horse! She was a good listener, but did not do well holding up her end of any conversations.

They were all anxious to reach Fort Sumner, sell the herd, collect the Yankee gold, and head for home. According to the Butterfield stage drivers, Fort Sumner was where the buying would take place. The U. S. Army has established it in 1862 as a supply and control station for the Bosque Redondo Indian Reservation. They would need cattle to feed not only those being held on the reservation, but also to supply the many Union army forts in the New Mexico Territory. John had been harboring some small personal concerns about riding into an active Union fort, given his previous departure from the Union Army. For the year since, he had done all in his power to avoid contact with either army, well except that time when he and Glenn had helped Mrs. Wagner break her Union husband out of the Confederate prisoner of war compound at Camp Ford. But then this New Mexico fort was so remote from Pittsburg Landing in Tennessee and the battles in southwestern Missouri that there was no likelihood of someone out here who would have known him before.

For the last two days he had been scanning the western horizon with his spyglass looking for Fort Craig, but could never find it, just too far away over on the Rio Grande. There was supposed to be very old lava fields there and he would sure like to see that. Just imagine molten rocks coming right out the top of a mountain… *nothin' like that in Iowa!* From the stories he had been told, Fort Craig held an important place in the history of this south central territory. The fort had been originally established by the Spanish as a way station on the *El Camino Real de Tierra Adentro,* The Royal Highway of the Interior Land, which for many years was the lifeline that connected Mexico City to Santa Fe. The U. S. Army established a garrison there in 1849 that was formally replaced by a fort in 1851. In 1862, Confederate Colonel Henry Hopkins Sibley had captured a number of the Union military installations in the southern part of the territory and led 2,500 troops up the Rio Grande to capture Fort Craig. Colonel R.S. Canby, the military governor of the New Mexico Territory had moved south to reinforce the fort. At about this time in February, 1862, John and the Iowa 14th Volunteer Regiment were fighting their way overland from the recently captured Fort Henry to the soon to be captured Fort Donelson in Kentucky; the Union and Confederate armies in the southwest had been engaged in battle at the Valverde Crossing, just north of Fort Craig. Both sides had taken heavy causalities and at the end of the day the Confederates held the field, but the Union still held the fort. That night Union volunteers left the fort located the Confederate supply wagons and destroyed them. What remained of the Confederate supplies were lost a short while later at the Battle of Glorieta Pass (east of Santa Fe) on March 28th; thus forcing the Confederates to retreat back to Texas and ending any Confederate push for the military conquest of the west.

Come dawn, John was in the saddle and moving to set his last trail marker before turning south to find the herd. On the return trip he had the chance to check the locations of his markers and when satisfied, he and the mare moved off at a mile-eating lope. After one more night on the trail, by mid-day of the second day he spotted the cloud of trail dust that marked his target. *God but he was truly getting good at this scouting!* He thought he hated the stench and the dirt of the drive, but today it looked damn good to him. As he approached,

Mr. Mc Cord waved him over for his report. John noticed the busted-horn Brahma was still out in front following Mr. McCord where ever he went, more like a lap dog than a 1000 pound bull. Too bad they couldn't take him back for their next drive, assuming this one ended well enough for there to be a 'next drive'. The men exchanged pleasantries and as his pa used to call it, the time-of-day, but decided they would finish out the day and bed the herd then do their talking after supper.

John couldn't remember a better meal in a very long spell. Cookie, with Pale Morning's help had fried venison steak from a deer killed by BC, boiled potatoes, and biscuits served with a never-ending pot of coffee to go with the dried apple pie. The men all agreed that they wished John would return to camp more often! Mr. McCord had even relaxed his practice of drink and allowed each man a generous drink of sour mash, or in the case of the Mexicans, tequila. John had explained the marked trail to Mr. McCord and told him when he returned to the trail he would go on into Fort Sumner and find who they would be dealing with. The herd would stop about a half-day south of the fort where there was plenty of graze and water, and where it would be easy to secure them. As they were lighting up one of John's cigars and filling their tin coffee mugs, Mr. McCord got to the next subject that was on his mind; Pale Morning. Not that there had been any problem...there had not. But Mr. McCord believed that with all the Indians being held on the reservation at Fort Sumner, it would be better to leave her there with 'her own kind'. John quickly pointed out that she was Lakota and that neither the Navajo nor the Apaches would accept her, point-in-fact, she had been held as a slave by the Apache when John had found her in the desert. "Well what the hell can I do John, we can't take her back to the ranch with us and as soon as this herd is sold, that's where we be a going?" While they were talking about this problem, Pedro had eased up by the fire and found himself a seat.

"*Patron*, the Indian woman can go with me. We have talked and we want to be together, at the ranch if you'll have us, or I'll take her back to Mexico and we'll start our life there. Either way, she is what I want and she seems to want to be with me as well."

"Pedro my friend, you just rode to San Angelo and back with me and told me you were as much as a confirmed bachelor, and would never marry. What has changed since then?"

"I had not seen this woman when I told you that. Now that I have seen her, she is what I want. Reminds me of the wisdom of my grandmother who always told the children that we should never say 'never'."

"Pedro my old and dear friend, it has been you and me against the world for such a damn long time and regardless how bad things got, you never left me. I could not deny you anything you ask me for. You are welcome to remain at the ranch, in fact if you left, it would be like my right arm was going down the trail; but you have to know that Miss Lucinda will never tolerate the two of you there without marriage."

"Then it is agreed. Pale Morning will stay with us and return with me and when we get to the ranch we will marry. I shall go inform her you said she is to marry me and thank you *Patron`*."

As Pedro left the fire, Mr. McCord turned to John and announced, "I am not comfortable with this new, quick love, and she is so much younger. This is so unlike the Pedro I've known for these many years."

"My Pa used to tell us boys, 'we don't choose love; love chooses us'. I think our friend Pedro has been chosen!"

"The concern I have for my friend is that he may be have been chosen by the passion of the moment rather than the love of a lifetime, but I can't protect him from that!"

"What's this *Patron'*, I've never heard you called that before?"

"Pedro first came to me a about the age of 7 or 8. I had a small camp and was breaking my back trying to grow some cotton on the piece of land Sam Houston had given those of us who fought for Texas independence. Pedro came into my camp, about half starved, so I fed him, and just like most strays, you feed 'em and they just stay. He worked hard for his keep and we just struck up a friendship and he never left. Whenever there was no one around, he'd call me Angus 'cause I told him he could. When anyone was within ear shot, I'd be Mr. McCord to him, but whenever he wanted to be taken serious on any subject, I was *El Patron'*. Whenever he called me that, we were in for a serious discussion. Pale Morning is a serious subject for him and he wanted me to know that."

"What's it mean in English?"

"Like many Spanish words, it has many meanings, but probably defender or protector comes close."

"If I keep hangin' out with this outfit, I may learn to speak me some Spanish."

"Hell John, we'd be pleased to be able to teach you to speak Texican English!"

John rode the black gelding working the herd for a day to give the dun mare some feed and rest, then at dawn on the second day, he and the big dun mare rode out again. This trip was much easier, in addition to being well fed himself and with a rested horse under him; he had to but follow up the trail he had already marked. Gave him some time to relax and appreciate the beauty of the country he was riding through...relaxed, but still alert for all of the dangers that might befall a man and a horse riding alone through hostile country. He checked each of his marked crossings on the Pecos to make certain the shifting sands had not gone soft where he was directing the herd to cross. Satisfied, he and the mare moved north along the waterway as they headed for Fort Sumner and the expected cattle buyer.

Away from the influence of the river which was now running slowly, the foliage was gradually changing as John rode north. Along the river there was still green grass and willows and an occasional stand of cottonwoods. But back from the water source the ground had flattened and the grass became shorter and had long since turned brown from the lack of rain. The trees were more like scrubs than any tree John had ever seen in Iowa, and with a solid, heavy and dark green leaf, and in some places, the stands were too thick to try to ride a horse through...or drive cattle through for the matter. Looked like hard country to try to scratch out a living from. About the time John first saw the low adobe buildings becoming visible on the horizon before him, he became aware of a very unpleasant odor riding the slight breeze that was in his face. He turned west again to return to the river, crossed the shallow stream, and rode up on to a low ridge line. Sitting his mare, he pulled the spyglass from the saddle-bag, extended it and began a study the fort laid out below him.

Fort Sumner was a sprawling place with some disorganized looking adobe and log buildings clustered to one side. There were a few trees, but the most striking thing about the trees was a corridor of young cottonwood trees that stretched out for more than a mile. John assumed this was likely intended to be the main entrance to the fort area from the north side. In about a 15 acre large, lightly fenced area were more Indians than John had ever seen before or even thought to exist. They seemed peaceful, almost dossal just wondering around the enclosure without purpose or direction. At least he now knew the source of the very bad odor; it was from too many humans in too small a space. Must be the prevailing breeze was down the sloping valley from the north as all the main buildings of the fort and, what he assumed to be a sutler's store, were all located on the north side of the compound. Well he couldn't sit here all day wondering, he had to get down there and make contact.

He stayed on the higher ground to the west and rode around to the north side of the fort, and then approached up between the long opposing rows of young cottonwoods...the trees at least, were impressive. The flag pole marked the headquarters building and that's where he headed. A few soldiers milled around in the shade of the buildings as they watched his approach, with some curiosity but little real interest. Most noteworthy were all of the Indians standing around, they seemed quite interested in either this stranger or his fine dun mare. Based on his recent experience with the Muscalero in the desert, John found this attention more than a little uncomfortable; besides, he wasn't really thrilled to be inside of a Union Army post again anyway. He looped the dun's reins around the hitching rail, hoping she would still be there when he returned, brushed the trail dust from his clothes and hat.

Fort Sumner had been named for Lt. Col. Edwin V. Sumner who in 1851 became the first commander of Military Department No. 9, which included most of the New Mexico Territory. He broke up the scattered garrisons and relocated them in posts closer to the Indians, thus completely revising the system of defense. As John looked the place over from his vantage point on the porch of the commander's office, he wasn't certain that having this place named after you should be considered an honor. He turned and entered the orderly room.

"I'm the trail scout for a Texas cattle herd coming up the Pecos; I'd like to talk with whoever is in charge of buying cattle for the army."

"Ain't no one here like that, we not be authorized to buy either cattle or horses at this post since the territory forces were reorganized."

"When'd that happen? I was told to come here to sell."

With that question, a Captain who had been leaning against the frame of the door to the next office straightened and spoke up. "Couple of things has happened; with the defeat of the only Confederate forces in the Territory at the pass up north, the mission here has changed from fighting the Rebels to protecting the white settlers from the Indians. And, with the establishment of the Arizona Territory to the west, between New Mexico and California, the headquarters for this territory needed to be closer to the capital in Santa Fe. So the headquarters for the entire New Mexico Territory is now located at Fort Union, and that's where you'll have to go to sell your cattle. I'm sorry to tell you that cause I could use some cattle to keep all the Indians we have confined here fed."

"So how'd I fine Fort Union?"

"Step out here with me and I'll point the way for you."

They walked out the back of the building into the bright mountain sun and the Captain extended his right arm and pointed off toward the northwest. "See those twin buttes over on the horizon; the ones that look like the breasts of a young woman lying on her back?"

"I've not had much experience with that, but I do yet hope to." Sighting down the Captain's arm, John added, "I do see where you're a pointin'. So that's what breasts look like?"

"There's a trail between the two 'breasts' you'll find it easy when you get closer. Then look to the straight north for a *Mojoneras* and head for that."

"What's a *Mojoneras*?"

"You're not from around here are you?" Then as though already knowing the answer, the Captain hastened on, "Back when Mexico owned all of this territory the Mexican sheepherders drove their flocks on long migrations to the mountain pastures for summer grazing; then in the fall back to the lowland pastures for the winter. The *Mojoneras* were six foot tall pillars of stones that the herders laid up without mortar that would serve to guide the sheepherders who would follow. They each had their own name and with that name went an instructional messages as to where to drive the herds to find the best pastures. It'll work for you as well. When you get to the *Mojoneras*, head straight north until you strike the Canadian River, then northwest up the branch known as the Mora River, eventually you'll cut the Santa Fe Trail and follow it up trail and you'll come right to Fort Union. If'n I was you, I'd position your herd north of here a few miles on the free range by the river; the grass is good, the waters better and the odor is a hell of a lot sweeter. Besides if the General wants to buy your cattle, he'll likely want some of 'em delivered here to Sumner."

"Thank you Captain, I best be a goin' as I've got a passel of trail markers to reset."

"Let me give you a letter to the General about what we need here and then we'll head to the sutlers and I'll buy you a drink. His whiskey ain't real good, but it's better than you'll find anywhere else around here!"

John didn't argue with his host, but he knew the German's good stuff from his under-the-bar supply was a hell of a lot better and it had been free. Hard to beat free!

Author's Notes…

Fort Sumner was established by the Union Army in 1861 as a supply and control point for the Bosque Redondo Indian Reservation. About 10,000 Navajo were forcibly relocated from the Four-Corner's region to the north during the tragic march, which would become known as "The Long Walk". About 500 Apaches, the natural enemy of the Navajo, were also relocated from southern New Mexico. Fort Sumner became for awhile an agriculture experimental station as congress set out to demonstrate that it would be less expensive to feed the Indians than to defeat them by force. The ill-conceived reservation would be closed in 1868 after approximately 3000 Navajo and Apaches had died from too little food and from water sources which had become contaminated. The Indians tribes returned to their natural homes and the fort was abandoned by 1870.

In 1866 Charles Goodnight and Oliver Loving saw a business opportunity selling their beef to the government to feed the captives and established the Goodnight-Loving Trail from Texas to just south of Fort Sumner, in part using the journal notes and maps from the McCord drive of 1863.

The Territory of Arizona was an organized territory of the United States from February 24, 1863 until statehood in 1912. The forerunner, however largely differing in size and location, was named **The Confederate Territory of Arizona** and existed from 1861 to

1863 when the territory was recaptured by the Union, following which the Territory of Arizona was created. As early as 1856, following the Gadsden Purchase, proposals were advanced to form a separate territory of Arizona by dividing the New Mexico Territory along a line of latitude (from east to west), rather than along a line of longitude (from north to south).

At the outbreak of the Civil War, sentiment south of the 34th longitude strongly favored the Confederacy. On March 16, 1861 a Secession Conference was held and the Confederate Territory formed. President Jefferson Davis envisioned this as providing a route to invade California to control the gold fields and provide the South with access to the Pacific Ocean.

On April 15, 1861 a detachment of Confederates known as the California Column moving northwest from the capital of Tucson, met a Union cavalry patrol out of California near Picacho Pass. The Union victory that followed in the Battle of Picacho Pass was the western most engagement of the Civil War and became known as the "high water mark" for the Confederacy in the west. There were two other Civil War engagements fought in Arizona near Stanwix Station and Apache Pass; all three were near remount stations of the Butterfield Overland stage route.

Map of the Confederate and Union Territories of Arizona and New Mexico

Chapter Fourteen

THE TRAIL TO FORT UNION

John hated this damn rain storm! It wasn't a nice gentle rain like he remembered from his days at home in Iowa…one that cut the dust, made the summer air less like standing too close to a wood stove and best of all gently watered the crops in the field. This was what the old timers would have referred to as a 'real gully buster' where the sky opened up and just poured out water. The rain was coming down in sheets, driven by a strong, cold wind coming down off the slope of the mountains, and full of lightening and thunder. If at this moment any living thing disliked it more than he did, it had to be the dun mare. She kept trying to change directions on him to get the wind and rain out of her face and eyes. John finally just gave up trying to ride back down his trail and headed for a stand of cottonwood trees above the now raging Pecos River. Keeping dry was no longer an objective, but just getting himself and his mare a little shelter was. He knew all of the warnings about not being under a tree in a lightening storm. No sir, you were supposed to get in a gulley or a ravine in the middle of a flat field and lay down. He just plain doubted he had the skill to get this horse to lie down in a ravine running bank full of muddy water. This was likely gonna mess up all of his river crossings as well, but he'd have to take care of that detail later. There was better protection on the west side of the river, but if it was raining this hard in the foothills, there'd be no way for he and the mare to get back to the east side by morning…this ol' river was going to be wide, swift and angry by daylight. It reminded him of the night crossing that he and Glenn, and two blindfolded horses made with Mr. Miller on a log raft over the Mississippi River. John was still carrying the gold piece with Mrs. Miller's tooth mark that he had taken off the dead Confederate renegade.

There didn't seem to be any dawn. It was dark and stormy one minute and then without seeing the sun, the sky was suddenly a dirty gray, but at least the rain slowed and then had stopped. His ma had called that color 'dirty dishwater gray'. That quiet little meandering stream these folks laughingly called a river, was in that first light a mad torrent. It was twice, no maybe three times as wide as when he last saw it and was now carrying dead trees and scrub brush, and occasionally a dead animal. Yes, he had a lot of work ahead redefining the trail for the herd and now avoiding the river crossings. John was finally able to make a small fire from some dead tree roots that were protected by an overhang. He had his coffee and felt better about the day. The salt-back bacon just got kind of warm; he'd call it 'body temperature bacon' but it never actually cooked. His ma would not have eaten it. She said that only if you could pick up a piece of bacon by the end and not have it bend, was fit to eat, but not till then. This bacon had lots of wilt to it! John cleaned up his camp and he and the dun mare started up their back trail to reset the trail and to find the herd. He hated to tell Mr. McCord that they had to go on to Fort Union clear up north on the Santa Fe Trail to sell these cattle.

He reset the trail markers staying on the east side of the raging Pecos. It was not the easy trail he had before nor did it have as good a graze, but it would be days before that river could be safely crossed by 1700 head of wild Texas steers. The herd was a little harder to find on this return as there was no big dust cloud for him to guide on.

But just before dark, he encountered the remuda grazing off to the east and from that worked his way over to the herd. That busted-horn Brahma was still out there in front following Mr. McCord like another one of his strays. The riders were just circling the herd for the night-camp when John rode in.

After the night meal, Mr. McCord gathered Glenn, Pedro and BC with them around the fire and produced a bottle to go with John's cigars. They decided they liked it when John rode back into camp to report; they not only had a better meal than usual, but Mr. McCord found a bottle to share and John always had cigars, darn good ones they were; but no one ask where they came from. John had truly enjoyed the meal after his mostly-raw bacon and hard biscuit of that morning, and he thought Pale Morning had given him a 'specially warm smile as she served him his plate; then perhaps it was just John seeing another human being. That was another thing; when John came back they were served their night meal, when he was not here they had to serve themselves.

No one interrupted as John explained the now rougher trail caused by not being able to cross the Pecos, but a little grumbling could be heard after. This had been a hard drive what with the desert crossing and the Indian attack and the stampede; the men were rightfully looking forward to this easier trail north to Fort Sumner. Then John also explained that Fort Union, not Fort Sumner was where they had to go to sell the cattle. And that if they sold their cattle to the army, they would likely have to be delivered all over the eastern half of the New Mexico Territory. John finally interrupted the now much louder level of grumbling to explain what he thought was their best plan, under these new conditions. And, as he pointed out, it was at least good news that it appeared the army needed the beef and that was after all, the reason they had come!

"John, this trail you've marked on your map will take us way out east of Fort Sumner and then have us circle back north of the fort. That's a lot longer, why not just drive straight up the valley to the fort and make our camp on the plains on the south side?"

"Mr. McCord, there are about ten thousand Indians confined in and around that stockade and the prevailing breeze blows down the valley from the north. The stench of human waste is so strong as to kill flies and drivin' straight at the fort that breeze will be in your face for miles. No, trust me on this, in spite of the extra miles, you want to drive around the fort and come back in on the north side for our holdin' area. I've picked a spot about 10 miles up with some good graze and the water will be a damn-site fresher on the north side as well."

"You got any thoughts as to how we need to be doing this?"

"When we get the herd settled, I think you; Glenn and I should ride on to Fort Union and make our sale; leavin' Pedro and BC here to manage the herd and the remuda. There's no use drivin' the herd up there cause that Captain at Fort Sumner thinks we'll have to deliver steers all over the territory anyway 'for we can get paid. He gave me a letter to the commander asking for at least 400 head to feed all the Indians they have confined here."

"Well I think that's a good plan, 'cept I want Pedro to ride north with us also. It's just the same as when I ask him to go with you when you went off chasing Roberts. Most of the people we encounter along the way will be Spanish, and we need someone they'll trust and talk to. BC, you think you and Juan and the cousins can hold the herd and the horses here?"

"Yes Sir, I'm certain we can. If the graze plays out we'll just drift 'em north further up the river valley and away from the fort."

"Alright, that's settled. We'll get 'em movin' again at first light. John, I'm assumin' you know how to get to Fort Union where we're a goin'."

It took two and the better part of the third day to move the herd around to the east of Fort Sumner and then back north to the river valley. On the second day the wind had picked up and the strong odor that rode those currents confirmed the wisdom of John's plan to avoid the south side of the fort. The trail was hard on riders and animals. The muddy footing was treacherous and tiring, and the steers would get down into the ravines and with the mud, not be able to get out on their own. Pedro modified his opinion of horses; they were not the dumbest of God's animals, steers were, making horses the second dumbest. But the exhausted herds and riders finally found the tall buffalo grass, the open range and the fresh water John had promised and were content to stop. The steers were looking a little lean from the trail and now would have time to put some weight back on. The next day the four men spent getting their gear ready for the 150 mile trip to Fort Union and what they planned as the successful result of this long dream of Mr. McCord's.

"John, I am just assumin' that you do know how to get where we're supposed to go?" But this time it was a question, not a statement.

"Out north of here there's twin buttes, I'm told on the horizon they look just like the breasts of a young woman laying on her back; Mr. McCord maybe you can help me with that. There's a trail between them and from there we head north for the Canadian River, follow it to the Mora River branch, follow that till we cut the Santa Fe Trail and follow the trail north again to the fort. The Captain told me there's nothing' to it!"

It had seemed like the entire ride was 'uphill' and the horses had labored the last few days as the altitude began to increase noticeably. The Butterfield drivers had told Mr. McCord that Fort Sumner and the Pecos River valley was about four thousand feet and Fort Union would be about sixty-five hundred. Yet on the fifth day out, the men and horses left the Mora River valley and headed straight north to begin their search for the Santa Fe Trail. As the four riders came out of the foothills around the Mora River, they crossed the Trail well below the junction where the two alternate routes rejoined into one. They were also well below the Fort and turned slightly northeast, following back up the Trail that stretched out before them.

There was no mistaking the Santa Fe Trail; it was deeply scared from the thousands of oxen hooves and the hundreds of heavily loaded wagons that had torn up this prairie sod since the trail had first been opened in 1821. It stood as a never ending gash through the belly-high buffalo grass. The grass was fully headed and now turning brown under the summer sun and in anticipation of the early fall that would arrive in these high mountains. The footing was difficult for the horses and the four riders without speaking, moved as one up on the unspoiled firm ground above the Trail.

The flag of the United States flying high on a staff well above the Fort, confirmed they were headed in the right direction. The ever present wind coming down off of the peaks and into the valley was snapping the banner against the bright blue of the high altitude sky. The scene invited very different, and very private thoughts from this cluster of riders; John was stirred with the special pride that can only come from having defended her with his life in five major battles… he was moved to, but then suppressed the feeling of his need to render a salute. Mr. McCord felt the conflict inside from having been born under this flag and then having defended her against the oppression of El Presidente General Antonio Lopez de Santa Anna, but he was now living under another banner. Yet here he was to do business with these people in an effort to save his ranch and all he had worked for. The most committed part of Glenn's young life had been served under the 'Stars and Bars' with the Arkansas 6th, in fact this was the first time he had even seen the flag of the Union since he had left the battlefield at Shiloh Church in Tennessee. It still reminded him of 'The Enemy'. Pedro was forced to again recall that these colors had twice in his lifetime conquered his homeland in the south of Texas. There were very different feelings about what was before each of them, yet each was here with a common purpose.

"Mr. McCord, how do you want to handle this?"

"I want you to do the talking, after all these are your people and they should understand that brand of English you use. The rest of us will just kind of sit back and try to blend in."

John laughed out loud. "You three will blend in like a fox at a county fair poultry judging contest! You got any idea what price you want for these wild cows?"

"The drivers from Butterfield said they had heard of the army paying about ten dollars a head. If'n we hung-on to as many as one thousand, six hundred that'd be goin' on sixteen thousand in gold. That's a passel of money in these times."

The entire fort was now fully in view and it was huge! Unlike the forts John had seen in the western War Between the States, this one had no walls. It was a well organized and laid out, a cluster of dull red, single story adobe buildings build around a large central parade ground. Most of the buildings were obvious as to what they housed. On the left was what looked to be "Officer's Row" with the largest and most prominent building in the middle of the row likely the Post Commander's office and quarters. On the opposite side were the company quarters large enough for at least six companies, corrals and repair shop, many storehouses and the ever-present military prison and exercise yard. Away from the cluster of buildings and well off to the right on the other side of the Trail was what looked to be the hospital. This place was a small city. As they approached the main street leading to the parade grounds there appeared a sign that caused John to quickly pull up the dun mare:

Welcome to Fort Union
Military Department of the New Mexico Territory
Brig. Gen. Thomas Moore, Commander

The other three rode past and then Mr. McCord stopped and looked back at John. "What's the matter, Boy?"

"When I was a minor bit player with the Union campaign in the Boston Mountains in southwest Missouri, there was a Colonel Moore in command. Wonder if this could be the same man?"

"Not likely, 'sides he wouldn't recognize or remember you. You had to be but one of ten thousand or more. Come on, let's go see this

General Moore and sell him some wild Texas steers to feed his hungry flocks."

There seemed lots of well-organized activity throughout the entire fort. Men and horses all looked to have a task and they were hard at it. John heard a soldier shout that an oxen train was coming down the Trail, probably arrive tomorrow with over thirty wagons. There seemed not to be a single blade of grass anywhere in the fort, mostly just brown clay. But the place was orderly and clean, John could imagine all of the soldiers out 'policing' the grounds; showed him it was well commanded, yep, that could be 'his' Colonel Moore. They turned left, rode between the Company Quarters buildings, around the flag staff and pulled up at the hitching rail in front of the Post Commander' office. There was yet another reminder:

Brig. Gen. Thomas Moore, Commander

The four hard ridden, trail dusted, well armed cowboys were considerably observed as they brushed some of the dirt from their clothes and hats and mounted the stairs to the office door.

"What's your business here at Fort Union?"

The other three looked at John, so it was left to him to respond to the Lieutenant. "We've driven a herd of cattle up from Texas and the Captain at Fort Sumner sent us here so's we could make a deal to sell 'em." He fought down the deep-seated 'training requirement' to add the, 'Sir'. "Who do we need to see about that?"

"Generally the Commissary Officer, but he's in Santa Fe. So in his absence the only other person would be General Moore, but he may not have time for you, unannounced as you are."

"Lieutenant, we've been on the trail for well over a month with about seventeen hundred head of steers so wild that some had never seen a man before we rounded them up. We've fought Apaches that outnumbered us ten to one, dealt with a stampede and floods along the Pecos, only to find that no one at Fort Sumner could make a buying decision. So we left the herd and our horse remuda on the open range and found our way here to talk to someone who could make such a decision. Through all of that it never once occurred to us that we had to have an appointment. Rather than worry about when you could work us in, I think we'll just go get our cows and take 'em on to the gold fields in Colorado. I bid good day to you, **Sir.**" And with his speech finished, John turned and started for the door, nodding to the other three as he passed. They were just getting ready to mount when the Lieutenant appeared on the porch.

"The General will make time for now."

"We would not want to be putting anyone out to make time for us."

With a decided change in attitude and voice tone, the Lieutenant added, "Please gentlemen, the General desires to talk with you about your cattle. Right this way."

Mr. McCord leaned over to John and said, "After all we've been through with this herd, were you truly just gonna ride away?"

"No. I just could never stand Lieutenants with a better-than-you attitude toward Volunteers, and I've just always felt the need to put one down. This just seemed like a good time."

"But Glenn was a Lieutenant."

"Yes, I know!"

The very moment that John stepped through the office door and saw the commanding General behind his desk, John knew that this General Moore and 'his' Colonel Moore from Missouri were one in the same…and the thought of what might lay ahead for him made his knees weak, and the beads of sweat pop out on his forehead! This encounter that had been in his mind and was never supposed to happen…was about to happen! The General introduced himself and looking them over, waved them to a seat. Was it just John's imagination, or did his gaze stay on his face a little longer? "Thank you for coming Gentlemen, I've ordered coffee and cigars. Who speaks for your group?"

Mr. McCord nodded toward John, "Mr. Kelley will speak for us, but we are all equal in this adventure; just equals among equals."

"Your accent makes me think you are indeed from Texas Mr. McCord. Were you Confederate Sir?"

"I am not political General, I've never been a slave nor have I ever held slaves. I am a Texas cattleman trying to exchange some cattle for gold so's I can save my ranch from what I believe is surely coming."

While Mr. McCord was explaining himself to the General, John again noticed the General's gaze resting upon him. "And what about you Mr. Kelley, where do you stand in all of this on-going unpleasantness?"

"Me Sir? I'm just a saddle tramp that these kind folks felt pity for and took in. They were such nice people and the cookin' so good, I just never left."

As the coffee was being poured and cigars passed, the General added, "From the way you carry yourself Mr. Kelley, the delight you took in twisting the Lieutenant's tail out there on the porch and the way that Colt is tied down, I'd pick you for much more than a saddle tramp. In fact Sir, you have a familiar look about you; have we met at sometime before today?"

"No Sir. I'm certain I would remember if'n I'd met a Union General before. Now Sir we have a little over one thousand six hundred or so head of cattle down on the Pecos, just north of Fort Sumner and if you're in need of some beef, well we'd like to make a deal and we'd of course deliver them here, if you wished. I have a letter from the Captain at Fort Sumner looking for about 400 head."

"Well I'd say you were smart to hold your herd on the north side of that fort. Is that not the worst damn offense ever conceived by man against man? The Bureau of Indian Affairs in Washington City ordered that experiment started before I took command out here. If it belonged to me I'd of set those Indians free and burned that damn eyesore and attack to the nose to the ground long ago. Some members of Congress, that had never been west of the Allegany's before, decided we could confine the tribes and feed 'em cheaper than we could support an army in the field fighting 'em, and in the process teach them how to farm and fend for themselves. For the sake of God, save us all from the politicians in Washington! This War of the Rebellion would have been over a year ago if the politicians on both sides had stayed out of it and left it to the military men to settle. Unfortunately wars are started by old men who never face the risk, but have to be fought by the young ones. Were it the other way around there'd be damn-site fewer wars. Sorry gentlemen, that's all a sore subject with me. Old Lieutenant Colonel Sumner would spin in his grave if he could see what they've created and then hung his name on."

"I couldn't argue with your assessment Sir, and I don't think the Captain there believes he has the west's best duty either; now about our cattle."

"Gentlemen, I have seven permanent locations where men are garrisoned in the eastern Territory, by the way, did you know all this area used to be part of Texas before the Mexican War; everything east of the Rio Grande was in what Texas had claimed? I need some of your cattle delivered to each of those seven locations. You think you have a little over sixteen hundred head; alright the army will take 'em all but I need them delivered by you as follows; I've got some good soldiers serving here but none of them on their best day could handle a herd of cattle:

Fort Sumner; 400 head
Fort Craig; 200 head
Fort Seldon; 200 head
Fort Bascom; 200 head

Fort Union; 400 head
Fort Stanton; 150 head
And to Camp Nichols whatever number remains, about 100 head
by my count

We'll mark up your map Mr. Kelley so you'll know where you're going and I'll give you letters to each of the post commanders. You bring me back the signed delivery statements and we'll make the payment here."

"Sir, I assume when you say make payment, you mean in gold? Also, there's one member of that herd that we just want to leave to pasture to live out his days. The herd was led all this way by an ugly, busted horn Brahma bull and he has earned the right to just retire in some long grass. We'd take him home if there was any way to get 'em back to Texas. If that's a problem for you, we'll just find him a nice spot up in the foothills with grass and sweet water and turn him loose."

"No Mister Kelley, I'll take your pet bull off your hands. We've got a good stand of buffalo grass down by the old fort which we now use as the armory. He can go down there and we'll even put a couple of heifers in with him on occasion. That suit?"

"Yes Sir, thank you." John noted that the General was back to giving him a 'study' again, and squirmed in his seat, the ash from his cigar falling on his sail-cloth pants.

"Mr. Kelley, I can't shake the feeling we've known each other before. I'm right good with faces and I feel that I've known yours from someplace. Have we met before?"

"No Sir, I can assure you we've not met, I would remember meeting a General."

"Well, I've not always been a General. Have you ever served in one of the units under my command, not out here, but further back east?"

John knew the General was getting close and decided he was not going to screw up this sale by lying to him, regardless of the consequences. "Yes Sir, I did serve in a unit that was placed under your command. That would have been during the campaign in the Boston Mountains, 'specially the Battle of White Mountain. I was a Private in an Iowa Volunteer Regiment."

"Now I've got it! You're that crazy Private that stood up on the top of the redoubt and returned the salute of the Confederate Colonel at the end of the battle. Hell yes I remember you; I'm the one that had you promoted to Corporal...should have commissioned you a Lieutenant."

"No thank you sir! I became a better than adequate Corporal and kept some folks alive, but to this day, I'd made a damn poor Lieutenant."

The General moved his eyes to the other three men across his desk ready to tell them a story. "The Confederates had us outnumber 2 or 3 to 1 and we'd been fighting back charge after charge from them all day. Finally in the mid-afternoon they'd stopped the battle to tend to their dead, dying and wounded. After which their Colonel rode out from of their position on this big dapple gray horse. He faced our lines, took off this big two-cornered hat with a big gray plume that he was wearing and in a salute swept it down in front of him and his horse. I'm told that damn plume was so long it touched the ground. He held it there waiting for someone from our lines to stand up and return the salute...but no one did. Then this damn Private lays down his weapon, gets up on top of the redoubt in full view of the Confederate lines, squares himself away, buttons up his jacket and renders the Confederate Colonel a return salute. Well they face each other across this battlefield now strewn with their dead and exchange that salute for about 15 seconds, then the Colonel turns that gray and rides back into the woods. To cover up the fact that none of my officers would stand up there and exchange salutes with this valiant, but defeated enemy, a Captain's orders that Private to take out a patrol, ambush the retreating column and kill the rest of them. Well, that crazy Private and this cowpoke Mr. Kelley here are one and the same person. So what happened on your patrol?"

"We followed at a good pace down their trail, found their column, but then withdrew. We all agreed we should let 'em go, they'd taken enough punishment. So we rested and then about dark I sent back word that they had gotten away and requested orders."

"There's something I was taught long ago in my career that the Confederate Colonel had plainly forgot; it's a very big mistake in war to think too much of yourself or too little of your enemy. I know what was left of your Regiment was called out shortly after that; where'd you go from there boy?"

"We marched to Springfield then on to Rolla to the train, then picked up new volunteers at Jefferson Barracks, and joined General Grant's new Army of The Frontier. Hit Belmont, Missouri and the Mississippi River islands, then Fort Henry, fought across the land bridge to Fort Donelson then after the surrender, down the river to Pittsburg Landing."

"How'd the army let a man of your experience get away from them?"

John took a deep breath and knowing what he was about to say might well land him in that military prison just over the parade ground, he watched as his young life flashed before his eyes. "I volunteered in March of '61 and at that time the tour of muster was only for twelve months. My muster had been long up before Pittsburg Landing, so after that fight I just moved on and went west to Texas."

The pause before the General responded was deafening, "Well you are mighty fortunate to have volunteered when you did cause in May of '61 the muster period became three years and shortly after became for the length of the conflict. By March of '63 the Union was filling the ranks by conscription…yes sir, mighty fortunate indeed! The General looked off at no one or nothing in particular, then said to those assembled, "What a time in history this is Gentlemen.

Perhaps the one moment in America's history when all of the best and the brightest are within the forces of either the Confederacy or the Union. Each side being unified in purpose with no distinctions for class or politics...or at least so we would like to think."

Then with his solemn gray eyes the General reacquired them and he said, "Now let's price those cattle." John now knew what the expression, 'dodging a bullet' meant. He'd felt like he'd dodged a many through the five or six major battles he'd been in, but never one that came this close. And he also knew from the look in the General's eyes that General Moore knew exactly what had just passed between them, and he was not going to revisit it again.

"I know you men likely have a price in mind for all your risk and hard work, but let me tell you my problem. The Congress is so concerned that the army and the Bureau of Indian Affairs will get into a bidding war out here over the few available head, so they gave pricing authorization to the Bureau and told me I can not pay any more than they offer. Course they've not been west, so they set the price based on eastern prices and we're not going to tell 'em different; today that's thirty dollars a head. Now I can authorize pay for you to deliver them to the seven locations where I need cattle, so suppose I add five dollars a head for delivery. That'll be thirty-five dollars a head in gold when you return with the signed receipt notices. That'll be a little over fifty-five thousand, depending on how many you deliver; that agreeable with the four of you?"

The four men sat in stunned silence, mouths agape. Finally Mr. McCord nodded his head in what the General took as agreement. "Good, let's shake hands on it. Lieutenant, bring me five glasses and a bottle of that good whiskey that came in off of the Trail. We've got us a deal to drink to!"

Four of those drinking shared a common thought, *"My god, fifty-five thousand dollars and in Yankee gold!"*

Author's Notes...

The Santa Fe Trail was first opened in 1821 by William Becknell, beginning first at the west bank of the Missouri River, then at Independence, Missouri and later at Westport on the Missouri/ Kansas border. It became the first international trade route between the United States and Mexico, even thought at the time Spain forbid any such trade. Later, in 1846 it would serve as the primary invasion route of northern Mexico by United States forces during the Mexican War.

The original (mountain) route was over 900 miles of plains, deserts, mountains and frequent attacks by the Comanche and Northern Apaches, requiring eight weeks of very difficult and dangerous travel. Rattlesnakes were also a constant menace and many travelers on the Trail died of snake bite. A year later, in 1822 the Cimarron Cut-Off was established as a more direct route to Santa Fe; trading the danger of the Mountain Route for deserts, unreliable water sources and very hostile Indians. However, it did offer up to a ten day reduction in the travel time and allowed for the oxen pulled wagons to travel four abreast for greater safety.

In 1825 Congress authorized $30,000 for Major Sibley to survey and mark the Trail from Independence to the international border. By the late 1860's, more than 5,000 wagons per year traveled the Trail. In a six month period during 1865, 4,472 wagons, 28,000 oxen and 6,500 mules traversed the Santa Fe Trail all heading to Santa Fe where the "Old Spanish Trail connected and then went west to Los Angeles and the Pacific Ocean and the El Camino Real connected and went south to Mexico City. By 1865, Santa Fe was the commercial hub of the southwest. In 1879 the Santa Fe railroad had reached across Kansas to Las Vegas in New Mexico Territory, and use of the Trail ceased.

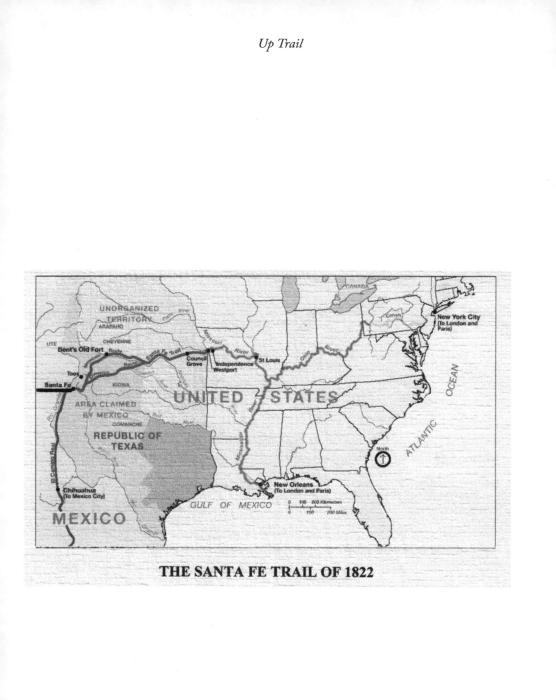

THE SANTA FE TRAIL OF 1822

Chapter Fifteen

THE DELIVERIES

The four men quietly left the General's office, walked casually up to the horses they had left tied to the General's hitching rail, mounted as though in no hurry and rode away at a slow trot down the street of Officers' Row. They eased out the main road and at least 500 yards back down the trail. Then what had just happened over came then and all four began to holler and slap each other on the back and arms. Mr. McCord whipped out his copy of the trail map, ran the stub of an old lead pencil over his tongue and did the numbers. "That's more than fifty-seven thousand in gold, hell that's fifty-seven thousand and another seven hundred fifty in gold. We gonna need that busted-horn Brahma just to pack all that gold back to Texas! I figured if'n we got seven, maybe ten dollars a head for wild cows that cost us nothin' we had a good deal, but thirty-five dollars!"

"Let's us go back down by the banks of the Mora, make a camp and get drunk, before we go do what we gotta do."

"No John, were a long ways from finishing this agreement, but we'll have us a drink and work out how we're gonna do this. I'll save the drunk till after we get home and I get the three of you married off. Hot damn, we've got us enough to buy Texas, secede, and go back to bein' independent!"

Everything seemed easier on the way back to the herd; the air was fresher and the sun and the sky brighter, the horses' frisker...and when they finally stopped on the banks of the Mora River, the sour-mash and the cigars were the tastiest they'd ever had. They had talked Mr. McCord out of a second drink all around, then he corked the bottle, put it back into his saddle-bag and said, "Alright, let's figure out how we're a gonna do this."

"Well, seems like the easiest first step it to cut-out 400 head and drive 'em over to Fort Sumner. Then we'll leave a crew with the herd and take the 200 head over to Fort Bascom. When we return from Bascom, we'll cut-out all but the 400 for Fort Union and whatever's left for Camp Nichols and drive the rest to Fort Stanton, Fort Craig and finally Fort Selden. After those are delivered and signed for, we'll come back and make the drive to the last two locations and take all our signed papers back to General Moore."

"John, you figure that Yankee General keeps that amount of gold at Fort Union?"

"From what I have seen of that General, he is a true and honorable man. If he says come back with the signed papers and I'll pay you... then when we get back with the signed papers, he'll pay us. A larger concern to consider may be how do we get all this new found wealth safely back to Texas, and what do we do with it when we do?"

It was decided that John would ride on down to Fort Sumner to advise the Captain that he had 400 head of steers coming in a couple of days. It was an easy ride, for a change. BC had drifted the herd only a couple of miles north of the original location to keep them in good graze. When John met with the Captain he strongly suggested that the army hold the herd north of the fort if only to place them close to the fresher water of the Pecos. Anyone with a nose could tell you that almost everything; water, air and likely even the ground south of the Fort had some level of contamination. As John warned him, you poison 400 head of steers with bad water and they start dying out here in this August sun, you will definitely have an odor problem. Likely they'll know about your problem as far south as El Paso. The tally taken and the delivery papers signed, the drovers returned north to cut out the 200 head for Fort Bascom and the small community that had grown up around the fort.

Author's Notes...

Fort Bascom was initially opened in late 1862 and enjoyed but a short life, being abandoned in 1870. It was plated by General James Henry Carleton and was one of a series of forts placed to protect against a feared Confederate invasion from West Texas. But a larger mission became the control of the Comanche and Kiowa Indians, and to halt the trade of stolen goods and captured white slaves by the Comancheros (a mixture of American and Mexican renegades who traded illegally with the Indians). In its later life, the fort also protected travel on the Goodnight-Loving cattle trail and the Santa Fe Trail. The new Fort was located on the south side of the Canadian River near the western border with Texas, closer to Amarillo than Santa Fe. It had a reputation as a hell-hole and some of the worst of the Union Army would eventually be garrisoned there following the Civil War. In November of 1864, operating out of Fort Bascom, Colonel Kit Carson with about 500 men engaged nearly 1500 Comanche, Kiowa and Cheyenne in the battle of Adobe Wells in the Texas Panhandle. After inflicting heavy losses, he ordered their settlements burned.

Fort Bascom was named for Lieutenant George N. Bascom who in February of 1861 lured Cochise, the principle Chief of the Chokonen Apache, into a trap in SE Arizona at Apache Pass. Cochise was wounded but escaped while his brother and five other leaders were captured by the army and hanged from trees. This became known as the "Bascom Affair" and was the primary event that triggered the brutal Apache wars which followed. For his action, Bascom was promoted to Captain but later was killed leading his command at the Battle of Valverde near Fort Craig.

* * * * *

John left the camp at first light to find and mark a trail for the 200 head that would follow. He rode between the twin buttes before he turned northeast to pick up the Canadian River, it really wasn't necessary to go through the buttes, but since it had been pointed out to him that they were just like the breasts of a young woman lying on her back; well he just liked going that way! He picked up the Canadian River, which was already back in its banks and but a quiet stream; it had however deposited debris as far as fifty feet above the normal bank. John found an easy trail heading east along the river and marked it for the herd to follow. He could have arrived at the fort just about dark, but decided it might be best to camp and go in when he could see details. Besides he didn't want to get soft from all of his recent camp living and the good meals being served him by Pale Morning. He was sometimes made a little uncomfortable by her attention to him, then Pedro explained in her culture when you saved a person's life then that life belonged to you; nice sentiment, but he was quite certain that would not fit comfortably with any of Sarah's culture. So he had finally explained to her that he had "given" her life to Pedro and she now needed to serve him. With that, the attention had slacked off a little, but he still got his meals served to him when he was in camp.

The 'community' that the General had spoken of that had grown up around the fort was, John thought, a very generous use of the word. It could have also been described as God throwing a hand full of small adobe huts at the ground and where they landed, they stayed. The buildings were all made of mud and sticks with straw thatched roofs. They were small, likely one room, but no more than two. There was no central street plan, you either rode around or just weaved your way through the openings left between the huts, sometimes ducking the wash lines and dodging a passel of kids along the way...John rode around the 'community'. Closer to the fort, there was a sutler's and a small general store, but that was all of the commerce available.

The fort was a much smaller and much poorer copy of Fort Union and John was surprised at the little activity he saw. Working his way toward the obvious command office, he looped the dun's reins over the hitching post, dusted his clothes with his hat, and mounted the steps. He was almost immediately confronted by a Lieutenant resting himself in the shade of the porch; *God, another smart-assed Lieutenant I am cursed with 'em*, demanding to know his business.

"I am John Kelley of the McCord cattle company out of Texas and we've been directed to deliver 200 head of cattle here. They are about a day behind me and I need to speak to the commanding officer to find where he wants the cattle quartered and to get my delivery papers signed for General Moore."

"The Captain is out on patrol looking for some of you rebels out of Texas and that would make me in charge here. I'll be damned if I know anything about cattle being delivered here and I'm sure as hell not gonna be signing any delivery papers for you or any other damn rebel."

"Don't make no matter to me **Lieutenant**, you don't want to sign for the cattle, I don't leave 'em…simple as that."

"Well perhaps I'll just take control of your herd and hold 'em until the Captain gets back."

John squared himself toward the officer and hitched up his Colt to a comfortable height. "So's we understand each other, **Lieutenant**, you are not takin' any control of my herd unless you first sign the delivery papers. You not prepared to do that, no skin off of me, I'll be advising General Moore when I get back to Fort Union and just sellin' 'em elsewhere…your call."

"I don't know how many drovers you got with that small herd but I suspect not many, meaning I've likely got you out-gunned about five or ten to one. If I want that herd, I'll just take 'em from you and your papers be damned."

"Perhaps you'd like to start that takin' control thing with me."

"No need for me to get my hands dirty, I can put 50 armed men out here on this parade ground on a few minutes notice."

"**Lieutenant**, fore you go ahead and make such a serious mistake in judgment, one from which neither you nor your career'll likely recover, let me tell you we've been months on the trail livin' with these wild cattle; we've fought Indians and floods and at this point we're ready to die holdin' 'em. You best ask yourself and your men, if you're all prepared to die tryin' to take a herd of wild Texas cattle. Cause I'll tell you the men that are comin' behind me with that herd are the closest thing to barbed-wire on two legs you've ever seen. They are mean sons-a-bitches and you'll get yourself and your command all shot to hell fore you'll take even one of them cows from 'em. Just so's I know for later, what's your name Lieutenant?"

"Why do you feel the need for that information, Rebel?"

"Cause I'm gonna turn and walk to my horse and ride out of here and if'n I hear the snap on that holster flap of yours, I'm gonna turn and kill you where you stand...where possible, I like to know the names of the people I kill!" John turned on his heel, spit over the rail of the porch to show his contempt and walked slowly to his waiting horse. If he had heard so much as a snap unfastening or boots shuffling, he would have turned and shot that Lieutenant where he stood. *Hate to shoot a fellow Union man, but he's been warned; besides he called me a rebel.* As he stepped into the saddle John heard, "I recon' since I'm left in command, I'm authorized to take delivery and sign your papers. You bunch your cows over there by the bend in the Canadian, and I'll send some men up to hold them in place. If you have your papers handy, we could take care of that detail now and then have a drink."

"I've got the papers handy, but I'll be passin' on the drink."

"What, a Texas cowhand that doesn't drink?"

"No, I'm a cowhand that's some fussy who he drinks with!" *Well, that went well!*

When the 200 head finally arrived the next day just after dawn, John directed them to the bend in the river and watched while the Lieutenant directed his men to hold the herd there. He did a quick count and rode over to John and without so much as a greeting being exchanged, signed the delivery papers for 200 head. That evening at their camp, Mr. McCord came over and sat by John as they both enjoyed their cigars. "John, I want to compliment you on your attitude in dealing with that Lieutenant. He was more cooperative than I had expected and took quick control of the herd; that would never have happened if you had been as surly with him as you were with the Lieutenant at Fort Union. Just like I've been telling you, John; just bring your attitude down a little and watch how well that works."

"Yes Sir, Mr. McCord, you are correct and I've decided I'll keep trying your suggestions, seein' how well they worked this time. Why he called me a Confederate rebel twice, and I didn't even take offense to that."

By the time the riders returned to their base camp, BC and his crew had cut out the next 550 head for the drive to deliver at Fort Stanton, Fort Craig and Fort Selden. Just before daylight the following morning, John left to start marking trail.

Author's Notes...

Fort Stanton was established in May of 1855 and named for Captain Henry W. Stanton who had been killed in a skirmish with the Apache Indians. The Fort's primary purpose had been to protect the white settlements along the Rio Bonito from the raiding Muscalero. It was briefly abandon by the Union army in 1861 to the Confederate forces invading from Texas, who after its capture had tried to burn the fort and the out buildings. It had been saved by a massive and timely rain storm and survived to become the Confederate Army headquarters for their forces operating in the southern New Mexico

Territory. Meanwhile, with the armies distracted by the Civil War, the Muscalero began to again raid throughout central New Mexico.

In1862, Kit Carson and his Union Volunteers recaptured the fort and with the Confederates now out of the territory, the Union army was free to open the campaign against the Apache and the Navajo tribes; eventually moving over 8,500 captives to the holding reservation at Fort Sumner. After 1865 the fort was headquarters for the "Buffalo Soldiers" as they rounded-up the remaining Apache Tribes. It would be decommissioned in 1896; but took on a new life in 1900 as a Merchant Marine tuberculosis hospital and later would become a German POW internment camp during World War II.

Fort Craig was established in 1854 after having been authorized by the 1848 treaty ending the Mexican war, the treaty of Guadalupe Hidalgo. Located on the Rio Grande and consisting of 22 buildings, Fort Craig was one of the more spacious forts in the Southwest. It was named for Captain Lewis T. Craig, a popular hero of the Mexican War who was later killed by deserters in California. A walled fort of adobe and rock, it was normally garrisoned by 1200 men who were awaiting the arrival of 2500 Confederate troops advancing up the river fresh from their victories in the southern New Mexico Territory. However, before their arrival, the defenders ranks were swollen to over 4000 with the arrival of Colonel Kit Carson's 1st New Mexico Cavalry. The Battle of Valverde on February 21, 1862, took place within the shadow of the fort on the volcanic escapement known as the Black Mesa. The battle was mostly a draw with the Union continuing to hold the fort and the Confederates left to advance on up the Pecos River.

Confederate General Sibley's forces were soundly defeated in their second major battle on March 28 at Glorieta Pass in northern New Mexico territory. Left without supplies or replacements they were forced to retreat back into Texas. The mission of the Fort Craig garrison then again became the control of the raiding Indians in the southwest. The fort was abandon in 1885. General Sibley later traveled to Egypt where he was made Inspector General of

Artillery and devised the plans for the costal defense of Egypt and Alexandria.

Fort Selden was officially dedicated in 1865, having been named to honor Colonel Henry R. Selden who had died of illness in February of that year while serving briefly as the Commander of Fort Union. At its opening the new fort garrisoned a company of Buffalo Soldiers and a company of cavalry, totaling 155 officers and men. The fort was built on the east bank of the Rio Grande, just 16 miles north of Las Cruces to fulfill the revised mission of the U.S. Army in the territory; to protect the Mesilla Valley of southern New Mexico from the marauding Indians and the outlaws and to guard the key emigrant ford on the Rio Grande. It stood astride the arid *Jornada del Muerto*; the Journey of the Dead.

Under orders from the Army Commander-in-Chief, William T. Sherman the fort was closed in 1877 and the garrison relocated to Fort Bliss in Texas. But it was quickly reopened in 1880 when the much feared Chiracahua Apache leader Geronimo bolted from the San Carlos Reservation and launched the final years of the Apache Wars.

In 1884 Captain Arthur MacArthur was assigned as the post commander. With him were his wife and two sons, Arthur III age 7 and Douglas age 4. The youngest son would become General Douglas MacArthur, one of the Nation's few five-star generals and a hero throughout three of this nation's wars. Fort Selden was permanently closed in 1890.

(Author's disclaimer: It will be clear to the reader that with Fort Selden not being opened until 1865 and the McCord Cattle Company drive into New Mexico Territory being made in the summer of 1863, these cattle deliveries to Fort Selden could not have been made as described in this chapter. However, after having walked the grounds and having studied the history and mission of the Fort, I felt including it added to the overall understanding of the Army's mission during this period and as such; it deserved to be part of in this story, and thus I exercised my "license" to make that happen.)

*   *   *   *   *

The last remaining 200 head of cattle having been delivered and most important, the delivery signed for, the men and spare horses turned north again to return to their base camp north of Fort Sumner on the Pecos. Their last remaining delivery would involve 400 head and the busted-horn Brahma to Fort Union, whatever remained of the herd to Camp Nichols, and then a bigger pay-day that any had imagined possible just a few months ago when the wild-cow hunt had started in The Breaks.

*   *   *   *   *

Between 1850 and 1891 there were three different forts in the area where the Cimarron and the Mountain branches of the Santa Fe Trail rejoin; about 75 miles northeast of the capitol of Santa Fe. Each was named **Fort Union** and they shared a common mission; the protection of the travelers and commerce on the Trail from attacks by outlaws and the Jicarilla Apaches and Ute Indians. The first fort was a collection of shabby log buildings in need of constant repair, yet as bad as it was, it survived for almost 10 years before being razed and an adobe arsenal constructed on the site.

The second fort was a massive earthwork designed to also defend the Trail against a threatened Confederate invasion. Poorly constructed, the parapets soon eroded into the ditch and the unbarked pine-log barracks rotted and became nesting places for insects. The troops refused to sleep in such hovels and camped in tents outside in all manner of weather. As soon as the Confederate invasion was turned back at Glorieta Pass, this second fort was abandoned.

The third and last fort became almost an adobe city in itself. Like most southwestern military posts, this **Fort Union** was not enclosed by a wall or stockade. It consisted of the military post and the Quartermaster Depot and served as the principal supply base for the

Military Department of New Mexico Territory and a service location for the many supply trains using the Santa Fe Trail. Shipments of food, clothing, arms and ammunition, tools and building materials were unpacked and stored in the massive warehouses; then distributed as needed to the other forts. The supply depot continued to flourish until 1879 when the Santa Fe Railroad replaced the Trail as the principal avenue of commerce. By 1891 the fort had outlived its usefulness and was abandoned.

Camp Nichols was established by the order of the Military Command of the New Mexico Territory and built by Colonel Kit Carson. It was supposed to have been located in New Mexico, however when Colonel Carson found the favorable commanding high ground he sought, it just happened to be four and one-half miles east of the territory border in an area know as The Nations (not until May 2, 1890 would it be organized to become the Oklahoma Territory). So, that's where he built his fort; on the Black Mesa the highest point on the Cimarron and Carrizo Rivers. It was positioned midway between Fort Union and Fort Dodge, in Kansas to protect the travelers on the Cimarron Cutoff from raids by the Indians and outlaws. A detachment would provide an escort eastbound to Fort Dodge, and then return escorting the next westbound train.

The camp was named in honor of Captain Charles P. Nichols of the First California Cavalry. It consisted of about 40,000 square feet enclosed by walls of native stone. Life at Camp Nichols was hard where over 300 garrisoned troops lived in tents and dugouts. The camp was abandoned in November of 1865 with the declining need for escort protection; the garrison was moved back to Fort Union.

* * * * *

John, BC and the two cousins of Pedro and Juan's had been sufficient to deliver the remaining cattle to Camp Nichols. The General had ordered a hundred head for the Camp but the final tally was only 78, so John said he and BC would make that delivery and the rest of the drovers, along with Mr. McCord and Glenn could go on to Fort Union with the 400 head. It was an easy drive for John, all he had to do was get the cattle on the Santa Fe Trail and drive 'em east till they came to the Camp. They had spotted Indians scouting parties twice, but both sides passed giving the other a wide berth. Now on the way back to the west, the ride became almost boring. For months John had either been scouting for the easiest trail to drive, or working wild-cattle, now he was doing neither. The Santa Fe Trail was so wide in this location that the men could ride four abreast without the stirrups even touching. The General had told them that the wagon drivers often came down this part of the trail four wagons abreast with a six-up or even an eight-up oxen hitch.

John thought the country here was simply god-forsaken; it was a dull orange, mostly flat, broken only by ravines where the hard rains would run off, and very rocky with no trees to speak of, just scrubby looking brush. Ever now and then he would see a cluster of what must had been grave sites of those who had died of the trail and had to be hastily buried and left behind by loved ones. As he rode alone, his mind quiet, John made up stories about the ones buried there. How they might have left farms, maybe in Iowa or Ohio, and had been convinced there was a better life to be found in the west perhaps even a gold strike. But for many only to finally settle for a small plot of orange clay beside the Santa Fe Trail; likely there were hundreds out here mostly unmarked. While he was dreaming, he noticed a single grave by itself just off to the side of the trail, and wondering about it, he left the group, urged Storm out of the depression they were riding in and over to the site where he dismounted. It was a small grave, covered over with stones to keep the wild animals from digging up the body. There was a weathered gray headboard with some carvings stuck in the ground and braced with more stones. John took off his hat and brushed the dirt away to read...

Girl Williams
4-days old
1857

How sad, she wasn't even in this world long enough to have a name and now she had to lay out here all by herself. And the parents, who had to leave her; that had to be a really hard thing to do knowing they'd likely never be back. John stood wiped away a tear before the others had a chance to see it, he spotted some sickly looking yellow flowers in the bottom of a run-off ravine, gathered a few and pushed the ends under the stones so's they'd not blow away. Then he replaced his hat, mounted and rejoined the other three.

BC thought he saw the dust streak from the tear and said, "That was a nice thing for you to do."

I just felt sorry, her being so alone and all and havin' no name. Nobody knowin' where she is…everybody otta have a name; even Joshua had a name before he was killed."

"According to the teachin' of the Priests at home, God knows where the sparrow falls and He also knows where she is. If'n that's true, then guess it don't matter about others knowing."

One of the highpoints of this delivery to Camp Nichols for John had been meeting the legendary Colonel Kit Carson, and to get the little girl out of his mind, he began to focus on his conversations with Colonel Carson. John had expected a big man, the legend being so big and all; but the Colonel was only about 5 and a half feet tall. He liked to sit when he visited so's he wouldn't have to look up at anyone. He was interested in the McCord cattle drive cause in 1853 he and some others drove 6500 sheep from New Mexico Territory clear up to Sacramento. He had made lots of money Kit said cause of all the hungry gold miners. He thought John needed to keep that in mind as gold miners had to eat and had the money to pay, and they'd likely take to cattle as well as sheep. Christopher had been the ninth of fourteen children and so he left home early to make his own way; had first traveled the Santa Fe Trail in 1826, only four years after it had been opened. He had more stories about the rattlesnakes than about the Indians. He had been a trapper in the western mountains and had scouted for General John C. Fremont. He had fought in the Mexican War in California and when the Civil War broke out, formed the New Mexico Volunteers and led them in the Battle of Valverde and the capture of over 8000 of the Navajo Indians John had seen at Fort Sumner. They had shared a few of John's cigars and the Colonel's good whiskey while they swapped stories, but mostly John just sat in awe and listened. Perhaps someday he'd be able to tell his grandchildren about meeting Kit Carson.

John's thoughts about Mr. Carson were again interrupted by BC, cause he wanted to talk about some gathering feelings he had about Suzanne McCord. Seems they'd had some conversations before the drive left and BC wanted to know if'n she would take 'em seriously. John looked at the concern written on BC's face, and then he imparted his very limited wisdom about men and women; "When a man talks to a girl, he's not always as honest as he might be; although most of the time he believes it all himself. Women have powerful imaginations when it comes to what a man says to them, or the way he says it. If they are interested in him, they tend to read things into him that maybe he didn't even know were there. Fortunately, after they have time to think about it, they throw most of it out. So she likely has no idea what you meant when you talked to her. Like me, what you really need is a beautiful woman with bad eyesight."

On the third morning the four came through the pass that looked down into Fort Union, and to John's way of thinking, it was even more impressive this time than the first. From this height he could look down into this small city and see all of the buildings and grounds. He could look beyond the fort from the direction they had come the first time and see the busted-horn Brahma and most of the 400 head that had been delivered. They were standing in the tall buffalo grass and could graze without even bending their heads down. As they rode down slope, John wondered why the Confederates had never thought to place some cannon in the pass; they could have raised some hell from there. Then John's attention was drawn to the Union flag rippling in the down draft of the mountain breeze. He felt such a stirring in his chest as though the Cornet Band from Springfield was playing *'Mine eyes have seen the glory...'* and they were again just marching in from the Boston Mountains. Just the plain joy of being alive and the intense pride he felt knowing both he and his pa had once put it all on the line in her defense; another tear to be hastily wiped away.

As they turned into the main street that went down Officers' Row, John saw Mr. McCord walking toward them. He fished in his pocket, found and waved the last signed delivery receipt in the air... "Mr. McCord, it's all done except the fun part!"

Chapter Sixteen

THE DRIVE OVER, THE DELIVERIES DONE... NOW WHAT?

It was done...the deliveries finished and after all the huggin', back-slappin' and hootin 'n hollerin', the men regained their composure and the four, Mr. McCord, Glenn, Pedro and John made their way to the General's Office and mounted the steps into the welcome shade the porch provided from the August sun. As John looked out over the parade ground he could see the heat waves already rising from the broad orange, grassless areas. The same Lieutenant that had been so 'helpful' before was there to greet them as they entered the Orderly Office, but with a decidedly different attitude than on their first trip. Mr. McCord had already decided that they were not to be distracted by any smart-assed exchange between the Lieutenant and John so he stepped in front, identified himself and requested the opportunity for a word with the General. The Lieutenant eyed John but then turned to be most polite and helpful to Mr. McCord.

They were announced, entered and shook hands all around. "Well Gentlemen, I assume all of the deliveries have been made as we agreed, or you wouldn't be here."

Again Mr. McCord took the lead, "Yes Sir General Moore, we've got the signed delivery papers right here". And with that he reached and collected the one from Camp Nichols that John was holding and proudly fanned them all out on the desk.

"I never doubted it would be done Mr. McCord, you impressed me as a pretty tough old fox."

"Well Sir, us old foxes **are** tough foxes, that's how we get to be old foxes!"

"Well let's see, I make that one thousand, six hundred and twenty eight head all together. You agree?"

Mr. McCord consulted his tally book, licked the tip of his stub of a pencil, made some scratches and announced, "Yes Sir. That's what we have also."

"The Bureau of Indian Affairs has re-adjusted their cattle prices since last you were here, so as I explained, I have to adjust our agreement to match their price. The explanation was they are now using Chicago Stock Yard prices rather than the east coast." Each of the four on the other side of the desk felt their fortune slipping away with a vast hollow place left in their stomach, John thought he might throw-up right there on the floor in the General's office. "Let's see, I've got that telegraph here someplace…yes, here it is. They are now paying twenty-eight dollars a head and of course our deal was another five for delivery, so that's thirty-three dollars a head for the 1,628 head delivered and signed for…um, that's fifty-three thousand seven hundred and twenty four dollars in gold. That sound about right to you gentlemen?"

Mr. McCord was the first to regain his breath and while nodding agreement finally got out a squeaky, "Yes Sir!"

"All right, you come by in the morning and I'll have it counted out and bagged for you. Now, I think we need a drink…Lieutenant, if you please. Mr. Kelley since you were here last and we finally figured out how we knew each other, I've been giving some thought to your circumstance and I'm wondering; you ever give any consideration to going back to the army? If you would accept it, I would be pleased to offer you an endorsement letter for entry into West Point."

"That's mighty generous of you Sir…but when my pa and I went to the small town up above the seven mile falls to sign me up the Army said to pa, 'we'd like your boy for twelve months' and pa and me we also agreed and that's the way that paper read that pa signed. They told us what they wanted, we agreed and I gave 'em more than we signed for, so's I kept the bargain and now we're done. I figure it like this", John caught his breath and took a drink of his whiskey, "If'n the Army comes for me again General, they'll likely lose two good men in the process…me and the good man the army selects to send after me!"

The General swiveled in his big chair and while focusing on a horizon that lay far beyond his office window, puffed his cigar back to life, killed the remaining whiskey in his glass in one large gulp, then said to everyone while looking at no one, "Can't say as I blame you son. There is a brutal and harsh reality to fighting a war, so brutal and so harsh that it can only be witnessed for what it truly is by the young men who must fight it, while those who started it in the first place remain faraway and shielded, their only glory being that which they make up in their minds for each other. A man only has so much time on this earth so he would be well advised to devote it passionately to the work and to the people that mean the most to him, so's he'll be left with no regrets."

"Many nights when I was alone out ahead of the herd marking trail and I could not sleep cause the nightmares keep coming to visit, I'd look at the black sky overhead and I think about God sitting there behind those stars looking down at us. What He sees is most likely some upsettin' to Him. Here's this nation that was created by His hand and grew through His guidance and what are we busy doing; we're digging the riches out of the ground…the iron, the coal and the gold so's we can use 'em to kill each other. I often wonder if it makes Him question why He did this at all! But there's more to it than that Sir, I've found me a beautiful woman, one fortunately with poor eyesight, who claims to love me and who started our acquaintance by saving my life. I intend to marry with her fore her sight comes back and spend the rest of mine tryin' to show her how grateful I am. She's a Confederate lady with a good Christian heart…lackin' that, both me and Glenn here would be dead. I had made an earlier promise before I met her, or I'd have not ridden away the first time, but that's satisfied, she's now waiting for me in Texas and I'll not risk askin' her to wait any longer. Sides we've got us lots of things to do… were gonna start us a ranch in the Hill Country and cross-breed our Black Angus cows with some strong Mexican cattle. Were gonna have us some kids and I've been thinking if this drive worked out, we just might put together another one and head for the gold fields in the Colorado Territory. Colonel Carson and I talked some about that as he had made his start about the same way in California. So you see, I ain't got the time or the inclination to start me no Army career, 'sides like I told you; I made a decent corporal but I ain't never gonna make a Lieutenant worth a damn. In the meantime, we've all got to get ourselves ready for what gonna be comin' down on the South after the Confederacy's done; don't know just when that'll be, but it's sure as hell a comin'."

"Son, I wouldn't try to talk you out of any of that. I think you've got it well figured out and good luck with that beautiful woman before her eyesight recovers!" Then the General broke into a rolling belly laugh at his own humor, but his hand was still steady enough to fill the five empty glasses before him. The pouring done he raised his glass in a mock salute and said, "here's to beautiful women everywhere but especially those with bad eyesight, otherwise all us men would be terrible lonely." He threw the amber liquid down his throat just as he started to again be overcome by his own humor and then he began to choke and cough, so much so that his aide came to the office door, but was waved away. "Corporal Kelley you're so damn funny, that must be why Mr. McCord loves you so."

"He don't love me, he just keeps me around cause I work hard, I don't eat much, and I own a compass."

"No Son; It's a whole hell of a lot deeper than that. I don't know what you did for him, but whatever it was he'd kill for you and never bat an eye. That's for damn certain!"

They made arrangements to all return at the next dawn and load the gold. The men were anxious to tie on a drunk, but Mr. McCord would have none of that. "You know, it may be the easier part that's over, holding this gold in this country and getting it home…that may be the hard part. That done, we'll have us a good celebration when we get to the Hill Country."

They loaded the bags filled with the gold double-eagles and $50 gold pieces in the false bottom of the chuck wagon that John had originally built to hide the guns and valuables for the trip he and Sarah made to Texas. There was still enough left over that they traded the army a broke horse for a big black mule, made a pack-rack and put the rest of the gold on the mule. They were loaded and ready. The Studebaker wagon and the four-up horse hitch had no problem, but Mr. McCord was concerned that the wheel tracks showed evidence of a very heavy loaded wagon; so they cut two small oak limbs and tied them with some brush off the back of the wagon for a drag. It did not completely cover the wagon tracks, but it did destroy the signs of a heavy load.

Mr. McCord directed that two men would ride about a mile ahead and two men would ride one to two miles behind. The rest would fan out in a protective shield around the wagon while he, Cookie and Pale Morning would always be close to the wagon as would the big black mule. They had already decided that they would not return by the same route. They moved southeast from Fort Union, then crossed the Mora River and a short while later the Canadian River and then stayed north of the Canadian after the river turned east. This would take them well north of Fort Bascom and on into Texas, but still close enough to the river to have a good water source and a route that would likely produce fewer Indians to contend with than the route over the desert and along the Pecos. For the most part it became a right boring trip. True to the plan they encountered few other travelers on that trail. As they crossed into Texas, an Indian scouting part picked them up and rode the ridge lines with them for much of the day. But late afternoon they broke off and disappeared as easily as they had appeared. That night Mr. McCord doubled the night guard. John was struck by the fact he had gotten up that day in Union territory and bedded down in a Confederate one…this thing made less and less sense to him every time he pondered it.

Where the Canadian River began to meander more north, the McCord Cattle Company caravan again crossed the river and began moving to the southeast. Crossing rivers with the loose stream beds and banks of wet sand proved more difficult with the heavily loaded wagon. Often the riders would have to put ropes from their saddle pommel horns to the wagon and help the big four-up drag the wagon up a wet bank. But like most things, after you do a thing a time or two it gets routine and didn't even much slow progress; course being back in Texas made it seem like home was getting near. They rode wide to the east of Abilene to avoid the town with its lawless reputation. There was a great and spreading lawlessness all over northern Texas even since the army had pulled out to fight the war. The Texas Rangers were a noble group but with just too small a force, and with too much territory to cover to have much impact on the peacekeeping. They spent an extra day in the old abandon fort at Breckenridge, another product of so many goin' off to the war, resting the stock and working to repair their gear. When they crossed the Pecan Bayou, it began to feel like home, they all knew the Pecan emptied into the Llano River and that led to the McCord ranch where the Llano met the Pedernales River.

At dawn, following their last night on the trail, Mr. McCord took BC and a bag of gold and the two riders broke off heading for Austin. Mr. McCord insisted that Doctor S. G. Haynie was owed a share of the profits for all the supplies he had furnished, especially the case of Henry rifles, and the advice he had given them; and there were the drivers and shotgun riders for the Butterfield Stage Line who had provided so much information on the lay of the land, and the water and Indian situation. They had sketched the first map and were certainly owed at least a steak and a good drunk. The rest of the caravan pressed on and late in the afternoon crossed the Llano at the Marshall Ford and came on to McCord land…home and in only ten weeks!

After the celebration of the arrival and catching up on a lot of missed hugging and kissing, it became obvious how the women had spent their time during the men's absence…planning a double wedding! The two dresses were made and ready, but the biggest change was in the house itself; the two sprawling wings which Angus and Lucinda had always planned to fill with their children and their families had been reworked and turned into separate living facilities for John and Sarah in the north wing and Glenn and Samantha in the south wing. The women had decided that when the newlyweds returned from their honeymoon they would all live in the same big house until the young men and their brides could set their plans and start their own ranches…that they would return had never been in doubt in their hearts. The only issue not decided was the date and finding a pastor who could come by on his circuit…they would leave that detail to Angus.

Angus did finally return home two days later and when Lucinda began a tirade of sharp words for his extended absence, he but held up his hand and said he would not discuss it until their family meeting at the fire pit that evening. Before his return, Pedro had taken Pale Morning and left for his family in northern Mexico. He believed as the first son to marry, he and his woman should be married before his surviving family members, but Juan did stay behind in his brother's stead until he would return

While the days of September had continued hot under the blistering Texas sun and the cloudless sky, the evenings were already turning cool as soon as that sun dropped below the horizon. The evening meal had been a masterpiece for the now fully welcomed home. Sitting around the big oak table laden with more food than could possibly be eaten, Glenn had caused some color to rise in John's cheeks when he suggested that now he would have to get used to filling his own plate at meals. When the color of embarrassment was obviously and suddenly replaced by anger, Glenn wisely decided not answer the follow-on question about what his remark had meant. Now the six were gathered around the fire pit, the men with their cigars aglow and their boots up on the bricks, and all six with at least a touch of amber liquid in their glasses. Angus offered thanks to their God for their safety and success and for the long happiness of the two young couples. It was a most special family moment and Lucinda knew she would hold it in her heart to be cherished to the time of her grave; through her moist eyes their images blurred.

"My good friend Dr. Sam Haynie, who's also the mayor of Austin, wants to furnish a few things as his gift for this up-coming happy occasion. He is sending out two rigs with teams, one for each couple to use as their get-away and he is reserving two suites at two different Austin hotels for each of the honeymoons…so you'll be in the same town, but not together. Now as to the question of a minister, rather than wait for a circuit rider to come by, Dr. Samuel has a friend who owes him a favor and he will come officiate on the date you set, not the date of his own schedule. And that my dear woman is what took me the extra day in Austin."

"Who is this friend of your friend and is he even authorized to officiate at the wedding of our two sons, or he just another one of your hard-drinking friends in that town?"

"Well I'd think he might be authorized alright. He is Dr. Rufus C. Burleson. He is a pioneer Baptist minister, teacher and currently President of Baylor College in Independence, Texas, although they are movin' the school to Waco. He graduated from Western Baptist Theological Seminar and the town of Burleson is named after him. Oh yes, he has a cousin who was the first Vice President of the Texas Nation under General Sam…but then that's about all I know about him."

* * * * *

The weddings were as beautiful as the women had planned for those long ten weeks that they would be…the brides were beautiful and the young men tall and dashing. Except for the color of the eyes the young men looked enough alike to be brothers, and indeed given what they had been through together, they truly were. Their similar looks caused Dr. Burleson some confusion and for awhile Lucinda was concerned he would marry the wrong young man to the wrong bride. With each of his stumbles she would turn and glare at Angus as if to say, '*I thought so all along.*' But Angus continued to ignore her while he savored these special moments, as an old man will tend to savor those special things that he knows may soon come to an end for him. He was so satisfied that he did not even get upset when he noticed the red-headed Irishman with one patched eye training the good eye on his daughter. What most surprised him was the loving look Suzanne returned.

* * * * *

Looking up, John noticed that the passion of their long awaited coupling had completely dislodged the beautiful canopy of multi-colored, silk scarves that had been draped across the frame of the high bed posts. Now in complete disarrangement, they hung limply like the Regimental flags in a dead calm. He rolled over next to the naked body of his beautiful bride. Each of them covered with a fine sheen of perspiration and gasping to catch their breath. Sarah reached out and found her new husband's hand and brought it to her rapidly beating heart. "I love you John Kelley" she whispered.

"I love you too Mrs. John Kelley!" John raised his head and looked over at the shadowy profile of his wife lying beside him and he suddenly understood completely the analogy that the Captain at Fort Sumner had been using to describe the twin buttes on the New Mexico horizon. "They do look exactly like he said they would", John informed no one in particular.

* * * * *

From a box canyon far to the southeast of the blissful couple, just beyond the little used stage stop at Ben Flicken, came the rapid echoes from the firing of a handgun. A young man of no more than 17 was practicing his quick draw technique while firing at the cactus scrub that grew in the canyon. He was good and the cactus was taking a hell of a beating, but no one was there to observe just how well Samuel Roberts, the oldest male cousin to the Roberts' brothers Eugene, Clint and Garth, had mastered the use of that weapon.

Author's Notes...

Gold was discovered in Colorado in early 1858 by prospectors on the Vasquez Fork of the South Platte River. The find led miners up streams looking, but without success, for the source. But even lacking that find, the area quickly became known as the "Richest Square Mile on Earth".

Georgia miner John H. Gregory and his wife Christina were in Fort Laramie, Wyoming with plans to mine in Canada and when the word of the Colorado find reached his ears, they immediately turned south. Gregory would follow stream after stream higher and higher into the mountains and on May 6, 1859, discovered the "Mother Lode" of the original Colorado find. In the next six months over $2 million in gold would be taken from that location...this at a time when gold was $16 an ounce.

Epilogue...

It was President Abraham Lincoln's inspiring words from his Second Inaugural Address that were intended to set the policies for the reconstruction: *"...with malice toward none, with charity for all, with the firmness in the right, as God gives us to see the right, let us now strive on to finish the work we are in to bind up the nations wounds."* March 4, 1865

Unfortunately these noble objectives would die with the assassin's bullet which would snuff out his life 40 days later on April 14, 1865. While the President's intent to bind up the nations wounds would be supported by the new President Andrew Johnson, he would be much less able to win support for the needed legislation in Congress. With the rise in the belief that Confederate President Jefferson Davis conspired in the assassination of Lincoln, had in fact perhaps even ordered it, the mood in congress became one of repression and revenge against the south.

The "Reconstruction Act of 1867" laid out the process by which the Confederate states would be considered for readmission to the Union. These included pledges of loyalty and the state's ratification of the 13th and 14th Amendments to the Constitution...later the 15th Amendment was also added to that list.

Initially the occupying Union Army by default assumed the civil tasks of the local governments as the Confederate National government had collapsed. The civilians appointed to fill the vacancies worked under strict military orders. The 250,000 Union troops that remained in the south were called upon to perform a wide variety of civil duties, often without any training. Also frequently with little supervision from commanding Generals, many of whom were not regulars and lacking specific directions, were often left to act on their own judgments. As a result the rules varied widely from military district to district. Not only had all commerce collapsed and the local money deemed worthless, crime became wide spread and beyond the army's ability to control. This frequently resulted in a confiscation of all firearms. Imagine living on the frontier in Texas without firearms!

By September, 1865, 45,000 Union troops remained in Texas. By the end of that year as troop strength declined, black regiments in the south outnumbered white regiments, and especially in the Territories where the focus again shifted to controlling and containing the Indians.

The "Reconstruction Period" in the south generally ran from 1865 to 1877. It officially ended on March 4, 1877, in a "backroom" political trade-off deal made by Republicans to secure the next presidency for Rutherford B. Hayes.

The Reconstruction period frequently brought Republican state regimes to power that were heavily inclined to use the military to enforce their civil rules

In the meantime:

On May 26, 1865, the 65,000 men of the Confederate Army of The Trans-Mississippi surrendered at Shreveport, Louisiana. This essentially ended any armed resistance by the Confederacy.

It was not until June 19, 1865, that Union troops, under the command of Major General Gordon Granger, arrived in Galveston, Texas, with the news that the Civil War was over and that all remaining slaves in Texas were freed.

On July 24, 1866, Tennessee became the first former Confederate state to be readmitted to the Union. President Grant signed the order readmitting Texas on March 30, 1870. Georgia became the last Confederate state to be readmitted on July 15, 1870.

President Andrew Johnson by decree formally declared the Civil War over on August 20, 1866. This, many months after all fighting had ceased.

The Posse Comitatus Act of 1878 was an outgrowth of the over reaching of this occupying military into the role of the civil governments.

On December 12, 1870, Joseph H. Rainey of South Carolina took his seat in the U.S. House of Representatives; to become the first elected Black Congressman.

Manufactured By: RR Donnelley
                              Momence, IL USA
                              May, 2010